MOUNT HELLFIRE MATES

Brewing Fire

Book 2

K.L. ANDERSEN

Cover made by K.L. Andersen using Canva Pro

Formatted with Vellum

Trigger Warnings

Please read the following trigger warnings. If any of these bother you, please don't proceed to read.

*Sexual Explicit Scenes
*Vulgar Language
*Alienation by a parent
*Assault (Not by MMC)
*Attempted Kidnapping

Acknowledgments

Thank you so much to my beta readers who have been with me since the beginning, whether you started as an ARC reader or dived right in as a beta reader. You three are my amazing support system, and I'm so grateful for each one of you! Love you, Lisa, Lou, and Kelly!

Mom, these last few months have been a rollercoaster for us. But, through it all, I have been there for you, and you have been there for me in return. Thank you, I love you!

And my hubby, whom I have dedicated this book to since I'm releasing it on our 15th wedding anniversary. You are always there when I want to talk about books and my characters, and even if you never read another book I write, I love you all the same.

Blurb

Viv is adamant she'll never marry or accept a mate bond—ever.

After a blaze breaks out at her best friend's bookstore, she finds herself in a dilemma when she risks her life to put the flames out, only to be thrown over the shoulder of a firefighter who seems to fan the embers of her absent desires.

Now Viv is faced with the one thing she didn't want—a mate and a persistent one at that.

Can Kit prove that their bond isn't something to fear, but rather a blessing, or will the dragon shifter learn what it feels like to get burnt?

Unfortunately, neither choice comes without consequence.

City of
Mount Hellfire
Mount Hellfire
Hellfire Park
Mount Hellfire Lake/Falls
Hellfire Hospital
Hellfire Festival Center
Flamed Bar & Grill
Bound in Fire
Kindling Cakes
Molten Java
Embers Lace
Charred Peaks Steakhouse
Inhuman Special Forces
Hellfire University
Crimson Lane

For my Husband.
Happy 15th Wedding Anniversary
May we celebrate another 15 years and more.
Thank you for supporting my dreams of writing XOXO

Chapter One

Viv

The Night of the Fire

My internal ward alarms were blaring like the dickens I haven't had in, well, for fucking ever.

Damn, whatever the hellfire was wrong with me lately needed to buzz off.

I couldn't seem to shake this feeling of foreboding, and that my impending doom was soon to come crashing down like a car being thrown by Superman or some equally fucked up strong male who I also wouldn't have any interest in banging.

Goddess, I needed to get laid and BAD; this was so unlike me.

But enough of that; this bitch needs to get the fuck up and find out why my wards are going crazy.

Talking to myself had always helped ease anything urgent, but tended to make me less compelled to get shit moving.

Those wards were pressing, tugging at my soul, which sent prickles of uncomfortable awareness and a pep in my step.

There was no time to change out of my black lace teddy, which I had just purchased from Mitsy at Embers Lace.

For all that she had been a bitch in high school, I found I really enjoyed her company and her taste in sexy things that could make even my less-than-desirably small breasts plump up like nobody's business.

I wasn't blessed in that area, but I made up for it in my libido, which at the moment seemed to be missing, like the adorable cat in the posters attached to several light posts around the city.

Fuck, focus.

My eyes caught on the long knitted sweater hanging on top of the pile of clean clothes I hadn't put away yet. And thank goddess for that because it was the best thing I could grab now that those wards were hollering like cougars in the woods.

There was no time to pay attention to speed limits, stop signs, or traffic lights as ringing started in my ears.

I had taken too much time getting to the building that housed my coffee shop, The Molten Java, and the bookstore I owned with Teags, Bound in Fire.

And on fire it was.

My tires squealed as I rounded the corner, and the flames and smoke came into view. I gritted my teeth, wondering how the fuck the bookstore caught on fire.

Across the street, I could see Teagan and Finn holding each other as they watched, horrified, while the place was ablaze.

I hoped they hadn't been in there during the start of this. Guess I would find out soon enough, but for now, I needed to get this shit under control because the slow-poke fire department had yet to show.

I was now flying across the sidewalk, and when I hurriedly left my car, still running because I had already wasted enough time getting here, my ears picked up the distant sounds of sirens.

They were still too far away.

Putting out this fire was a job only a witch could handle without further damaging the structure or the shit show inside. But, I couldn't very well walk through the front of Bound in Fire, seeing as the flames flickered and rolled along the top edges of the front window and began seeping at the top of the closed entrance door.

My only option to safely access the starting point was through Molten Java's partition.

Teagan's scream with my name rolling from her lips nearly made me pause. Unfortunately, there was no stopping me from taking care of business. Literally, our business, in fact, because fuck someone did a number in here.

Coughing through the smoke that had snuck its way into the coffee shop, I tore the partition away after casting an unlocking spell, which I most certainly never used in any way possible when I was a teenager to get things I wanted. *Nope—never did.*

I was through the opening, and when my senses heightened, I could see the pulsating from where the fire had started. That's where I would focus most of my magic while simultaneously pushing it outward like a beating heart pushes out the blood through the veins.

It was the best option because, holy fuck buckets, it was a disaster in here.

Slowly, that beating and pulsating magic rippled through my arms and out of my fingers in an invisible flow to anyone else, but to me, I could see the shimmers glittering like water dousing every inch of the store.

What started as uncontrollable scalding flames now trickled into embers as the last wisps were snuffed out. And since the fire was now gone, the smoke remained, demanding to be let free as most of it was sucked out the window.

The front doors of both businesses needed to be opened so we could get them aired out, so I went to open the bookstore's front door first, only for it to crash open, slamming against the wall.

"Son of bitch, you motherfuckers are going to pay for a new door if my magic can't fix that shit," I screamed, thinking about all the work my magic would already have to do and the exhaustion this would cause. It appeared I would definitely need to call in backup due to the damage that became visible as the smoke escaped through the now-open door.

"Does your mother know you use that sort of language?" A smoky, sinfully silken voice said behind a helmet. I couldn't see who was beneath, but my body sure didn't care as it ramped up her fucking motor for once.

Maybe my dry spell would finally be broken, and I could break my bed with this sexy fireman.

Goddess, I was a sucker for a man in uniform.

That was until he approached me and rudely tried telling me what to do, "You need to exit the building. It's not safe for a little thing like you to breathe in the smoke. Now get."

His tone was authoritative, and even though he said it in not such a nice way, I couldn't help what it did to me. And then I started to get pissed because he should have realized I was the one who put out the fire, since it was gone, leaving only ash and lingering smoke.

I reared back to respond, "I just did your job, asshole. Do you still see any flames flickering? No? Yeah, because I'm the one who put it out. A little thank you wouldn't hurt."

Crossing my arms, the hem of my sweatshirt rode up my thighs, showing my alluring skin that I had hoped to use on this fire boy to get him into my bed when all this was over. Now, I was rethinking that.

Suddenly, I was thrown over said fuck boy's shoulder and brought outside.

"Put me down, you prick!" I yelled while pounding his padded back that I knew he wouldn't be able to feel anyway, since these things were made to keep them safe from fire.

A warm hand that felt like the glove was missing slid up the back of my thigh, just under my ass cheek, lighting a new fire in my veins that shot straight to my pussy, making me squirm enough that his helmet fell off.

When that barrier fell, he froze on the sidewalk, turning his face and placing his nose against my outer thigh, inhaling.

What the fuck?

"Hey, fuck boy, put me down, or so help me, I'll make sure the goddess rains down her wrath for being a twat and manhandling me." I spat, hoping my bluff would entice him to get his hands off my overheating body. "I said, put me down and get your claws off, you bastard!"

And it worked because I was being lowered gently, albeit fucking sluggishly, to my feet.

When he was about to move away, my sweatshirt caught on his belt and rode up, showing the world the goods I kept hidden away until it was time to get down to business.

This asshat saw said goods, and the visible smoke billowed out of his nostrils while his incredibly dreamy Adam's apple bobbed, a growl rolling off his tongue.

When my eyes finally found his golden-ringed ones, I gasped; my alarms were blaring and throwing fucking confetti behind my lids. An imaginary neon sign was pointed at the top of his light golden hair, reading in all caps, 'MATE.'

Oh, hellfire to the fuck no.

I didn't want a mate, let alone a fucking shifter one at that.

He had to be a dragon shifter because there was no way any of the other animals could spew smoke from their face.

I'm in a fuckery pickle that I needed out of.

"Mine—" He growled, reaching for me.

Before he could grab hold of me, I backed off, ripping the bottom of my sweatshirt from whatever it had snagged on.

And now I was pissed that one of my favorite oversized cardigans was ruined.

"Fuck, that," I muttered.

Luckily, before anything further could happen, Finn and Teagan had crossed the road and were there. Teagan wrapped me in her arms, blubbering as if I had been about to die.

The manhandling firefighter was still there in my bubble, an apparent rage on my face that he could clearly see; it was as if he wanted to poke me further. "Calm down, woman."

I couldn't help or stop the uncontrollable seething anger from hitting him when I slapped his padded chest while sneering, "I had it under control, you overgrown beast."

My outburst only seemed to amuse him, as his eyes never left mine.

"Yes, well, the real professionals are here now to take care of the fire."

"I already put the fire out, asshole. So why exactly are you still here?" I spat, wondering what the hell was going on and why he riled me up so easily.

"Well, princess, now there's going to be an investigation into how it started, and you could have potentially contaminated the crime scene."

I could have what now? My eye twitched at the implication I hadn't been more careful, but the only thing I did was snuff out those damn flames. My magic hadn't touched anything to repair the damage that was done.

"I didn't touch anything. I'm not stupid. Anything that was

done in there was to put out the fire, and I took care of your job. So a little thanks wouldn't hurt you." For some reason, my feelings were beginning to get hurt. I had done a good job, hadn't I?

Those old wounds of my father's hurtful words and the shunning I received when I refused to do the duty of the eldest daughter resurfaced.

I thought I had long dominated and locked those thoughts away, but this asshole's words pushed them forth.

It was like he could see the hurt written on my face when he tried to smooth it over, "I suppose you are right, princess, so thank you." The tenderness was woven into the nickname this time, rather than used as an insult. It still didn't take away the fact that he was a jackass.

"Yeah, whatever—bastard."

I went to walk away, but his hand gently gripped my wrist. "My name is Kit, not bastard or whatever else you have called me."

"And I'm just some witchy bitch who couldn't care less what your name is, fire boy."

I pulled away and turned my back to him, where Teagan reprimanded me like a mother hen, calling me crazy, which wasn't new. I thrived on chaos, fuckery, and debauchery.

When Teags and her man, Finn, my people's king, were busy speaking with one another, I took out my phone. The first person who came to mind who could help with the magical cleanup was my baby sister.

Although she was less than a year younger, I still treated her as if we were years apart.

"Hey, sis," Liv answered sleepily. "Why are you calling me at this hour? Everything alright?"

Her concern was warranted, but it shouldn't have been meant for me. No one should have to worry about what was going on in my life.

"Yeah, everything's peachy keen. Except if you count someone trying to burn down my building with Teags and the King still inside."

Muffled swearing and scrapes sounded as Liv likely fell off her bed when I announced what happened.

"What?! Is Teagan alright?" She asked, more concerned over our mutual best friend than the king, which I found hilarious. But, then again, she already knew he was Finn, and it had all made sense why he had up and moved without a word to our girl.

"She's fine, so is Finn. They're pissed; well, Finn is; Teags is our strong girl, though. She can get through anything. But, I'm here and put out the flames, no thanks to the fire department." I muttered, still seething from my interaction with the dragon shifter, Kit.

"Thank the goddess. I'm relieved to hear they're both alright, and you're there to take care of things. That answers that now, big sis; tell me, what do you need?" Liv already knew I had only called lately when I needed something, which was either me complaining about my sex life or needing her to placate our strict parental units.

"There's some major damage control that needs to happen, and I can't fix everything myself. I already exhausted the magic within me tonight, putting the flames out—"

"Say less; I'm already booking a one-way ticket; be there in a few hours. Pick me up from the airport?" She asked, rummaging around in her room, likely packaging a carry-on with her essentials.

Liv didn't need much since we were the same size; she could borrow whatever I had in my closet. Or whatever she usually left behind when she visited.

"Shoot me your flight details, and I'll be there with bells and party hats," I said.

"Will do. Love you, Viv, see you in a few hours. Oh—and give Teags big hugs from me!" Liv hung up the phone before I could respond, so I shot her a quick text, replying with an 'I love you' back.

I only needed to contact one other person before going home. And while I was speaking with Liv, Kit had decided to hover nearby, listening to my conversation.

A devious plan was hatched before my fingers flew over the screen while I texted my cousin, Dom. I warned him that I needed to speak with him, telling him he just needed to play along and that I would explain what was going on later.

He replied to go ahead and call him, and that he was down for whatever fuckery I was up to since we had played this game before.

In the past, I would text him a warning about my call, and he would pretend to be a distraught boyfriend or husband, which would scare off any guys I wanted out of my bed the next morning or even that same night. He was just as devious as I was, and I loved that he matched my vibe.

So, with that, I leisurely headed inside the Molten Java to see if Kit would follow like a love-sick puppy. And when I was alone or pretended like I thought I was alone, I hit Dom's name, placing the phone to my ear while I waited for him to answer.

Chapter Two

Viv

I was halfway through my coffee shop, headed toward the back, when my cousin finally answered, "Hey, babe, what's going on?"

He knew the drill, always. Pretend to be a doting boyfriend, which he loved playing into just to fuck with people. I was sure he got off on being a dick to everyone except those he kept in his close circle.

"Dom," I whined, putting on a little extra pazazz, knowing Kit was lingering in the shadows of my shop. "I need your help, can you come by tomorrow? I miss you."

My cousin let out a breath, while behind me, the light scrapes of Kit's movement edged closer.

I was playing a dangerous game, knowing that the dragon was my mate, but there was no way in hell I wanted one.

Men were good for one thing only.

To fuck and then leave me to my peace.

There was absolute certainty that I didn't want anyone to sniff and stick around and claim what freedom I had fought so hard to achieve. I had climbed out of the trenches that my stuck-up parents had erected, and to this day, they still refused to leave me alone.

"Yeah, sure, love. What's going on?" Dom asked.

Face-palming myself, I had forgotten that I hadn't even told Dom about the fire over text. "Someone tried burning my building down with Teagan and the Demon King still inside. There's a ton of damage, and I managed to snuff out the fire, but I need a boost in the magic juice."

My cousin snorted, "Viv, sweetie, drink some of that Serpent wine, and you'll be good to go in the morning."

I rolled my eyes, knowing damn well he couldn't see me doing it, but it still felt great nonetheless. "Yeah, that doesn't work for me, Dom, and you know it. And it would leave me with a hell of a hangover, which wouldn't help. Please," I cooed, twirling a finger along the counter as I slowly walked to the back, putting on a show for the lurker.

Dom let out a breath, "Fine, you twisted my wrist. I'll be there bright and early. I have shit to do in the afternoon."

"Oh?" I inquired. Now my curiosity was killing the cat, because Dom usually didn't have much going on, and this was the first time he actually had plans.

"Horace called and asked for some help with the winter solstice planning."

I winced at my father's name. Just the mention of my sperm donor was like a dagger to the gut while someone twisted and turned it in jerky motions.

"Of course he did." I seethed through clenched teeth. The reminder that my father loved to use and abuse people for his gain was the worst kind, especially since he was roping Dom into whatever he was after.

"Sorry, Viv. I know you don't like hearing his name, but you asked." He had been contrite enough that I knew I shouldn't take it out on him.

My father was known for persuading anyone and everyone into doing his bidding. And wouldn't take no for an answer. He was a master at manipulation. And once upon a time, he had held me in his snares and whims.

I leaned over the counter, resting my elbows on it as I peered into the open shelves that held tea bags in metal-lidded containers, contemplating what to say next. I didn't want to know, but I had to. "He hasn't mentioned anything about me to you, has he?"

Dom was silent for a moment before chuckling, "No, he knows not to ask or talk to me about you. Dad made sure to let him know he wasn't allowed to meddle in anything having to do with you and me. I'm just helping as a favor."

"Alright, good. I don't want that bastard knowing about anything that I do. Just promise me you'll be careful."

"I will, Viv. You shouldn't worry so much about others."

The front entrance of my shop whooshed open, and the chime dinged a moment later. I didn't turn to see who it was, but knew someone else was among us. Kit was still out of sight, or at least I thought he was.

"Miss Woodward, a moment when you've finished your conversation." A male's voice called out, making me turn my head. When I glanced over, I saw a man whose body was flickering in and out like he was here one moment and gone the next.

He must be the new detective I keep hearing about.

"Gotta go, Dom, baby. I'll see you tomorrow." I said, with a smile on my face, knowing damn well this next bit would rile the dragon shifter up. So I put a little more breathiness to my voice before provocatively saying, "I love you so much, big boy."

"Ew, Viv–ahem, I mean, alright, see you tomorrow. Love you too, buttercup." Dom nearly forgot we were playing a game and almost gave us away. He could have still done it, but

I would worry about that later. I had another matter to attend to.

Shoving the phone in my back pocket, I turned and smiled at who I thought was the detective for the Inhuman Special Forces. A separate entity from the human police here on Earth. Looks like Finn, our king, decided to bring them over after all. And thank goodness, because this mess with the fire was sure to draw a lot of attention to the fact that humans were targeting businesses owned and run by supernaturals. I owned the building that housed not only The Molten Java but Bound in Fire, which hadn't even opened yet, and I was very much a part of the Inhuman community, being a witch and all.

It was a hellfire shit show, and I didn't even want to comprehend what it would bring once people found out I had abilities. I hadn't been open about who I was when the Veil was revealed.

It could have been the years of having to hide ingrained in me, or just that I didn't want those around me to see me differently.

Guess the cat really is going to get let out of the bag, now, though.

Couldn't worry about that, as I needed to figure out what the flickering ghostman wanted.

"What can I help you with—?" I drawled out, not knowing what his name was since he didn't have any clear identification on him.

He smiled, and the flickering lessened. "Miss Woodward, I'm Detective Rayth with the ISF, and I just wanted to speak with you about what happened this evening. Do you have time?"

I shrugged, "Sure, but call me Viv. And, I don't have much to tell you other than my wards woke me up, I drove here like a bat out of hell, and then saw the fire, put it out with my magic until the fire department showed up and rudely removed me from the building. I didn't touch anything, but I did notice a broken glass bottle on the ground with a rag hanging out. I'm guessing that's what they used to start the fire."

The detective brought out a notepad and jotted down a few thoughts. I mentally smacked myself in the face, realizing I just admitted to breaking the law.

"I mean, I totally made sure to go the speed limit to get here, I didn't actually miss any stop signs or red lights." I smiled sweetly, lacing my fingers together in front of me and batting my eyes.

Maybe I could persuade him not to give me a ticket for admitting to speeding.

My fingers itched to graze the hem of my sweatshirt up my thigh a bit more, but I stopped at his movements and coughed.

He clicked the pen and closed the notepad, keeping his eyes above my neckline like a true gentleman. "No need to worry, Viv. I'm not the human police. While we should certainly follow their rules and laws, I'm not here to uphold them. You know as well as I do that we have different laws among our people."

Nodding, I bit my lip and let out the breath I had been holding. "Okay, great, because I totally drove like a fucking mad woman to get here. If I didn't, my wards would have likely driven me to the brink of insanity from how insistent they were being. And for hellfire good reason, too, it seemed all things considered."

Detective Rayth started flickering again but smiled. "Well, that's all I have for now. I'll be by in the morning when the adjuster gets here." He glanced over near the partition that separated the two businesses before turning back to me. I also peered over and saw nothing, and I definitely didn't see Kit; I no longer felt him directly in the room with us.

"Perfect, well, Detective, I suppose I'll see you in the morning." He tipped his head in a nod before vanishing from sight.

Hellfire, he really was a ghostly fucker, wasn't he?

I was too wound up from the events early in the night that I knew sleep was a long shot to achieve.

Teags had texted me earlier, saying Finn was too eager to get her out of there and back home. So, I swaggered behind the counter and took out several tea pouches.

My witchy specialty was liquids. That's why I became a coffee shop owner. I could turn even the most basic of drinks into something that would have someone want to come back again and again, without the addictive side effects that human drugs had. My drinks were safe, unlike the fuckery the humans liked to get up to.

Pulling out the chamomile, lavender, and valerian root, I mixed the three before steeping them in hot water. Then, I let the tingling sensation ripple through the tips of my fingers over the steam. My magic was nearly tapped out for the night after using so much of it to smother the fire, but I had just enough to give the tea a boost of sleepy goodness that I would gingerly sip on my way home.

Satisfied enough, and completely depleted of my magic, I stirred the water, added a dash of honey, and covered the cup with a lid.

I hummed as I cleaned up my mess by hand, taking my time since I had to let my tea steep for a while before I could add ice, making it more bearable to drink.

And once everything had been cleaned and ready for my arrival in the morning, I gripped the cup and rounded the corner of the counter.

My eyes were glued to the floor as I walked, counting the tiles as I went, before a pair of boots came into view. My gaze shot upward, and an involuntary yelp left my mouth along with my right hand, which had shot up on instinct, letting a shock of magic that had apparently not been completely depleted leave my fingers.

A hissed curse left Kit's throat before I dropped my hand swiftly.

"Shit," I cursed myself, placing a hand over my chest, ensuring my heart wouldn't ricochet out of it with how rapidly it was beating. "What the fuck are you doing sneaking up on a witch, *dragon*?"

He had the gall to chuckle, "You're quick with your magic, princess. I'll give you that, but you could have waited to see who it was before using it on me." He rubbed the back of his neck while smirking, giving me a look like I was a lollipop for him to lick.

And even if I found him incredibly irritating at that moment, I wanted him to use that tongue on me, tracing my skin and delving between my thighs. But! That would certainly never happen, and could never happen. I had to stay far away from the man who was making my body react so strongly.

Switching my thinking quickly, I tsked, "I would have still used it on your ass, *dragon*."

"Kit." He muttered, making me pause.

"What?" I asked, confused, why he was repeating his name. I already knew it from earlier.

"That's my name, princess."

If there were a way to roll my eyes all the way inside my head so I wasn't looking at this smug bastard, I would have done it just then. He wanted me to use his name, but wouldn't use mine?

"And my name isn't princess, *dragon*." I sneered, knowing damn well he'd heard my name being spoken enough tonight.

Kit's face was a mask of amusement as he slowly perused my body from head to toe, stopping briefly on my exposed thighs, courtesy of a ripped sweater and my haste to get here from the blaring wards nagging at me.

Thanks, wards, you dicks.

"Who's Dom?" Kit's question threw me off, as I had forgotten about my earlier call to my cousin and the shit stirring I knew was brewing.

"Uh, why?" I set my tea on the table next to us, making sure to keep both hands free in case I needed to use them to poke his eyes out because fuck all, I knew my magic was for sure tapped the hellfire out now when I gave him a little jolt.

"You were speaking," He paused, considering his words. "Very forward with him. Is he a boyfriend? Husband?"

I snorted, loving how he couldn't contain his dragon's growl as he spoke. I knew that it would rile him up, not knowing who Dom was to me. Maybe I would play this game just a little longer to fuck with him since he'd upended my 'no mates for this bitch' motto.

"He's none of your business," I said, shrugging, ready to go home. I wanted desperately to strip out of my torn sweater and mourn over the fact that I didn't know if I could mend it, although I would ask Liv for help; she'd always had a knack for fixing shit with her magic.

My hand gripped the cup of tea again, but I was stopped when Kit's big, incredibly warm hand enclosed over mine.

The heat crawled along my arm and shot straight down to my pussy, making my lace panties dampen instantly. I cursed when I watched Kit's nostrils flare a moment later. A fierce glare crossed my face, "Let go, beast."

His eyes didn't leave mine, and neither did his hand when he pulled me into his scorching, thick body. "I said, let go!" I seethed, ready to dump the still wickedly hot liquid on his head. Not that it would do much since he was a dragon, and I certainly didn't want the scalding tea to splash on me. So, instead, I pinched the backside of his arm with my nails as hard as I could.

"Ow, what the fuck?" He angrily muttered, letting go and rubbing the back of his arm where I had dug in.

"You didn't want to listen to me, so I had to use force. You made me do it." I sneered. "Now, if you don't mind, kindly fuck all the way off and get out of my building so I can lock the doors and go home."

"You didn't have to pinch such a sensitive place, Viv." He said, still rubbing the spot and looking like a kicked puppy.

"Fuck for a dragon, you sure are a baby." I pointed out, brushing past him to open the front door. He followed like the puppy, er, dragon I knew he was.

Finally, he relented and left my shop, allowing me to lock the door. My car was parked on the side of the road, its engine shut off, unlike when I'd left it running earlier. Either someone was kind enough to turn it off, or I ran out of gas. However, it was likely the first option because I had just filled up earlier that day.

"I turned it off for you," Kit whispered into my ear, making me jump. It was almost like he could hear what I was thinking as I assessed my vehicle just now.

"You have got to stop doing that." I shrieked, swatting his arm before quickly walking away, leaving him standing at the edge of the sidewalk. Before I entered my car, I glanced over and saw that someone had already boarded up the door and window, but people were still coming and going. It was a relief, though, because I was done with this burnt marshmallow until the morning after I got some much-needed sleep.

Forgetting about Kit, I sat in my driver's seat, ready to close the door when his hand held onto it. I noticed his arm had scales that were starting to pop out of his skin, unlike earlier, when it had been as smooth as a baby's butt.

I pointed, "You should probably have that checked out." No idea why I had said it when I knew it was his dragon, likely trying to show off for its mate, but I was in no mood for his titivating.

Kit glanced over at the arm I pointed to and smirked, "No need, my dragon is readying himself for your acceptance. I have no control over the scales showing now that we've found our mate."

A laugh sputtered out of me, "In your dreams, fire boy. Have a shit night."

Then, without glancing at him, I wrenched my door out of his grasp as it slammed against the body of my car.

Without looking back and not belting myself in correctly, I took off, speeding all the way home while the pounding beat of metal music blasted through the speakers.

As I pulled into my long driveway out in the country, I let out a breathy chuckle. Put the car in park and slogged my way inside, all while downing the remainder of my now cold tea.

Soon, the concoction would kick in, and I could forget all about this hellish day and the fucking misery it had brought into my life.

Now, if I could only ensure a certain scaly big bastard would stay away, then I could forget all about mate problems and what that would bring if my parents ever found out.

Chapter Three

Kit

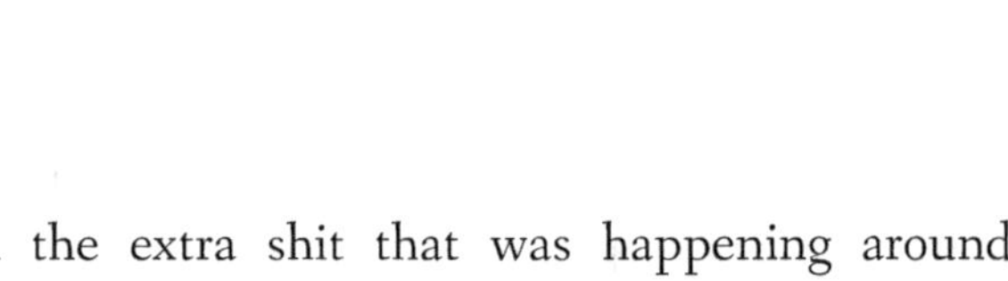

With all the extra shit that was happening around Mount Hellfire lately, I could hardly believe what my dragon was roaring to the skies.

Our mate.

That declaration alone left me staggering after hoisting her in my arms to get her to safety from the still-smoldering building, regardless of whether she had indeed snuffed out the flames or not. The smoke was still an issue and caused my hackles to raise, but when I smelt her after she knocked my helmet off with her incessant wriggling.

I knew.

She was mine, and I had been waiting for her for what felt like lifetimes.

She, however, did not feel the same. Which wasn't ideal, but I wouldn't let that deter me, especially with my dragon bouncing and clawing inside, urging me to chase after her. Find her, hoard her, and make her ours. And of course, get rid of whoever the hell Dom was. But that was something for another day.

In due time, my Neesha, my mate and eternal life partner, would walk into my arms and never escape.

Until then, I would remind her that whenever possible, I was here and not going anywhere.

I watched as she sped away from the building. My coworkers were busy ensuring the fire was indeed out as the investigation wrapped up. It was clear arson and was done by the ever-growing 'human only' group that had popped up when the Demon King, my best friend, revealed our world.

Thoughts of the dangerous group spurred me to shift before Viv's car was entirely out of view. I took to the skies and flew high enough that she wouldn't notice my ginormous golden form trailing behind, but close enough that I could still follow her home.

She lived just outside of the city in a quaint little cottage that was nestled in a clearing surrounded by pines and oaks. It gave her enough privacy without being too far away from the bustling and ever-growing city, now that Inhumans had begun showing up.

Mount Hellfire was considered the hub of supernatural activity and had been steadily growing these last few months. The need for new housing was rising, as many unmated males from several species expressed a desire to join humans and find mates.

That had been the ultimate goal for Finn, too, since his mate was human, and she was the reason that spurred the meshing of our worlds.

No one regretted our King's decision aside from certain humans that we had yet to confront.

Still flying above in the skies, my mate parked her vehicle and, without glancing up, stormed into her house, muttering under her breath.

"Stupid fucking dragon. How the hellfire did I get paired with such an arrogant scaly bastard?"

My dragon huffed his annoyance at her irritation with us, but I was amused that I had gotten under her skin so easily, and I vowed to dig my way in until she couldn't resist us any longer.

Calm, Vero. We'll win her over; have faith.

YES, BUT I WANT HER TO LIKE US, AND RIGHT NOW SHE DOESN'T; IT HURTS.

We will only suffer for a little while. Let me work magic on our witchling.

My dragon said no more. He was clearly sulking, and I didn't like it when he got in this state, but for now, there wasn't anything more I could do. Tomorrow, I would have to start my wooing and show Viv that fate had bound us for a reason, and that I was good enough for her to be with for centuries once we gave her our firebrand.

The fire branding was common among any paranormal that wielded fire magic or the flaming element, and it would prolong the lifespan of whoever their fated one was, especially if they had a shorter lifespan than them.

I knew a few Inhumans who possessed the fire trait, and they were all good males and would make good mates to whoever the fates had destined them with. My hope was now that we were all out in the open, several more pairings would happen, and it would open a whole new prospect to those who had remained mateless.

After circling Viv's home a few times and the surrounding area, Vero and I had determined that our mate was safe, so we headed back to Bound in Fire.

When we reached the building, the smoke had drifted into a haze along the darkened horizon. My crew was still lingering around the building. We usually stayed for hours after a fire to ensure that no embers remained and could be relit.

I could also see that Detective Rayth had remained at the scene. He was standing in the street, gazing at the building, clearly lost in thought.

Vero snickered, and without him even uttering a word, I knew already what he wanted to do with our unsuspecting ghostly friend.

We soared through the sky stealthily and then dove straight down. The speed at which we plummeted was increasing as our hearts raced. The adrenaline coursing through our veins intensified as the ground drew closer.

No one knew we were coming in hot, especially not Rayth, who still seemed to be consumed with his thoughts. The joy at scaring the shit out of him rocketed through the mutual harmony between Vero and me, and at the last possible minute, our wings shot out, slowing our descent exponentially.

We landed hard in the middle of the street directly behind Rayth. His shoulders scrunched up as his body jerked, then his skin flickered like it usually did when he was deep in his emotions.

Rayth slowly turned to face us; his expression was murderous. We knew he wouldn't do anything to us, so the look was amusing.

My dragon huffed out a trundle of smoke in laughter before I shifted to my human form.

When I transformed, I was left in my birthday suit, which I couldn't help; it happened every time I switched from dragon to human.

A few of the human bystanders shrieked when they saw me. My smile widened, and deranged laughter left my chest.

"Put some fucking pants on, by the Veil, you're going to give some poor old woman a heart attack with that swinging around!" Rayth's skin flickered rapidly with his emotions as he shielded his eyes before turning around. "Vizek, bring Kit a pair of shorts before he scares the entire city."

I chuckled, standing proudly as some of the spectators gawked. I wasn't ashamed of my nudity; frankly, it was normal for most shifters, but humans tended to shy from such displays.

Too bad my mate left already, and she didn't get to view this magnificent body.

Vero snuffed at my absurdity. He was the more logical one of us. Direct, but modest in the cultures and manners of Earth.

A flicker of cloth was thrown in my direction as Vizek unceremoniously threw shorts at me.

"He's right, put that shit away, man. No one wants to look at your one-eyed snake." My friend chided. It wasn't as if I wanted to come out of my shift butt-naked. It happened to every shifter, Vizek should know, considering he was one as well.

A sly grin formed as I thought of a clever retort, "You're just jealous of this monster cock, which is a one-eyed dragon, not a snake, mind you. Since, you know, I'm a dragon."

No one laughed; instead, both Rayth and Vizek gave me incredulous stares before they departed in different directions.

In that moment, I decided to leave my friend alone; I would catch up with the shifter later and join the detective.

"Wait up, Rayth." I huffed, acting as if it was treacherous to jog after him when, in actuality, I was just being lazy after my flight.

The detective blew out a breath and halted, "What do you want, Lieutenant?"

"Aw, come on now. I feel hurt that you don't use my name. I am more than my rank, *Detective.*" I goaded, loving the fact that, while I might have held a higher rank than most due to my association with the Demon King, I still preferred to act as if I were still a strapping detective myself.

He eyed me, his skin still flickering but in a more languid succession. "What is it you need, Atticus?"

Quirking an eyebrow, I would have loved to have known who in the Veil spilled the beans on my real name. "Now, who told you my full name? Was it Finn? It was, wasn't it? Did you know his full name is Finnick? He doesn't like it much, so feel free to do with that tidbit as you like. But, please just Kit."

Rayth uttered nothing, patiently or maybe impatiently waiting for me to answer the question he had asked twice now.

"Anyway, I just wanted to know what you found out about the fire? Anything other than how it started?"

He grunted, walking toward the blackened building, standing in the doorway of the bookstore, gazing in. "The only new lead we have, which isn't necessarily a lead, is that the glass on the bottle was etched with a symbol."

"Interesting, do you recognize this insignia?" I asked, curious as to what it could have been.

"No, but it's incredibly unremarkable and quite bland for the humans who have formed their human-only organization." He paused, sporadically disappearing and reappearing, lost in thought, before I cleared my throat, waiting for him to continue. "It's of an 'H' inside an 'O', like I said, completely mundane, which isn't a surprise."

Rayth's phone began ringing in his pocket, and an exasperated sigh left him before he answered, "What is it, Azazel?"

He listened just as intently as I did, because with my shifter ears, I could pick up most conversations and was a nosy bastard.

"You need to get to the Queen's parents. There's a knife and a note lodged in the front door. The King hasn't touched a thing." Azazel said, piquing my interest as the evening grew more mystifying.

"Be there shortly." Rayth hung up the phone, turning toward me. "I presume you heard everything?"

Nodding, I crossed my arms and glanced around at all the personnel who were still milling about. "What do you need me to do here?"

"Take a look around and see if you spot anything that I might have missed. A second pair of eyes is better than one. I must go. I'll be in touch in the morning." Rayth answered, and before I could respond any further, he blinked out of the area.

He was a great detective, and I hoped one day he would be made Captain, since the current Captain was often absent from his duties. Finn was made aware of that fact, and the sly vampire's whereabouts were being tracked, or they would be, but he slipped out of the hunter's grip often. We'd have to call in the best tracker in the Veil soon. Usually, that belonged to the gargoyles, as they could hide high in trees and had wings on their backs at all times, making tracking easier when you could see from a vantage point.

The current Captain's activities were drawing unwanted negative attention from human government officials who frequently stopped by the ISF.

That was a problem for another day, though, and one I wasn't willing to take on by myself, even if I was the next highest ranking member.

So, I did what Rayth had requested; I walked the inside of the bookstore, this time with different lenses than the ones I had used earlier as a firefighter.

Only, I didn't find anything aside from piles of ash that were likely books and charred bookshelves.

There was nothing further I could have looked for. The only solid lead we had was that this was the work of the human-only group, which had become quite bold. They nearly burned our King and Queen in the blaze they set.

Speaking of which, I needed to contact Finn and let him know I had found my mate and needed some time to woo her.

AH, YES, "WOO" IS THAT WHAT YOU'RE CALLING IT, ATTICUS?

My dragon taunted. Clearly unamused with how we handled our fiery little princess earlier.

Just you wait, Vero, she'll be crawling on her hands and knees, begging to put her mouth on us. And then, when that time comes, I get to say I told you so.

My dragon remained silent as he lay to rest in the recesses of my subconscious. The use of my full name didn't bother me when Vero spoke it because we had a harmonious existence together.

Mostly.

I wouldn't be me without him, and he wouldn't exist if I didn't. But, he was the part of myself that I had needed, especially now with a mate who would need the more logical and attentive side as well as my goofy, obsessive one. Vero would help push me in the right direction.

I *hoped.*

Making my way out of the bookstore, I jogged to the firetruck I had ridden in on, where my personal belongings had been stored. Mainly, what I needed was my phone, which, *ah, there it is,* was found stuffed in the pouch behind the passenger seat.

Pushing Finn's name on the phone, I called my King utterly besotted and giddy like a schoolgirl, er boy, at the thought of romancing Viv.

"What?" Finn's growly voice ruptured through the speakers.

"Well, hello to you, too, cupcake. Hey, I'm calling because I know a lot is going on with the whole 'you were almost burnt to a crisp' situation, along with our soon-to-be Queen, the lovely

Teagan. However, there are a few things I wanted to discuss with you. Firstly, I can look after the house and see if anyone suspicious shows up." I quickly said.

"Perfect, thanks, Kit. Yes, I would like you to keep an eye on her place and put up security cameras on her parents' property and yours to catch anyone coming after Teagan, and I leave the place." He paused briefly and then said. "She's coming home with me after we pack some of her things."

I snorted, knowing damn well that this was as good an excuse as any for him to get her to move in permanently. He had been trying to make it seem less sudden, but they had known each other since they were teens. There was nothing sudden about his approach.

To me, though, I was hoping things would progress rapidly with my mate. Although I wasn't sure it would be as easy as Finn's predicament.

"Perfect, I will get on that; however, I also need some time off to woo my female." He remained silent on the other line, which, to be fair, I hadn't given him enough time to speak anyway. "She's the coffee shop owner. Oh, I suppose you already know who that is since she's friends with Teags, but anyway, I'm getting off subject. I plan to visit her coffee shop every day until I convince her to give me a chance."

"Good—good. You have fun with your female. I'm sure she'll come around. And don't worry too much about being at home. You can review the footage and then report to me if you see anything suspicious." Finn said. I was aware of the urgency to ensure her safety. It was for the benefit of our people and humanity. So, I would take my duty as a Lieutenant very seriously.

"Cool—cool. Is Teagan doing okay?" I asked because I was genuinely concerned for our future Queen.

"Goodnight, Kit. I have a mate waiting below me to get off the phone." Finn said impatiently.

I stared at my device in shock that he would have answered my call with his mate beneath him, "Did you answer the phone balls deep in—"

Finn had clearly wanted to end the conversation and get back to business. Thank the Veil I didn't hear any moaning in the background; otherwise, my ears would have been traumatized and would need therapy.

I saw Teagan as a sister, just as I saw Finn as a brother, and picturing them in coitus was something I didn't want to imagine.

Instead, I daydreamed of my mate—my Viv and what I would do to her when I got her alone. Would she allow me to touch her? How would she like to be touched? I could be gentle, or I could be rough; spank her endlessly until her ripe ass was a pretty pink and then kiss the sting away. Maybe she'd like to be choked, to be controlled, and give her pleasure over to my hands.

Those thoughts were enticing, but would need to be tamped down until I got home, where I could stroke my cock to the memory of her beautiful, fiery hair, those stunning, different colored eyes, small, perky breasts, and an ample ass and thighs made for gripping and pushing into.

Chapter Four

Viv

"Why did it take my building nearly burning to the ground for you to come fly out and see me, Livvy?" I whined, even if my heart soared seeing my baby sister walk through the doors of my little coffee shop, *finally*, after months and months of video calls and texts.

She had moved across the country to be near our parents for a brief time after my falling out with the people who brought me into this world. And even though I knew it was to keep them off my back, as I was the 'high honor expected eldest daughter turned black sheep' of the family, it still hurt for her to be far.

We may have been Irish twins, spread out by ten months, but the universe could suck a big fat cock because the connection we shared was like we had grown together in our mother's womb.

Nothing and no one could stop the love and protectiveness we both shared for one another. I would cut a bitch if they so much as touched a single strand on my baby sister's head, and I knew she'd do the same for me.

"Hey, Viv. Sorry, I know, trust me, I would have come sooner, but you know, Dad, he keeps me busy with the extra shit he likes to do for the Coven. If someone doesn't placate him, he'd be on the first flight here, convincing you to move back in and do your 'eldest daughter' duties." She explained, "So I make sure to appease his controlling tendencies so he doesn't bother you, and you know that you are forever grateful I do such a thing." She pointed out.

Liv gently swept a lock of my bright red hair behind my ear. I was speechless with gratitude, and she knew it without me needing to say a word. Giving me a cheerful, vivacious grin as she took in the Molten Java, tapping her fingers against her thigh.

"So, are you going to make me a cup of Jo before we get to work? That flight kicked my ass, and I could use a pick-me-up."

It was as if she had read my mind, knowing my magic was rejuvenating but itching to pour into her drink, giving her a boost of what I did best.

My witchy powers had grown throughout our younger years, and while my father had hoped I would gain a 'more useful' skill, nothing else lingered further than my knack for liquids, which he had taken advantage of years ago with disdain.

The magic I was born with had definitely come in handy last night, when I was able to mimic water without the damage it would have caused to put out the fire.

If the fire department had its way, shit would have been soaked. Not that they didn't need any help with that when I thought back to the one who definitely made my panties drip.

No, bad girl Viv. He whose name shall not be spoken, shall also not be thought of.

It was bad enough my dormant libido suddenly roared like a fucking tsunami thinking about that man, who was my Veiled fated mate. She sure was a funny bitch for throwing him at me now when I had sworn off falling in love with men. She could have sent me a woman, and I would have happily taken her over the smoke-filled, cinnamon scent of the firefighter dragon shifter.

And the swearing off of men *mostly* all came down to one man in particular, who haunted my life no matter how far I moved myself or how much I ignored his calls.

Horace Woodward, my father, was a piece of work. He despised how I spent my free time and how I used my magic. He wanted me to return to being a bartender in the small, dingy bar he oversaw and used as an interrogation center for the Coven. His approach to gathering information was cruel, as the person he extracted the data from was an unwilling participant.

No matter, I was fortunate to have a sister who kept him off my back, especially since he wanted to use me to merge our family with another. That was only because he couldn't utilize me for my water magic in his sick twisted ways like he had when I was younger underneath that bar in what I called his 'chamber'.

"Don't burn the milk, Viv," Liv shouted, rousing me from the dream-like trance I had put myself in whenever I had thought about our sadistic father.

"Shit! Sorry, Livvy!" I said, pulling the milk down from the frother and setting the heated metal pitcher on the counter. With a damp cloth, I cleaned the steamer wand, then dispensed ground espresso beans into the portafilter and tamped them down. Once I had the grounds securely back into the machine, I pressed a button to dispense the single shot, then poured it into a cup and added heated milk, topping it off with a smooth, heart-shaped froth.

Every little bit of liquid that went into the cup as I poured took a little bit of my magic with it, as I dashed luck, love, and healing to my sister in preparation for everything she would do that morning.

When I was finished, I handed over the now enchanted coffee and admired my sister's blissful smile as the magic exploded her senses.

"Goddess, I love you." She said, smirking over the lid. "Thank the Veil you inherited the gift to manipulate my coffee because I am already roaring to go. You are truly astonishing."

I waved her away, "Ah, shucks, you know how to butter me up. There's more of that go-go juice whenever you want it while you're here. You have no idea how much this means to Teags and me that you're helping."

Liv took another sip, sighed, and then asked, "Where is Teags?"

"She's still sleeping. I messaged Finn and told him to let her sleep as long as she needs it. They've both been through so much. We need to speak with the detective and insurance adjuster anyway before we can do anything." I paused to glance at the time on my phone. "Speaking of, they should be here any moment."

"Already here," Rayth grumbled from the front of the store, eliciting an unsavory screech to leave my lips.

I clasped a hand over my chest, "Hellfire, you can't sneak up on a witch like that, Detective. What would have happened if I had used my magic on you in defense?"

He disappeared only to reappear next to the counter, "Move?" He deadpanned.

Detective Rayth sure wasn't one for theatrics or for many words, for that matter, but I had to admire that he was very punctual.

The front door opened, alerting us to the chimes, and we realized the adjuster had also miraculously arrived nearly at the same time as the Detective. Luckily for him, he had used the front door to announce his arrival, unlike the detective. "Knock, Knock."

"Over here," I called out, rounding the counter to greet the insurance company representative who had arrived. "Welcome, I'm Vivienne, but you can call me Viv."

"Nice to meet you, I'm Greg, the Inhuman Financial Resolution and Insurance Department sent me over as soon as I arrived at the office, so I haven't been able to view the files of complaint yet." He said, shuffling through his backpack clumsily.

"Let me take you over to the main event, and we can go from there. Coffee?" I asked, already grabbing another cup to butter up the man who would determine the worth of the damages.

We only needed enough to cover the cost of the lost books, and I wanted to set aside a few months' worth of mortgage payments to give Teags more time to order a new shipment and reset the shelves. Hopefully, in that amount of time, her stalker and our arsonist would be caught, and things could go back to normal, or as normal as we could, with Inhumans walking around Mount Hellfire now out in the open.

Greg sipped on the black coffee I had poured while walking through Bound in Fire. A giggle left my throat as I thought about how it was on fire the night before, and it was an apt name Teags had picked out.

The adjuster quirked an eyebrow before moving onto the outside. I could tell he was nearly finished as I followed him around.

"So, my supervisor said you have a proposition for all the damage." He said, ending the silence aside from the scrapes of our shoes on pavement and the clicking and clacking of his pen as he pushed the popper in and out.

I gripped the back of my neck as the sound sent me into a whole other orbit, but I needed to remain calm and collected. Once he left, I could lose my shit. I hated dealing with mundane adulting, and right now, having to negotiate anything was awful and just reminded me of my father.

"With my sister's abilities and my magic to help boost her, we can repair everything in the building. The only thing she can't mend are the books that were lost along with the time it's going to take to re-order and restock the shelves, leaving the business closed for longer than we hoped." We walked back into the store, where he had left his backpack in safekeeping behind the counter.

Even though I had decided to remain closed for the majority of the day, it never hurt to be cautious, considering all things.

"Okay, that sounds like a fantastic idea. So what are you expecting in compensation? You do have a deductible of," He flipped a few pages before he found that information. "Looks like it's $1,500 and you have great coverage."

"Yes, so for the books, I'm thinking enough to cover what we had already ordered in the first place, Teagan has those receipts in her office, which were untouched, and then at least four months of mortgage, electric, water, and sewer payments."

Greg jotted a few things down while Liv and Rayth sat near the fireplace. They had stayed behind to give us space to go over the logistics and the boring shit.

When he was finished, he spoke, "I'll have to get this approved, but I shouldn't see why that wouldn't work. It's less than I expected you to ask, given the cost of completely gutting, remodeling, and bringing in new furniture and bookshelves, along with the existing books. We'll help cover all other expenses for the four months you requested while the arson investigation and hopeful arrest take place."

Receiving this news was such a relief, and I smiled back at the insurance adjuster. "Thank you so much, you have no idea how much that will help." I turned, heading back behind the counter to grab him another cup of coffee before he could leave. I wouldn't take no for an answer; he had been extremely helpful in making this process go smoothly, unlike normal human adjusters, who made you go through extreme hoops, from what I was told. "Here, take this to go. I'm sure you have a long day ahead of you."

He took the cup, nodded, and then packed up his bag. "That's great, thanks. You'll hear from us in a few days or so. Have a good one, Ms. Woodward."

Liv stood from the table and smiled brightly, "So? Good news, I suppose? Since you're not hurling the cup of coffee at him, that is."

I smacked her arm lightly, "Hush, you, I wouldn't ever throw a good cup of coffee at anyone. Unless you're a cocky dragon shifter that is." I mumbled the last part, but Liv caught on when her head snapped up.

"What's this about a cocky dragon shifter?" She asked, suddenly curious when my cheeks heated, making me walk away to hide from her.

However, it was of no use as she followed.

"Vivienne Lynn Woodward. You answer me right this second. No one has ever been able to turn you three different shades of pink." Liv gripped my arm when I wouldn't stop walking toward the back. "Please, Vivvy, tell me about him."

Her eyes turned pleading as she stuck out the bottom of her lip.

I groaned, knowing I wouldn't be able to keep this secret from her, but first I had to swear her to secrecy.

"I'll tell you about him, but you need to promise that this doesn't get back to mom, and especially not to dad. The last thing I need is for him to haul ass and kidnap me just so he gets his way, even if I wouldn't give in regardless of the situation." I said, waiting for her assurance.

She gripped my hand, squeezing while she spoke, "I promise on the Moon Goddess, may she guide us through our trials and tribulations and take us on the correct path to our true futures."

Blowing out a breath, I knew her oath was solid and unbreakable, especially when she swore to the Moon Goddess we communed with.

"The dragon shifter I mumbled about is one of the firefighters who were here last night."

"Okay, I'm definitely liking where this is going—dragon shifter, check; firefighter, check; what else?" Liv ticked off each point on her fingers, making a list of pros, but what she didn't know was what I told her next.

"Yes, well, all those things definitely rev my dry engine up; however, I can't get involved with him. You already know I swore off any kind of commitment." I reminded her of the pact I made after leaving Kash behind with my parents and ending things with him years ago, once I found out what my father had conjured up behind my back, that is. I still wasn't sure if Kash had known or not, but I had an inkling, considering my father and his were chummy.

She waved her hands at me, "Boo, you and I both know that's no fun, and it's been years since all that went down. You have to let go and live a bit, if you happen to fall for the guy, well, then it takes care of the little problem with mom and dad and everything, Kash."

"I don't think anything would 'take care' of that mess." I left Liv's side and started making a tea for myself out of habit whenever I got too jittery. "Well, it is worse than anything I could have conjured up. The Moon Goddess sure has a fuckery sense of humor because that gorgeous, sexually desirable, dripping with danger, smells like he could fuck up your whole world and then put it back together, man. Is my mate."

It was an imaginary record scratch when Liv froze, stared at me, slack-jawed but sputtering, "Oh—shit."

"Yeah, tell me about it." I finished putting together my calming tea (not the one that would put me to sleep) and walked around the counter toward the bookstore, where Rayth was waiting for us. "We'll finish this convo later, kay? And don't say a word to Teags, she has no idea, yet."

Liv nodded, grabbed her own drink, which she was nursing, and followed.

Rayth smiled tentatively when he saw us enter, "Everything alright?" He asked, jotting something down in his notepad before putting it away.

"Peachy keen, Detective. So, you've stuck around after all that," I waved behind me, indicating I meant with the insurance guy. "I'm sure there's a reason you're still here?"

He nodded, body flickering, which I presumed was some kind of emotional response. Once he started speaking, I knew I was right. "Look, I don't want to alarm you ladies, but with your affiliation with Teagan, our soon-to-be queen and the king, it's pertinent that you know that there have been some significant threats against the supernatural community."

I shrugged, "I figured, I mean, hello." My arm swung around, reminding him that just last night my building had been on fire. "All of this gives me a big neon sign of, 'watch your witchy bitch asses.'"

Rayth didn't smile or give any kind of emotion as I sat there giggling to myself.

Raising my hands, I continued, "Okay, not funny, but just a teensy weensy bit. But I appreciate the concern, Detective. I'm already going to be placing some precautions after getting the place cleaned up."

Liv stood silently next to me, bobbing her head in agreement, as she knew her job was temporary. After I shared my plans, I hoped she would stay longer than just a few days.

"I plan to put new wards up over the one already in place that would make anyone with malicious intentions unable to enter the establishment or property. That means both the coffee shop and the bookstore. It's the only fix I can make to keep Teags, any paranormals that come in, and myself safe."

Liv turned to me, her eyes wide with shock, "Were you going to tell me about this little plan or just have a go at it by yourself? You already know how much magic needs to be expelled to do such a ward!"

I knew all too well that my first ward was a solo experience, and it took me a week to recover from the dizziness before the room stopped spinning.

Blowing out a raspberry breath, I turned my attention toward her, "I was going to bring it up after Rayth left, but if you don't have anything going on, maybe you could join Dom and me?"

"Have you asked Dom yet?" She questioned, and the answer was simple: I hadn't.

"No, I was going to do that today, whenever the hellfire he decides to get his ass out of bed."

"Uh, huh—right. Well, you and I both know that kind of ward will take weeks to be fully impenetrable. I have to go back home in a few days, but I can help at least get it started." Liv chewed on her fingernail without breaking it, contemplating and tapping her toe.

Rayth watched our exchange with interest, even though he was a man of few words.

"Well, I just wanted to ensure you both knew the potential dangers. Anything suspicious, give me a call." He pulled a wallet out of his pocket and handed me his card. "My direct line is on the front, and if I can't be reached, on the back is Azazel's number. He'll get in touch with someone if I'm unavailable."

Placing the card in my back pocket, I smiled, "Thanks, Detective. If you need a cup of Jo before you head out, go ahead and serve yourself. I'm gonna stick here and go over a few things with my sister."

He shook his head, "No thanks, I have somewhere I need to be. Have a good rest of your day, ladies."

And then, as if it was nothing, he disappeared. That was a handy ability; he didn't even need to use the front door or have a gas-guzzling vehicle to travel from place to place.

Liv stood, glancing around at the bookstore's damage; it was charred, with remnants everywhere. The bookshelves were impeccable, aside from being blackened and filled with dusty remnants of the books that had occupied them.

All of Teagan's hard work had literally lit up in flames, and my heart ached thinking that if she didn't have an awesome friend as a witch, how long it would take to mend everything to the way it had been.

And that brought me back to last night, after I had extinguished everything, the abrupt tilting of my world. Quite literally and figuratively, with Kit's grip that had been tight across the backs of my thighs. Rekindling the Sahara into the Nile River with a single glance at his impeccably handsome, crisply lined jaw. The way he felt when my body slid down the front of his uniform, and the way he smelt of fire, wood, and cinnamon rolled into a delectable, muscularly man-shaped form.

"You're deep in thought over there," Liv called out, and thank goodness for that because I was diving into no-no territory and that needed its own caution tape with signs pointing and stating 'beware, will cause a surge of panty melting fuckery.'

"Yeah, sorry—just thinking," I replied like a tweedle dumb.

Liv chuckled, "I figured that's what you were doing, since you had this dreamy stare. Lost in thought about a certain hunky firefighter?"

She could always read me best, and at times it was a gift, while at others it was a blasted curse.

"Maybe," I drawled out. "I'll figure my shit out eventually," I said, waving my hand at her. "But, for today, I just want to see Teagan, spend time with you, and get this place back in order, and then open up the coffee shop to keep my mind busy."

Liv nodded, taking off her sweatshirt and placing it, along with her mini backpack, down near the partition.

And just like that, she started her low humming to get a feel for all the damage that had been caused before the real work would begin.

Chapter Five

Viv

Teagan had left hours ago, after Liv and I worked on repairing everything in the store.

Things were back to order, for the most part, aside from the burnt, crispy books, which couldn't be fixed.

My baby sister was incredible, and anytime she used her magic, it left me in awe. She could take anything that had been destroyed and essentially repair it as if nothing had ever happened. It was a thing of beauty, especially when the bookstore went from drab, blackened soot to sparkling, spanking new as it had been before.

I couldn't help but have a big sister proud moment when everything returned to the way it was, aside from the books, of course.

Once Teags left with Finn, I set off to secure the bookstore until the new order of merchandise came in, which wouldn't be for a while. But, right now, Liv needed more go-go juice as the bags underneath her eyes deepened, while her golden red hair, a few shades lighter than mine, looked limp and in need of a serious wash.

"Here, Livvy, you did amazing today," I said, sliding the tea over to her. I had put in an extra energizing boost, watching her sway as she reached for the cup.

She smiled weakly, "Thanks, Vivvy. I love you, but your king mattress in the guest room is calling my name. I'm so zonked, I'm just going to soak in a hot bath and turtle crawl my way to bed."

"Okay, I'm going to stay until close, just make sure that things are taken care of. Don't need my workers coming in in the morning and seeing nothing has been prepped."

Every night, whether I had done so or another employee had, we ensured that the first shift opening went smoothly, as it was usually the busiest.

That meant the chai tea was prepared with the bag of spices as it steeped overnight, while tea bags were restocked in their respective metal containers. And any beans that needed to be roasted were ready in bins next to the roaster.

"Night, sis, see you in the morning before I head out again," Liv said, grabbing her bag and the tea I had made her.

I went to the back rooms while she exited, and the little chime above the door dinged, telling me she had left.

Letting out a heavy breath, I could finally find some semblance of a break from it all. The fire, the magic, the heaviness surrounding Mount Hellfire since Finn had revealed we were real, and some of us were hiding in plain sight.

I went and scrubbed the remaining dishes from the day before.

The front door's chime, delicate little twinkles clanged together, telling me someone had entered. Either Liv had forgotten something, or a patron was looking for a caffeine fix, which, even though we had closed for the day, I would absolutely ensure they got.

Rounding the doorway to the counter with my customer

service smile plastered onto my face, I was ready to greet the patron or ensure my sister didn't know the mental drain of the last 24 hours had on me.

But when I saw the person standing in my store, I stopped in my tracks.

It wasn't my sister.

It was Kit.

And when his eyes found mine, they burned a deep gold as he took in my disheveled hair, a mischievous grin spread on those delicious lips.

I wasn't trying to impress anyone, but for a fraction of time, I had wished I did something more with my appearance.

But then I shook myself out of that thought because I couldn't and shouldn't want this man, this beast.

He stood near the counter, his hands in those tight front pockets, one hip leaning against the edge. He looked like a delicious ooey gooey sticky lollipop that I wanted to drag into my mouth, to suck and lick until he exploded his goodness across my tongue.

Fuck, this was bad. I can't even keep him out of my mind for one second!

I was entirely out of my marbles. Kit needed to leave and stat before I gave in to my dry spell upheaval and slacked my lust with his dick.

"We're closed for the day. You need to leave." I went to turn back and escape those knowing eyes when he opened his mouth.

"I came by to make sure you were alright after last night," Kit said, oblivious to the fact that I wanted him gone.

Or maybe he knew and was just ignoring my rudeness, a concept that was new to me.

"I'm just peachy. Now you can go." Pointing toward the front door didn't do anything when Kit rounded the corner of my counter. "Hey! You can't come back here. Employees only, bud."

He wasn't listening; I wasn't sure anything I said would make him see reason as his arm looped around my back. I should have stopped him, I really should have, but instead I leaned into his touch as his fingers brushed along my cheek.

His whispers were like wings of a butterfly, effortless and enchanting.

"Don't you see, Neesha, I can't leave you alone. Not after finding you and knowing that you complete me and my dragon. We long for your surrender." His face lowered to mine, tilting to the side so he could continue his lyrical assault in my ear. "Give in, my mate, let me show you how good I can be."

Oh, how I wanted to, desperately. However, I would surrender to no man. Not my father. Not my ex and certainly not for him.

I was the one who made men surrender and then broke them where they stood.

I pushed away from him, or tried. His grip only tightened, and a growl left his throat as his very visible, very unnecessarily attractive Adam's apple bobbed. And goddess damn it all to the Veil, did that sound do absolutely everything to my pussy.

Whimpering, I crossed my legs to lessen the throbbing ache that began just from the sound that came out of his body. But nothing was helping, and I desperately wanted to rub myself on his thigh, like a fucking heathen, anything to relieve the torture I was going through.

And it was just about to happen, too, except the bell above the door chimed and in walked my cousin, Dom.

"Fucking hell, Viv, I have had a day. I need a pick me up with your go-go juice pow—er." Dom was peering around the furthest end of the counter, his brows lifted as he took in the proximity of my unwanted guest. "Am I interrupting something?"

His hand waved back and forth, while he stayed rooted, unsure if he should indeed disrupt what would have been a break in my recent sexless life.

"Don't worry about it, Kit was just leaving." I gazed up into his eyes, which had darkened. He was likely pissed about being interrupted, but I was relieved. "Weren't you?" I asked Kit. It was a challenging question that resonated with a 'you better bud.'

"Actually, I was going to ensure you made it home safely, considering everything that happened last night." Kit still hadn't moved away, and it only grated on my nerves further. He was dangerous, not only to my libido but also to my sanity.

"I'm a big girl, I can handle driving home. And anyway, I have someone else here now that I trust impeccably." I said, smugly, while ducking under the arm he had extended over my head against the wall.

Dom moved cautiously toward me as I went to work, bringing out the freshly cleaned equipment.

"What do you want to drink tonight?" I had aimed the question at Dom, but Kit answered.

"I'll take your favorite."

I snorted, clinking the pitcher on the counter. "I wasn't asking you."

Kit shrugged and sidled closer, watching what I was doing like he was fascinated with anything regarding me.

Dom moved in on the other side, keeping his eyes fixated on Kit, trying to gauge if he was a threat. "I'll just take a caramel latte, make it a triple shot."

Glancing over at Dom, I raised my brow. "For what? It's like ten o'clock."

His left shoulder lifted briefly. "Your dad has some late-night things I have been tasked with doing."

That had my attention. My father was hundreds of miles away from Mount Hellfire, and I prayed to the goddess that it stay that way. However, he still had businesses in the city from when he had moved us here when I was in my teens, and he was always asking Dom to do one thing or another.

I didn't want him to get sucked into the bullshit my father tried to con me into doing.

"Is this something—" I peered over at Kit, who was still so close and so attentive to what my hands were doing with the milk and frother. "Legal?"

"No idea, Vivvy. He said he'd call me later."

Kit perked up at the nickname he used and narrowed his eyes, standing up straighter. His dragon must have insisted he assert his dominance over my cousin, which, if this kept up, would become exhausting.

"What's your name again?" Kit asked.

Uh oh.

The conversation from last night quickly replayed in my mind with Dom, and I inwardly winced, forgetting to warn my cousin about the overbearing dragon shifter who was still sniffing around.

Dom, being the nice guy he was, smacked the side of his head like he had forgotten his manners.

It wasn't his manners I was worried about, though.

"Sorry about that, man. I'm Dom, you are?" He held out his hand, waiting for Kit to shake it, but all I could feel was the shift in the room.

Before I could stop his momentum, Kit was on Dom. He shoved him clear across the floor, making Dom slam into the side of my roaster.

"Kit, stop it right now," I yelled, quickly setting down the heated milk. It was no use, though; he continued to advance on my cousin. Kit was fast, and I couldn't stop him in time.

A screech left my throat when he gripped Dom's neck and started squeezing.

I ran forward, gripping Kit's arm, trying to tug him off.

"Stop, Kit, you'll kill him!"

"He's the bastard who dared touch what's mine."

Not this again. I wasn't his, and if he killed my cousin, I most definitely wouldn't be. *Was I really thinking there was a possibility in the future? Did I even want that? No, I need to refocus; saving Dom was my priority right now.*

"You big dumb idiot, he's my cousin!"

Dom nodded the best he could, and his choked response came next, "I'm. Her. Family."

That seemed to have shaken the red haze of violence from not only Kit but his dragon as well when he suddenly let Dom go as he crumpled to the ground.

I was on my knees instantly, checking over his neck. The crimson marks of Kit's sized hands were already bruising. I would have to add a bit of healing to his drink, along with boosting his energy.

Glaring up at Kit, he stood tall, unmoving, and unremorseful.

"What the hell was that? Do you just go around trying to kill people all willy-nilly?" My heart was hammering frantically inside, the pulsating beat drumming in my ears as I tried catching my breath.

"You think I wanted to do that? My dragon demanded retribution against anyone who touched our mate, and I had to listen to his call."

Dom gasped for a different reason than trying to catch his breath from being strangled.

I brought my palm to my face, smacking my forehead

lightly. "Really great—nice. Let's just scream to the whole world, I'm your mate when you know I don't want anything to do with you."

"You say that now, Neesha, but you'll change your mind. You just need to open yourself up and let me in. I can take care of you and treat you right." He pleaded, albeit aggressively.

I scoffed, "And I've already told you I don't want a mate. Period. Why do you think I was pretending like Dom was someone I was romantically involved with?"

Kit turned, and the crimson haze of anger flickered in his eyes once again. "You shouldn't play with a dragon and come between him and claiming his mate. Even if the person coming between them is the mate herself."

"Yeah, yeah, yeah. Blah, blah, blah." I said, gesturing with my hand like it was talking for me.

Dom hissed when I prodded a particularly sore spot on his neck. "Sorry," I muttered.

He waved me off, "I need to get going, I'll let the two of you sort shit out without my presence."

"That would be wise." Kit snarled.

I snapped my finger at him, "No. Bad dragon, you don't get to talk to him with that tone. Only I can."

That shut him up.

Turning back to Dom, I glared. "If you tell a fucking soul, I'll cut your tongue out myself. I need to figure some shit out, and I don't need word getting back to my father. Got it?"

He nodded, "My lips are sealed, Vivvy." He moved his fingers like he was locking his mouth shut to show me he meant what he said.

After adding healing to Dom's drink on top of the triple-shot energy booster, he turned to leave out the front but stopped at my words.

"Don't think I forgot about you ditching Liv and me this morning, by the way."

"I hear you, Viv. You can yell at me tomorrow after I've got some sleep." Dom sipped his coffee, humming. "You sure do know how to make a fixer-upper drink. I'm already feeling less achy."

His gaze lingered over Kit before he left.

I went to lock the door but paused, gesturing, "You can leave now. I have to clean up and get my duties done for the morning shift."

Kit approached slowly. The anger had faded from his eyes, and I caught a glimpse of the wounded dragon that lurked beneath the surface. It momentarily made me ache to comfort him, but the memory of him attacking Dom resurfaced.

"Let me stay until you're done."

This could have been a colossal mistake I was about to make, but I couldn't help my mind screaming at me to listen to him, to give him a chance at redemption for the small upheaval he caused tonight.

Chapter Six
Kit

My mate was trying to push me out the door, and I wasn't going anywhere. Her safety was my priority, my dragon demanded we hoard her, protect her, and mate her senseless so she forgets this silly notion that we aren't hers and that she isn't ours.

"I mean it, Kit, you need to leave. I can't have you in my bubble. You or your dragon, who keeps peering out by the way."

My head tilted, a question formed on my lips, but she answered before I could utter a word.

"When he's peeking, your eyes turn a golden shade. It comes and goes. More so prominent when you're being a dick." Viv returned to cleaning the espresso machine after making Dom his drink.

I didn't dare ask her to make me one. The edges of exhaustion were taking hold, and I knew she still needed to drive home.

An idea formed. I could convince her to come to my place.

It would be so much easier to woo her in our space than

anywhere else. But, then again, the safety of her home might make her more open to us.

Another idea, stacked on the first, clicked into my mind. I just needed to voice it and see where things led.

"Look, I know we got off on a rocky start, but I want to talk. I think we both need to speak about this and get to know one another better." For someone confident most of the time, this scared the shit out of me. The idea that she was our mate and could completely obliterate our bond was unsettling.

She was a witch after all, and anything was possible. I wasn't aware of her strengths or weaknesses. And I wanted to know it all, everything that made her tick. What I needed to protect her from, and the parts where I could help elevate who she was.

Viv rolled her eyes, and I couldn't help but be mesmerized by the difference between them. One was green, like that of an aloe plant, and the other was brown like a warm honey stick. They captured my attention and offered solace from my aching heart, if only she'd used them the way I knew she could, and free me from this cycling unknown territory.

"Yeah, fat chance, Romeo. I've got better things to do this evening than sit around and look deep into each other's souls, pouring our hearts out." Her voice took on a mocking tone; she certainly wasn't finished with her rant either. "That's not me and has never been me. I know myself and don't need anyone else sniffing around waiting to discover who I am."

Sighing, I was beginning to understand that it would take a considerable amount of effort to get her to relax and let her guard down.

I was absolutely up for the challenge, too. Vero was as well when his grumbled agreement echoed in my mind.

Viv had been facing away from us, and then she suddenly turned, "Did you just purr?"

It could have happened. Although usually anything inside my mind from Vero stayed that way. Did I inadvertently make a sound?

"It was Vero, my dragon. Don't mind him, he's just as anxious as I am to get to know you."

Our mate was making her way around the coffee shop, shutting off lights and straightening pillows as she moved to the front. I followed closely behind, not wanting to be too far from her.

"Well, you should probably let him know I'm not interested and will never be." Viv flicked the last of the lights and exited the building with me right behind her.

"Viv," My hand lightly gripped her arm as I gazed upon her. "Come to my place, you're tired, and I know that driving while exhausted is the same as driving intoxicated."

She snorted at the suggestion, "No way, dragon, I'm not coming to your place. I'm going home where I can unwind."

"Then, let me drive you, and I can stay. I'll behave and sleep on the couch."

Viv pulled her arm, and I let her go. Her head tilted back, and a booming laugh echoed in the silent night sky.

"You're definitely not coming to my place. I don't need your ass knowing where the hellfire I live. You'd for sure stalk me."

This was true because I'd wait until she left and take to the skies. Making sure that when I did achieve the height in my ascent, she wouldn't be able to spot me, even though I already knew where she lived.

Viv continued to laugh as she rounded her car, getting in, cranking the music to an unacceptable level that made my dragon's ears ache, and sped away from the curb while her tires squealed their protest.

She was headed in the direction of the main highway outside Hellfire. I stood watching her car get further and further away because, although she didn't take me up on either of my offers, I had a mate to protect.

At the stop sign, Viv turned right, and when her vehicle was finally out of sight, I shifted in the middle of the street.

A horn blared, catching my attention. I glanced over to see an angry older man flinging his arms into the air and pointing. When I still hadn't moved quickly enough for him, he started blasting his horn yet again.

I had no time for this.

Every second I spent here, analyzing this angry human, the further my mate traveled from me.

So I took off, and Vero was in control the moment our feet left the asphalt as he soared into the black starlight-speckled sky.

His excitement was evident in the way he beat his wings against the invisible field of wind as he barrel-rolled, drawing them in, bringing them into his body, and then snapping them back out to level himself.

On the invisible threads of the wind, we picked up our mate's scent easily enough.

We flew past the Hellfire festival center and park, closing in on the bright neon red lights of our mate's tail end as she kept driving in the darkness, outside of the city limits.

Trees began to deepen, clustering closer together, making it more challenging to spot Viv's car, but I could still smell her in the air, still feel her anger and defiance linger between the faint bond that had started the moment our eyes met.

Soon enough, she turned onto a gravel driveway, the crunch beneath her tires the only sounds before she stopped and turned off the engine.

I spun in circles in the sky as I waited for her to exit so I could swoop down and make my presence known.

She had no idea I was above her, watching, keeping guard, and waiting for the chance to be near her again.

This time, my dragon was eager to meet her. Not just flickers here and there in my eyes, but on full display.

SHE TAKES TOO LONG TO EXIT HER METAL CONTRAPTION.

It's called a car, Vero. And who knows what she's doing in there. We'll wait for her until she's ready. And then you can show off and impress our mate.

He snickered in my head, pleased with this suggestion. I knew, and he knew, that we would take her by surprise when we dropped from the sky into the open area of her lawn next to the house.

It was Vero's favorite approach when taking someone by surprise. It also gave me a good chuckle when we'd scare the shit out of the person.

My mate was no different; I wanted her reactions. All of them, including her fiery hot temper that made my blood zing and cock harden.

Viv's house was nestled in an open section of the ever-crowded trees that took up space to make up Mount Hellfire's surrounding forests.

No one knew exactly who or what resided in the vast span of land, but Finn, the Demon King, ensured that no one was allowed to touch that part of the city. He was as much in control of these lands as he was in the Veil. And of course, the human government bent over backward to ensure he was happy and had anything he asked for.

They sought information and an advantage, but Finn, being more intelligent, outsmarted them. He only gave them enough to placate and slake their lustful violence of war and destruction against other countries.

The click and screech of a car door opening brought me out

of my diplomatic thoughts and back to the woman who held everything in the palm of her fiery hand.

Viv slammed the door and sighed, dangling her keys as she leisurely strolled to her porch steps.

She was nearly stepping onto the first one when Vero suddenly dipped from the sky like a bullet ricocheting out of a gun.

We landed in the grass and gravel of her driveway with a loud vibrating thud.

Our mate's scream penetrated the soundless property as her keys flung in our direction. Those small, dainty pieces were like a feather grazing our scales as she hit us in the chest.

Vero huffed a chuckle, taking a claw and dragging the clanging metal closer to us.

We both knew she hadn't unlocked the door, and these were her only solace in entering her home.

She turned toward us, her face crimson, jaw tightening as she flexed her clenched fist.

"What the actual fuck!" She seethed, "You nearly gave me a fucking heart attack, you overgrown behemoth."

I didn't shift yet; instead, we opted for remaining in our beastly form to see how truly remarkable and brave our mate really was.

Did she know it was me behind the dragon? She had to. No one else would dare come near her.

She continued to glare at us. Vero didn't like it, but I calmed him down, explaining that this was part of the plan to get her to let us in.

He gripped the keys more tightly against our body.

Viv narrowed her eyes at our shifting.

"You going to shift? Or should I continue this one-sided conversation? Because it's apparent you've come here for a reason. Other than, of course, to figure out where I live." She paused, tapping her finger on her chin, thinking, before something clicked. "You followed me to make sure I made it home safe, didn't you?"

I continued to remain silent. While that was true in part, I had a more selfish reason. I wanted to be near her, spend more time with her. Make her see reason that being our mate was essential not only for our souls but for hers, too.

After a while, she'd start to feel that aching hollow loneliness and missing piece that I was already beginning to feel.

It was inevitable, and I only wanted to ensure she didn't suffer the emotional numbness that came when mates refused to complete a bond.

Our mate threw her hands in the air, an agitated groan left her enticing lips, and all our senses were attuned to her while she lowered those arms and placed her hands on those even more delectable hips.

I wanted her. Wanted to claim her and keep her from leaving our side.

"You're such a dick, you know that?" She scoffed, her eyes hadn't left mine, and with her keys still clutched in our claw, we took a step toward our mate.

Viv narrowed her eyes at the movement, "Uh—no. You can stop right there, fire boy. Don't come any closer until you've shifted back to a human."

We didn't want to yet, but as we watched her gaze roam around the yard, we knew what she was looking for and what we still held.

She turned around, bending over while her light from her phone illuminated the grass as she searched for the keys that were nowhere but with us. It was an alluring sight that I longed to experience in my human form.

"Where the fuck did I fling my keys?" She muttered under her breath.

And while her back was to me, I quickly shifted.

Vero willingly let go of his form so I could emerge and encourage Viv to let us in for the night. His excitement only made my cock harden at the thought of getting our pretty little mate beneath us.

Oh, the things I'll do to her.

WE NEED TO MAKE HER OURS TONIGHT.

Hush, Vero, I'm working on it. Let me work my human charms on her.

Vero grumbled in my mind. I knew he only wanted to help move things along quicker; however, faster wasn't always better.

I stood naked as the day I was born, watching Viv continue to scramble around for the keys she wouldn't find.

And while it was enjoyable to watch her bend over and whip her bright red hair out of her face, I wanted her attention.

Clearing my throat, my voice raspy from the shift, I interrupted her search. "Looking for these?"

Dangling the ring from my finger, my smile spread further when she turned, her eyes widening as she took in my impressive physique.

"Oh my Goddess, why are you fucking naked?"

It wasn't what I wanted to come out of her mouth, but I knew I had her as her gaze remained on my thick, hard cock, making me groan and nearly forget my plan entirely.

Chapter Seven
Viv

Kit had shifted at some point while I looked for the Goddess-damned keys that I flung.

His dragon scared the absolute dickens out of me, and I couldn't help but throw my hands up. But, in the process, those little metal, jangling suckers were now missing in the darkness.

And, there was a monstrous golden dragon eyeing me like I was the whole fucking cake ready to be devoured.

The thought was infinitely appealing; however, I wasn't touching Kit with a ten-foot pole.

Most paranormals had their own mating traditions to bind the other half of their soul to them.

I hadn't a clue as to what dragons did to tie their mates to them, but I wasn't going to take any chances if it was purely just sex. Although I suspected there was more to it than just the big ol' schlong taking a trip down the fun hole, I was still staying away from that activity if I could help it.

Only time would tell if I was strong enough to resist his sinfully clean cut jaw line that I could lick like an ice cream cone, or that plump bottom lip, or the way his Adam's apple begged to be sucked on.

Speaking of sucking on. My eyes roamed over his impressive, toned arms, chest, and abdomen as they dipped down to a majestic dick that was standing at the ready, waiting and begging for me to touch.

I swallowed the spit that wanted to dribble out the side of my mouth as it watered, thinking about what he would taste like, feel like against my even more demanding tongue.

I shook myself out of those thoughts and smacked my cheek hard.

Kit winced as I hit myself, the ring of my keys was dangling on one finger, as he stood naked as the day he was born.

His smile returned after he observed where my eyes had wandered.

"Notice something you like, Neesha?" He purred, making my insides quiver and tighten as his voice took on a husky note on the name he had given me. I was curious what it meant, but I didn't want to ask, not that I was too scared to, I just knew it was likely I wouldn't like the answer.

"No," I muttered, half-heartedly. "Can you put some damn clothes on and give me my keys?" I asked, then reconsidered, because I needed to make it clear I wanted him gone. "I mean, just give me my stupid keys and bugger off."

I hadn't meant it to come out like I wanted him to stay as long as he was dressed, but then again, I wasn't thinking clearly.

I was a sex starved woman, ready to pounce on the more-than-willing dragon shifter.

Not fucking happening.

"Come and get them, princess." He taunted.

That smile that spread across his handsome face was panty-melting, but right now I wanted to smack the shit out of it.

Exhaustion was drifting into my limbs, and I was in no

mood for his teasing bullshit tonight. He had done plenty of that in my coffee shop.

So, I stomped over to his glorious naked body, which stiffened the closer I got, and tried snatching them from his finger.

He was faster than I was, though, and lifted them higher into the air, making me put my hand on his shoulder to steady myself while I jumped up and down like a damn bunny.

Kit chuckled as he kept them just out of reach, "Now that I have you closer," His other arm snaked around my waist and pulled me into him. A breathless gasp left my throat. "Let me take care of you, my mate. I could smell your arousal when I first landed."

Unfortunately, he was right, and even if he had scared the crap out of me, it did something dangerous. Delicious but absolutely forbidden to someone like me.

So, I had to come up with something enticing to get him to lower his guard and bring my keys closer to allow me to snatch them from his grip.

Tilting my face toward his, I tantalizingly brushed my lips along his jaw, speaking all the way until I reached his ear, "You want to take care of me?" I whispered before nibbling on his earlobe, which made him groan. The vibrations from his chest rubbed against mine, making my nipples harden involuntarily, so I continued as his hand, which he had held in the air, lowered painstakingly slow.

"How badly do you want to do that, Kit?"

The last remaining distance of the keys closed in as he had forgotten the little game he had been playing in favor of savoring what was transpiring between us. I took the opportunity to snatch them from his finger as he went to put that hand on my hip.

I had successfully acquired my target goal.

Then, I swiftly pushed myself out of his embrace; the

growing distance helped clear the lust-driven haze from consuming my dwindling self-control.

Kit hadn't moved as I backed away from him. The growing separation cooled my heated skin after being encompassed in his arms and the warmth of his dragon.

Something inside twinged at the sudden loss I had created, but I shook that away as I kept my gaze on him while I walked backward toward my steps and home, which was my sanctuary from this absolutely absurd evening.

"Well, Kit. It wasn't a pleasure. Now that I have my keys back—no thanks to you, of course, since you were the one who snatched them—"

"I didn't snatch them, Neesha. You threw them at our chest after we had landed."

"And the only reason I threw them, *Kit,* is because you and your dragon decided it was a good idea to drop in on an unsuspecting woman who is alone at night. And what is that name you keep calling me? Neesha?"

A growl left his throat, and he advanced.

Just as he had almost reached me, I had turned, running up the stairs and fumbling with the keys. Unable to get them into the fucking keyhole before the dragon's hand gently wrapped around my upper arm, turning me around.

He caged me against my door. Backing me further into the wood panels.

"I don't like the thought of you being all alone out here by yourself." He rumbled, deep, low, and it was so sexy that it made my head spin. He came closer, his face mere inches from mine, "And Neesha is a term of endearment meaning eternal partner."

I was breathless, caught in his trap yet again. "It's nothing new being alone. And—and." I couldn't finish my sentence or respond to what his nickname meant. Deep down, my body was surrendering to the thought of being his eternal partner, but my mind had been made up, and that's all that mattered in this moment.

His eyes roved over my body, those now brightly lit golden globes, which I knew to be his dragon coming out, intently perusing every bit of my features, just as I was taking in him.

This close, he was truly magnificent and every bit the type of man I would fall to my knees for.

But I couldn't and wouldn't let myself fall into that trap again.

Just as I was about to protest that he should leave, all sense of reason blew up like a bomb as Kit's lips gently and hesitantly skimmed mine like he was afraid to chase me off.

But it was too late.

The unfortunate events of my dry spell caught up with me as a torrent of lust gushed and overflowed, short-circuiting my decision-making as I leaned into the kiss harder.

I needed more, wanted it even. Kit had made the first move, but I would take over control.

The keys slipped from my fingers as I forgot about them in favor of sliding those digits into Kit's hair, gripping tightly and bringing him further into my body.

He groaned, obeying my silent command like a good boy, and I delighted in the power he was giving over to me.

Kit's hands slid to the backs of my thighs, and he lifted my body easily off the ground, assisting in wrapping my legs around his waist as he pushed himself against my center.

I was still clothed, but fuck I could feel the hard ridge of his dick rub so wonderfully against my pulsing clit in a torturous rhythm.

What I wouldn't give to be free of the barrier. The thoughts flowed as I languished in his lips and enjoyed the freedom and the broken spell of no libido.

Kit's tongue licked against the seam of my lips, and I greedily let him in, moaning at the connection and building tension.

He rocked against me, slow at first and then harder, faster. His lips left mine in favor of trailing kisses and nips along my neck. Kit spoke huskily against my skin, "The things I want to do to you, Neesha. I would worship you all night long, my pretty little mate."

That word. *Mate.*

It was like ice being poured into my bra and down into my panties at the mention of being called that forbidden word.

I wasn't going to be anyone's mate. That much I was determined to keep.

How foolish I had been to let myself enjoy some sexy mingling when I should have known doing that with Kit would only lead to something I didn't want to give over.

My life. My single, carefree, mate-free life.

Even though I very much hated to cock block myself and get the girl version of blue balls, it was necessary.

My hands flattened on his chest, his impossibly hot and sexy pecs, pushing him away the best I could, considering he was much stronger and larger than I was.

"No." I managed to say as the haze of lust started to clear.

Kit reared back, his eyes narrowed as he roamed my face. He saw what I had decided and straightened. His brows furrowed deeply before he spoke in a low, gravely voice.

"No?"

"I can't be your mate, Kit. I won't tie myself to someone."

"Someone? Or me?" Hurt crossed his face for a brief moment, and for a fraction of time, I regretted it. I wanted to go back to kissing him and forget my vow. But that wasn't how my life would go, and he was tempting.

A very naked, scalding hot temptation.

"Anyone," I replied, sighing, I stepped to the side so we weren't so close, bending over to grab the keys I had dropped onto the porch floor. "It doesn't matter who it is, Kit. I won't let another person control what freedom I have fought so hard for."

He didn't understand the battles I had to go through after high school. The emotional toll it took on me when my future had been decided against my wishes. The late nights I spent magically exhausting myself at my father's behest, and the horrendous things he made me do.

I was lucky I got out when I did, even though I still feared I would be dragged back into the fray of my father's less-than-desirable approach to convincing people to tell him what they knew.

Kit's growl brought me out of the rolling memories.

Even though I had stepped to the side, he was right back, pushing me up against my home.

His hand snaked into my hair as he held my gaze to his.

"Who was it?" He snarled. The agitation wasn't meant for me, I knew it deep down in the back of my mind, when something was sneaking in to push whatever was going on between us further into an entanglement.

"It's not important. There's nothing you can do to change my mind." I blew out a breath, needing to create space again that he had made vanish. "You need to leave."

Kit was reluctant to let me go, but he did. Nodding as if he was deciding something that he didn't divulge.

"Sleep, my sweet Neesha. And dream of me." He paused, and a sultry grin appeared. "Dream of my thick, hard cock, pistoning in and out of this sweet, hot pussy while you scream my name into your room."

A shiver ran through me, and my already heightened arousal flared again.

By the Goddess, if he didn't fucking leave now, I was going to pull him into my house and shuck all the restraint I had gathered, throwing it away.

My walls needed to be rebuilt. He had barreled his way in, too quickly for my liking.

Shaking my head, I frowned, rolling my eyes. "Very astute of you to think I would do any dreaming of you. Fat chance. Now—get, I have things I need to do."

"Mark my words, Viv, I'll have you under me soon enough. Not only will I show you how pleasurable it can be with me, but I'd be the best mate and show you how a man should treat his woman outside of the bedroom. You won't be able to resist for long. I'm a patient man, along with Vero. I'll see you around, princess."

My mouth gaped open and closed. He sure had a way to turn that sexual prowess to a million degrees.

Kit didn't say another word as he backed away into my open front yard, where he had first landed.

I was admiring his ass when he turned around, smirking when he caught me gawking.

My arms folded over one another as I tapped a foot against the wood of my porch floor.

He shifted quickly. It was instantaneous, and a gasp left my throat as I watched his big golden dragon emerge. Vero was now out, and he was absolutely glorious. I couldn't help but appreciate the intricate scales, his enormous wing span as Vero spread them out, and the glint in his eyes as Vero and Kit were present as one but separate.

Then, he took off into the air silently—the complete opposite of how he had entered.

Muttering under my breath at the night sky, his golden form slowly getting smaller and smaller as the distance began to broaden. "Stupid dragons and their need to claim what doesn't want to be claimed."

And then when I couldn't see him anymore, I unlocked my home, rubbing a finger along the column of my smokey quartz tower that I kept at the front door. It gave me the strength to ground myself when I returned, while keeping negativity at bay.

After rubbing the crystal on regular days, the sense of foreboding would be washed away in the currents of the spirits. Today was different, though. As I waited for the relief that would blanket over my soul, nothing came. I felt the same as I had all day long.

At least nothing negative attached itself to me today. I thought. It was an unusual occurrence, but the store had been closed, and the only people I had been around today were ones I considered safe, aside from Kit. He was far from secure in many different aspects.

I wouldn't dwell on that, though.

Deciding I needed to soak in a hot bath filled with lavender Epsom salt before I crashed out, I got to work prepping my bathroom for the relaxation I so desperately needed. Adding candles and the soft melodies of ambient music.

And so when I stripped, dipping my entire body into the scalding hot waters that would soothe my muscles, I couldn't help but linger on what would happen next.

Kit kept popping into my head, even when I didn't want him there. This was possibly a losing battle of my will, but I had to hold out as long as possible. Hoping and praying to the Goddess that my parents, especially my father, wouldn't ever get the knowledge that I had a destined mate already picked out for me instead of their precious choice in a man that they had made long ago.

Chapter Eight

Viv

"Of course he's back again," I mumbled.

Saige glanced up from her kneading. Tilting her head and giving me a questioning frown.

She had taken up residence at a mostly unused counter where people could walk by and watch her mix and create delicious treats through a glass barrier.

The mysterious baker had opted to work in the coffee shop instead of her mobile bakery for the last few days. We held a verbal agreement. She could use my space and oven, sell whatever she makes in treats for the day, and I'd get part of the money.

The only thing was, she didn't know it, but I was stashing the portion I'd taken out to give her as a gift later on. I was convinced she wasn't going anywhere. She may have been a traveling baker, but she was enjoying Mount Hellfire too much, especially now that the paranormal community had emerged from the Veil.

And even though almost everyone was out and about, I

tried remaining incognito. The threat of my father demanding I do my duty as the eldest daughter weighed heavily on my shoulders. If he knew I was forward with who I was, he'd be down my throat and hauling me back to do his dirty work.

That wasn't happening. So, while I wished I could shout to the world, 'This bitch is a witch,' my lips remained sealed.

Saige knew what I was, though, and I think part of her was drawn to this town for one reason or another. But, ultimately, with all her traveling, it gave me a sense that this short, curvy goddess who can make panties wet and dicks hard with her goodies was running from something or someone.

What that was, I hadn't a clue. The baker was tight-lipped about where she came from.

So, I would give her that space, and when the time came and she was ready to open up, I'd be there. I had even told her so every day.

"You okay, Viv?" Saige questioned. She hadn't felt what I did; her eyes scanned the patrons and came back to me. "Is there someone I need to get rid of?"

The question made me laugh. Even for a short girl, she was fiercely protective and was ready to go toe to toe with any man who stepped out of line.

"No, you're good, Saige. Nothing I can't handle." I winked at her and went to the back, where my office was and where I was currently escaping.

I mean, I know I said it was nothing I couldn't handle. I just didn't care to handle it right that second. I'd round up the courage to look Kit in the eyes again, after that intense make-out, without wanting to shuck my panties in the middle of my coffee shop and face him.

Just later.

The air in the coffee shop shifted as I rounded the corner to the back room. Kit had likely watched me walk into the back before entering. It was a game he had been playing for the last two days, ever since our porch encounter.

He'd come in, I'd think I was getting away with him not seeing me, but then he'd approach the counter, and ultimately I'd come back out from the back.

"Morning, Saige, anything ready yet?" Kit's voice was like a siren's song. Candy in the form of a golden dragon shifter. And all things that were addictive.

This was becoming a problem.

He just kept showing up, and when I thought I had a handle on my impulses and inner monologue, he just had to come and explode like a firework in my face. All those pep talks didn't do shit for my self-control.

"Hey, Kit, fancy seeing you here. Again." Saige mumbled, which Kit ignored completely. "I'll have some lemon poppyseed muffins out in less than five minutes. They are perfect while hot. You want to wait for them?"

"Sure, I'll just have the cashier ring up the muffins with my coffee." He said jovially.

She went back to work, and I knew I couldn't hide forever. The dragon shifter could probably smell me back here, and I didn't want him to make a scene.

So, I came out and went straight to making his drink before he even finished making his order. It wasn't like I had memorized his preferred coffee. He ordered it every damn time, and it was the simplest thing.

A double shot of espresso in that day's medium roast.

He never strayed.

Just like he never abandoned watching me work. Always quiet while he was in, but always a blaring sign of his interest.

And then, usually around lunchtime, my sister, Liv, would

stroll in. They'd strike up a conversation until I could free myself to wrench her from whatever the hell they spoke about.

"What do you and the dragon shifter always talk about when I'm busy?" I asked one day, curiosity killed the cat, and all that shit.

Liv smiled, her eyes glittered mischievously before she shrugged, "Not much, just what's going on with the weather. If he's had to put any fires out lately, among other flames."

My eyes narrowed, "What do you mean, other flames?"

She shrugged again, "Not sure, he didn't really go into details." Liv turned, waving at Kit, and giggled while turning back to me. "Shall we get the last of the spell done until I can make it back?"

I groaned. My baby sister was leaving tonight to go back home and pack up her apartment. She had decided to move to Mount Hellfire so she could help strengthen the wards around the building.

It would take months to be permanent, which is why she was moving back. I was ecstatic to have her around more often now. However, that also meant our parents would most definitely be coming back to Mount Hellfire to visit.

Liv, being the youngest, was treated vastly differently from how I had been growing up.

While she could slack off, I had to ensure everything was perfect, and if I roamed, dire consequences followed. Usually, our father doled out those punishments, and they were more severe than those our mother would administer. I had much preferred her punishments to his. She was softer on us and usually said she punished us, even though she never did.

That was the least she could do for us—well, mostly me, considering who the man she had decided to have kids with was.

"Viv?" My sister's voice penetrated through.

I gave her a tentative smile and nodded.

"Yeah, let's do this. I have to run a few errands afterward for Saige before coming back here for a late night."

And as per usual, Kit stayed. He watched as we etched small symbols in different spots around the coffee shop and bookstore, chanting under our breath and infusing each area with a small amount of our energy.

Although once we were in Teags' store, he remained on the other side of the invisible barrier, just watching and sipping his coffee until we returned.

As if he took up the unpaid position of an unwanted bodyguard.

Liv didn't mind.

I did.

When we were finished, I gripped Liv's wrist lightly and brought her to the back room. "When will you be back?"

Even before she had left, I was anxious to have her nearby. Something deep down told me some shit was going to happen, and I couldn't put my witchy finger on what it was.

Better to have her close so I could keep an eye on her than have her across the country where I wouldn't be any help.

"Maybe a month," She lifted one shoulder and smirked, "Shouldn't be too long. You going to miss me?" She asked, clearly ramping up to some kind of comment that likely involved a certain male who couldn't stay away.

"Of course, I get lonely when you're not around."

"You know, there's a certain tall, golden, handsome dragon who can keep you company better than I can."

Rolling my eyes, I huffed, "Fat chance. Stop trying to play matchmaker. I'm fine without a man in my life. I have you and Teags for company."

She blew out a breath, cocking her hip and crossing her

arms. The ever-present little sister attitude was shining brightly, "It's not the same, and you know it, Viv. You're going to regret it one day when you're old, wrinkly, and gray to not have an equally old, wrinkly, and gray man by your side."

I waved her off.

The idea of growing old with someone put a bitter taste on my tongue. To lose oneself to another and have them dictate your life while you dictate theirs wasn't appealing.

I was better off alone.

Liv pulled her phone out and checked the time. Clicking her tongue as she shoved it into her back pocket.

"I've gotta run, my plane leaves in four hours, and that only gives me an hour or so to pack and be on the road."

"I wish you didn't have to leave so soon." A tinge of a whine left my throat before I cleared it.

"You and me both, sis, but if I don't go now, then I'll have to pay an extra month's rent and take even longer coming back." Liv gathered her keys, jacket, and purse. She slipped the jacket on and then threw the strap of her purse over her shoulder.

I wanted to stall her as long as possible, so I pulled her in for a hug and tried one last-ditch effort. "Want me to make a drink for the road?"

"No, Vivvy, I have to go. I'll call you when I land and see you in a month, okay?"

"Yeah, okay," I grumbled. I let my sister out of my hold as I watched her leave the back room and out the front of my store.

Sighing, I glanced around and saw Kit wasn't around anymore.

Huh, I wonder if he finally got the hint.

That thought, however, was wishful thinking after I got back from running around getting ingredients that Saige had asked to be stocked.

Kit was waiting in his dragon form on top of my roof.

Before I entered to bring all the items inside, I glanced up, glaring at the enormous golden inconvenience.

"Better not scratch my roof, fireboy. One puncture hole, and you'll be paying for a brand-new one. Got it?"

He didn't answer, and I knew he wouldn't, but he did blow a cloud of smoke in my direction.

Annoying man.

Ignoring his incessant presence, I brought everything inside. Put it all away and then went about my anxious organizing in the back rooms.

It was dark out by the time I felt it was good enough. What I needed right about now was a bottle of wine, a hot bath, and a good book to unwind.

So, I locked up for the night; my workers had already left, and I headed to my car.

Of course, there Kit was still perched on the roof. His big body was hard to miss in my peripheral vision, but I ignored him all the same.

The drive was quiet; I left the radio off tonight. Wanting to ease my mind or work through my thoughts of the wards, my sister leaving, and Kit's never-ending appearance wherever I had been.

I pulled into the driveway, and there he was, lying down like a cat with one claw over the other, watching, waiting for me to exit as he remained in his dragon form.

It had reoccurred the last few nights since our kiss. Only now did he stay on the lawn and never shift. He also never dove from the skies, scaring the shit out of me again.

His golden eyes followed my body until I closed the door and locked the deadbolt before he took off into the night.

Kit was a mystery. One minute in my face, trying to convince me to be his mate, and the next only observing my everyday activities.

It was irritating.

I needed someone to talk to about it without revealing he was my mate, since Liv was no help. All she wanted to do was sing 'Viv and Kit sitting in a tree,' *and you know the rest.*

And one person who came to mind was my best friend, Teags.

Chapter Nine

Viv

"Ring, ring bitch." I sing-songed when I knew Teags had answered after only one ring and a brief silence on the other end, not giving her enough time to speak. "I fucking miss your ass so much, you have *no* idea!"

I was sure she had, but I needed to say it anyway because Teagan was my ride-or-die. The ying to my yang—jelly to my peanut butter—all sorts of analogy shit.

"Hi to you, too, Viv." Teags giggled on the other end.

In the background, there was some shuffling, a scraping across the speaker, and low whispers.

"Oh ho, did I interrupt some fun time?" The gasp was all I needed to hear when my best friend's embarrassment crawled through the phone.

"N-no." She stammered, clearly busted. "Finn was just—um."

I rolled my eyes, even knowing she couldn't see me, I tittered, "You don't have to hide what you and Mr. Can't Keep His Claws Off You are doing. Sex is a natural thing between a man and woman, you know, Teags."

"I know, but he's your King, it's weird to talk about with you." She muttered.

"And? He's your King, too. Just in a much more different way, that's fun for you. And that I want nothing to do with." I giggled.

"Oh, stop, Viv! My cheeks are hot from this conversation. And Finn can hear everything you're saying, too." She tried mumbling; he had fantastic hearing, as did most supernaturals, when I heard his distant voice next.

"Don't worry, Viv, I'll make sure my touching resumes once you're off the phone."

"Oh, my goodness, I'm going to die of embarrassment," Teags said. Her footsteps echoed through the phone while she moved away from her mate.

It was adorable how the two of them came back together after all this time. I had always had a good feeling about both of them back in High School before Finn up and disappeared (for good reason, too).

Now they were making up for lost time. Of course, also while a psycho stalker was still out there lurking around and probably waiting for their opportunity to get Teags alone.

That was one thing I was worried about.

Ever since the fire, Finn refused to let her leave the mansion, and the only time I could see her lately was if I went there. Which is precisely what my goal was today.

After she and Finn got their bonking out of the way, of course.

"Anyway, what's going on, Viv? I feel like it's been forever since I've seen you." Teags' voice took on a sad tone like she was a bird stuck in a gilded cage.

"Oh, the usual. Work, work, staving the heart of a man whom I want nothing to do with. But that's neither here nor there." I had hoped she wouldn't see through my bullshit and the desperation and war that tugged within myself of who I had been speaking about.

"Want to come over and talk about it?" She asked.

Teags always knew what I needed. That was the best thing about her. Even when there were times when it was hard for me to ask for things, she had a knack for knowing what I didn't speak of.

"You have no idea how much I was hoping you would ask."

"Well, come on over," She paused, breathing heavily into the speaker before continuing, "but maybe in a few hours?"

I laughed heartily.

"Text me when you're done playing snake charmer with a dark gray serpent."

"Oh my goddess, Viv! You and Finn are both incorrigible." She hissed.

"You love us both, and you know it."

"I do. I'll text you after a while."

"Don't hurry on my account, enjoy the noodle taming," I said, hanging up before she could chide me for my sexual innuendos.

I couldn't help myself. I loved teasing Teags; she gave the best responses. So innocent without being a virgin and all that.

And it wasn't for lack of trying either. Teags had gone on plenty of dates and had a few men she had tried sexual encounters with, but ultimately her body and soul knew Finn was out there, and he was meant to be her forever.

So, while I waited for Teags' text, I left my home and went to the only other place I spent most of my time, my coffee shop, The Molten Java.

The weather was growing colder as Mount Hellfire and the people around the city prepared for fall to end and winter to begin.

While I wasn't ready for my favorite season to end and snow to dominate everywhere you walked, I loved the cold. It meant more customers sought the warmth from my magical drinks and the cozy setting of my store.

When I first bought the building that housed my shop and, later, Teags, it was run-down. The walls crumbled, and the high ceilings leaked where the roof needed to be replaced.

I transformed this building into what it is today, mostly without magic. I wanted to earn the right to have it.

To prove to my father that I was so much more than my abilities.

So, my blood, sweat, and tears went into what I could physically do, and when I had no other choices, that was the only time I used my magic freely.

"Hey, Viv! What are you doing here on your day off?" Saige asked when I walked through the front. The bells ringing as I quickly stepped into the warmth, closing the door behind me so those closest wouldn't feel the frigid air rush in.

I smiled at my newest friend and fantastic baker. "Just coming to make a couple of drinks. I'm going to visit Teags today."

She grinned back at me, nodding. "Is she doing okay?"

"I think she's going stir crazy being around Finn 24/7, so I'm giving her different scenery even if it's in the same four walls she's been in the last while."

Saige was rummaging around her station, pulling out a sheet she had stored in the sanitary display. She plucked a few savory muffins I'd been eyeing but never took the time to indulge. Placing them gently in a pastry-decorated paper bag, she handed it to me.

"Here, this is for you both to enjoy while you're together. Don't let Finn get any, though. He's already scarfed down more than his fair share when he was in earlier."

That had my ears perking up. I could have sworn that Finn was with Teags right now. When did he have time to come to my shop?

"What time was that? And was Teags with him?" I asked.

Saige shook her head, "No, she wasn't here. Finn was here right at opening time. Oh! But that handsome dragon firefighter was with him, and they looked like they were in a pretty serious conversation."

"Oh?" I asked, trying to sound disinterested, but she saw straight through me.

"Something about getting advice on how to woo someone." Her brow rose, "Anything you want to divulge?"

"Nope." I said, popping the 'P' while simultaneously walking away to make the drinks I was going to bring.

"If you say so," Saige mumbled. She was used to my abrupt endings to conversations as she returned to decorating cooled cupcakes, and luckily, she didn't press further.

Shortly after my brief conversation with Saige, I left with the bag of goodies and two hot, very caffeinated, slightly magical drinks. It was the perfect blend of sugary spices, all swirled with a dash of calming euphoria that I knew Teags needed, considering her overbearing mate.

And I needed it as well, since there was this unmistakable hollow that kept getting bigger, little by little, while I had chosen to ignore Kit, my own mate.

I drove up to the ornate cast-iron gates, waiting for entrance into the Demon King's layer, aka his mansion. It was late afternoon; the sun cast golden rays through the front windows, deceptively hinting at warmth when, truly, the fall air held a tinge of chill.

Soon, snow would fall, and all traces of warmth would wither away. Just like how I fear I would if I didn't do something soon about the dragon shifter and his insistent presence nearly every day at my coffee shop.

If only my magic could make him leave me alone.

My thoughts only twisted and turned. One moment, I didn't want anything to do with him, and the next, as soon as I even considered it into existence, something tugged, and a horrible ache formed around my heart.

Something was wrong with me. And had been ever since the night of the fire, when something clicked between the dragon shifter and me.

I had no idea how we had lasted so long without running into each other sooner, but I suspected it had to have been because most supernaturals hid, no matter how human they looked, until Finn came out of the Veil.

I blew out a breath, my lips vibrating against each other as I remained in my vehicle long after parking, just staring out the front windshield.

Glancing over at the mansion, I spotted Teags standing in the window, peering out. She was likely waiting for me to emerge and tell her what the hell was going on. I wasn't sure how much I wanted to say to her, but under no circumstances was I going to tell her Kit was my mate.

That was something I wanted to keep to myself for a while longer.

Gripping the pastry bag and our drinks, I left my car and walked up to the front door. It immediately opened, and Teags was already reaching for her drink.

"Oh my goddess, I love you so much. Finn told me he was at the Molten Java this morning and he brought me a chai latte, which I'm grateful for, but it was missing your touch." She gushed, bringing the lid up to her nose, inhaling before sighing.

"I love chai's, but I desperately needed coffee, and this smells divine!"

I chuckled, "Glad to be of service, Your Highness."

Her smile dropped, eyes widened as she opened and closed her mouth before speaking, "Viv. Just because I'm with your King doesn't mean I want you to treat me differently. That also means titles. To you, I'm not your Queen; I have no right to that title. I'm just Teagan."

"You're my Queen just as much as Finn is my King. Once you two are officially mates, of course. But, you're damn right you'll always be just Teagan." I fingered her wavy dark chocolate hair, pulling lightly before smiling playfully and continuing, "But, don't think for one second I'm not going to at least have some fun with your future title. You'll just have to deal."

She groaned, latching onto my arm, pulling me further into the foyer before dropping it once I was fully inside.

"Whatever, as long as you promise not to act like I'm royalty."

I crossed my fingers over my heart as I made the oldest and most sacred of promises, "Cross my heart and hope to die that I'll still be a pain in the ass and will always give you shit no matter the setting."

Teags grinned, her eyes twinkling as they widened, and then turned teary.

I pulled her into me, wrapping my arms around her shoulders while hers came around my waist.

"I love you so much, Viv, I don't know what I would do without you in my life. Thank you for always staying my constant, even when I had moved hundreds of miles away."

We stayed like that for a while, and I forced the lump in my throat to lessen before we parted from one another.

Teags wiped her cheeks free of wetness before declaring the best thing we could have been doing while she was holed up in the mansion, "Alright, enough of the sappy heavy shit. Let's get our swimsuits on and get in the jacuzzi."

"Oh my goddess, yes! I've been dreaming about soaking in there forever!"

With working later and longer, my muscles had been sore. Trying and failing miserably to tell myself I didn't want to see Kit, only knowing he would eventually show up and stay until I left.

Also, knowing damn well the dragon shifter would follow me home each late night to ensure my safety.

I didn't want him to know that I looked forward to seeing him, and that, slowly, he was cracking my iced heart even without speaking to me.

It was a problem I would have to fix another day. Those brief moments were like feeding a small flame, just enough to keep it going without growing.

For now.

Chapter Ten

Viv

My fingers rubbed along the edges of my bikini, pulling the fabric to cover my cheeks more and out of my ass, snapping the cloth on my skin.

I turned in the mirror, admiring the way it hugged my form.

Wondering if Kit would enjoy the view if he were with me. Would he trace the edges just as I had? Dip his fingers beneath to feel how wet he could get me?

Sighing, I rolled my neck; all these thoughts were deliciously dangerous.

"You okay in there, Viv?" Called Teags, while she lightly knocked on the hardwood.

Shaking my head and clearing my throat, I croaked out an answer, "Yeah, just a minute."

Goddess, save me.

Would I ever escape the thoughts of that infuriating, but absolutely ruggish, handsome dragon shifter?

I was afraid I knew the answer to that all too well. He certainly dug those claws into my thoughts and had yet to relinquish his hold.

When I unlocked the door and went into the warmth of the swimming area, Finn was sitting in a lounge chair, caressing Teag's hair behind her ear. She was smiling dreamily at him while his eyes devoured her.

I cleared my throat, needing to interrupt the building sexual tension before it exploded.

Was I slightly jealous? Possibly. But I knew Teags was extremely happy, and while I wished a certain someone would leave me alone, I couldn't help wanting the same devotion.

They both glanced over, and Teags immediately left Finn's side.

"Sorry, he just strolled in here, and I figured you needed a moment." Teag's cheeks were pink, making me tilt my head back and laugh.

"You're so fine, Teags. I get it." And I did.

When you found your mate, your one true love, it was hard to shake them.

I should know. I couldn't shake mine.

The difference between her and me was that she wanted her mate wholly, whereas I didn't. Or I didn't think I did.

She glanced back at Finn and waved; he returned the gesture before doing the same to me. I rolled my eyes, walking toward the male who made my best friend happy and who ruled over our people.

I reached his spot, smiling sweetly. "Look, I know you want to be near Teags and all, but you have to bugger off. We desperately need girl time."

He hadn't moved from his spot, just laid back idly. So, I crossed my arms, glaring at him. "That means you leave, Finn. That's not negotiable. You have your Queen in the castle. She's not leaving the premises."

Finn let out a chuckle, "You just want me to leave so I don't hear all the dirty things you want to tell Teags regarding my best friend, Kit."

I glared harder. This motherfucker might have been my king, but he was bold to bring up my mate. The question was, did he know Kit was my mate or just an obsessive male looking to get into my panties?

Finn winked, leaving the lounge chair, "No worries, Viv. I'll leave the two of you to giggle and spill secrets. She'll just tell me them later anyway."

"Finn!" Teags shrieked, "I won't, Viv. He'll try to pry it out, but whatever you don't want me to tell him, just let me know."

I waved my hand at her, "It's alright, you can spill the juicy details to your mate if you want. I have nothing to hide."

Even though I did, I hadn't even told her Kit was my mate. But that was for another day. I wanted it to be all about her, not me. This deep need for connection was ingrained in me by being around her.

She was incredibly special to me, and as witches, we needed our familiars. Whether that be an animal, another person, or people, it was essential to have a community.

Before Finn left, he swooped in and gave Teags a scorching kiss that even left me breathless. When his lips left hers, she was dazed for a moment, making him chuckle again.

"I'll see you at dinner, Firefly. Behave while you two are in here." He kissed her cheeks briefly and turned to me, "Good to see you, Viv. Don't be too harsh on Kit the next time you see him, will you? He's been through a lot. He could use a smile or two in his life, and I think you could give him what I give Teags."

And those few words left me speechless. What did Finn mean by that? What happened to Kit?

Shit, now I was left wanting to find out about Kit's past and who he was. What made him tick, what his pleasures were, his fears, everything, I wanted it all.

And then I glared at the back of Finn. *The sneaky bastard did that on purpose! He knows Kit is my mate. Has to.*

I wanted to be mad at my king that he put those thoughts in my head. But I couldn't because he wasn't the one who kept thinking about the dragon. Didn't wonder where he was. If he was keeping himself fed or letting himself sleep.

It was becoming a problem. I had one job, and it was to keep my heart guarded, but the longer I warred with myself, the harder it was becoming.

"Let's get into the hot tub, shall we?" Teag's reprieve was welcome, and I nodded, still keeping my eyes on Finn's retreating form before he was entirely out of sight.

Hopefully, he would keep his mouth closed, because without a doubt, he knew.

We sank into the hot tub's heat as the jets kicked in. Teags had a remote that controlled how much and how long the soothing pounding of forced water would last. It felt fantastic, as if she knew we needed the extra zing in our flesh, and all my worries started to fade.

"Oh my goddess," I moaned, "This is so good, Teags. I should think about installing one of these fancy ones at my place. I could use this every damn day."

She sputtered a laugh, "Yes, you should, because then I could come over and we could do this over there instead of here." Her voice took on a wistful, almost sad note.

My eyes popped open, and I glanced over. Teags had her eyes closed, but I knew just by watching her she wasn't fully happy.

"Want to talk about it?" I asked.

She nodded, already ready to spill all her worries and frustrations, "I love Finn so much, you know."

"I do, you don't have to convince me. You guys almost consumed each other just a bit ago in front of me."

Her already rosy cheeks turned a deep crimson, her hand covered her mouth, "I'm so sorry, Viv. Sometimes we forget people are around." She flicked the top of the water towards me. "But, as I was saying. I love him so much, but some days are so smothering."

I quirked an eyebrow, waiting for her to continue.

She blew out a breath, making her lips vibrate against one another before spilling her guts.

"He won't let me leave the mansion, not with the stalker out there and everything that happened with the fire. He's convinced someone is out to hurt me. Which, okay, I understand, but like I just want some freedom to get out and see people who aren't just him and his men. Do something with my bookstore, even if I can't do much right now. Anything, I'm literally going stir crazy over here, Viv."

I nodded; she did seem a little more on edge. Maybe I could help her in that regard, but it wouldn't be for a few more weeks.

"I know you want out. And that's also why I'm here. The book order should be here in a few weeks." Before I could finish, she groaned, but I held up my hand. "I know you want out now, but with the fire just happening, give Finn some time to smother you some more, and then when the books arrive, I'll convince him you have to be the one to put them how you want them."

"I don't think he'd let me out of his sight if he has meetings with the government. They seem to be more frequent as of late." Teags turned silent, likely contemplating escape.

And I could help with that. Steal her away one day, get drunk, and make fools of ourselves at the Flamed Bar and Grill.

"Well, no worries, my bestie, I have a plan, but you need to not act suspicious. Got it?"

Teags eagerly nodded, swimming over next to me while she held my hand. "Anything, I just need out!"

Chuckling, I flicked some water at her. "Then, have faith and be ready when I come to get you in a couple of nights."

Her smile widened, her shoulders relaxing.

We lay our heads back against the edge of the hot tub, letting our bodies float while the jets jumbled us around.

There was a long, comfortable silence that surrounded us, and I thought Teags had fallen asleep. I knew I was almost there, with the laps of water against our skin.

"So," She drew out. "Want to talk about something else?" She asked sheepishly.

I sighed, knowing where this was going. She'd been curious about my dynamic with Kit, and it was likely eating at her that I hadn't spilled the beans yet. So I played naïve.

"Sure, we could talk about the birds and the bees and the wildebeest." It was a lame distraction that failed.

"There's not one thing you want to talk to me about?" She tried again, this time a little differently. "The specific reason why you wanted to come over in the first place?"

"Hmm—no, I don't think so."

Teags sat up, splashing my face. I followed, glancing at her incredulously.

"What the fuck was that for?" I was getting annoyed, for no reason other than she didn't just spit it out.

"You know what, stop hiding it from me, Viv." She grasped my hand in hers when she saw the slight movement of my escape. "Please, you don't keep things from me this long. Does it have to do with Kit?"

My eyes widened. It shouldn't have surprised me, but it did all the same. I wanted to keep him in mind for a bit longer.

Before I could respond, she explained why she needed to know.

"People talk, Viv. Especially to my mate. It's kind of hard not to hear bits and pieces when I'm in the same room as Finn, and especially when Kit calls to talk about you." She squeezed the hand she held, letting me know this wasn't an interrogation and I was free to tell her if I wanted. "Is he bothering you?"

I huffed out a laugh, "Bothering is an understatement, Teags. He's almost like Finn—smothering."

She goddess, honest giggled, "So you know how I feel, except Kit isn't keeping you locked in a pretty prison."

I squeezed her hand back, "It's not a prison, Teags. He's keeping you safe, even in his own fucked up way. But, if Kit had it his way, I'm sure he would also try to keep me locked in a pretty prison, only I don't have a stalker after me."

"That's true, and I know. It's just I saw the way his eyes were practically fucking you the night of the fire. I don't think I've seen another man look so enamored with someone." She said wistfully. Almost like she didn't realize her mate did the same.

"Oh, I don't know, I can tell you there's definitely another man, or should I say demon, who has that same look."

She giggled again. "He does look at me like I walk on water, doesn't he?"

I nodded, feeling better about telling her a little more. "Kit has this uncanny way of showing up everywhere I am. Almost like he's my shadow, he likes to hang out at the coffee shop every single time I'm working the evening shift."

"Do you like him?"

I sure did. I more than liked Kit; hell, he was my mate. But, I wasn't ready to admit anything out loud to anyone, her or the man himself.

"I suppose I do. I don't want to with everything from my past, but there's an undeniable attraction there." I wanted to say more. I really did, but it stuck in my throat. There was no escaping the reality that the goddess's will was more powerful than my own.

Teags let go of my hand and sighed wistfully. "I think it's romantic that he comes to the Molten just to sit and watch you work. You should give him a chance, Viv. No matter what happened before. Not every man is like your father."

She was right. Kit was nothing like my father. I knew that, I could tell by the way he was more attentive to my moods and what I liked and didn't even if he was observing from a distance.

"I know Teags. I'll figure it out one day." I smiled, but it wasn't genuine. I couldn't truly be happy for now.

A knock on the pool doors distracted us, and Finn stuck his head in.

"Hey, ladies, it's nearly dinner. I have a surprise for you, Nocti. I'm taking you out for tonight instead of ordering in or making something."

Before Finn could fully finish, Teags was shrieking with joy and already climbing out of the hot tub.

Guess that was my cue to get the hell out. I grumbled to myself.

But when I glanced at Teags, she was beaming. Joy radiated, and I knew I wasn't going to be a buzz kill.

She came running back over to me, hugged me tightly, and squealed again. "He's taking me out of this house!"

I couldn't help the laughter that bubbled out. I lowered my voice so Finn couldn't hear. "Well, why don't you get ready. I'll show myself out, and I'll get you in a few days. Deal?" I winked.

"Deal." She wrapped her arms around me and squeezed. "Love you, Viv."

"Love you too, Teags."

I watched her skip to the pool doors and leave with Finn, who waved me goodbye as well.

They trusted I would find my way out on my own. The mansion wasn't a giant maze, at least.

So, I took my time in the showers, knowing I had nowhere else to be. I cleaned the chlorine out of my hair, so I didn't have to when I got home. All I wanted to do was curl up on the couch, turn on a movie, snack on popcorn for dinner, and guzzle some fuzzy liquid goodness before falling asleep.

Thankfully, it was all that was on my mind on the drive home until I pulled into the driveway.

And there on my porch stood the golden dragon shifter. I had forgotten about him for just a little while, but there he was, rushing back to the forefront of my mind and soul. Trying to break the chains and ice I had formed.

And damn, did he look delicious, standing there with a bag of food and flowers. His button-up plaid shirt was rolled up, showing off those irresistible forearms as he flexed them while holding the items.

Drool left the side of my lip before I wiped it away, staring at him.

Guess I couldn't just let the food go to waste since he's already here.

And so I left my car and slowly, tortuously walked up the steps to the man I couldn't get away from.

Chapter Eleven
Kit

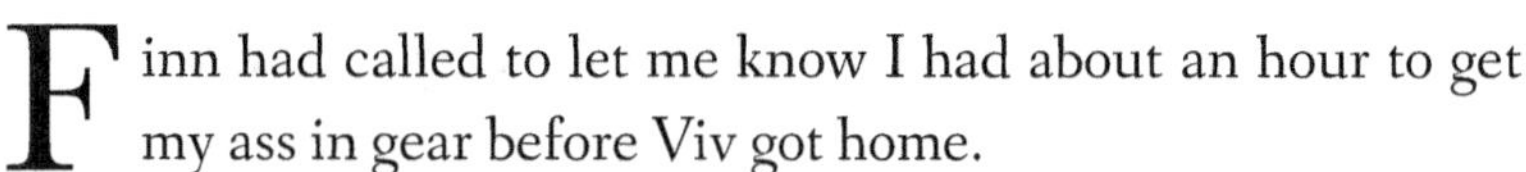

Finn had called to let me know I had about an hour to get my ass in gear before Viv got home.

I was dead set on waiting for her to arrive in the cold. To stand on her porch with food and convince her to let me in. My dragon was itching to get to know our mate and had been so pushy lately.

He was gnawing on his own claws in anticipation while we waited for her to drive up the road. Our excellent hearing indicated she was nearly here, and Vero stalked around in my mind like a cat waiting to pounce on its prey.

Vero, calm yourself.

I CAN NOT. OUR MATE IS ALMOST HERE, AND I CAN'T WAIT TO SMELL HER AGAIN, TAKE HER IN OUR CLAWS, AND NEVER LET HER LEAVE.

Pinching the bridge of my nose, I let out a groan.

She is her own person, Vero. We must respect her wishes. I will help her see the need for compromise. Soon, she will start to feel the bond tug harder.

Vero remained quiet after reminding him she needed time,

as we continued the slow crawl of waiting for Viv to make her way home.

It was a chilly night, and I had worried the food would grow cold while I waited for her. I had requested a heated bag to keep it warm, for an extra charge, of course, so the worry had vanished, but other insecurities usually popped up.

Just as Viv pulled into the end drive, the breeze picked up, as if the goddess were welcoming one of her children home. The scent of our mate carried on the wisps of the fall evening, bringing her intoxicating aroma and slowly calming our racing hearts.

I stiffened, preparing myself for her rejection as I watched and waited for her to leave the car. She sat there staring at us. Vero was just on the edge of shifting so he could show himself to her.

Enough, Vero, or I'll put you in my mental cage.

He grumbled before lying back down in my mind. I didn't want to threaten him, but I was trying desperately not to fuck anything up with Viv tonight.

Our mate's chest lifted and lowered before she left her car. She didn't make eye contact with me until she was on the steps, directly in front.

"Kit."

My name on her lips was like an aphrodisiac; my cock started to harden while Vero perked up again. I cleared my throat while situating the Charred Peaks bag in front of my groin to hide my growing attraction.

"My lovely, Neesha. I've brought us food for dinner. Would you allow me to come in?" I questioned, staring at her, hoping and praying to the goddess and the Veil that she'd allow me just a sliver of her time tonight.

Even if I saw her almost every day, my dragon and I wanted

more. We wanted her words, her touches, anything she'd give. We were love sick and would give her the world.

Viv shuffled her feet, kicking at something imaginary on the step before answering.

"I don't know, depends."

"Depends on what, Neesha?" I inquired. Waiting desperately for her approval and invite.

She nodded her head toward the black paper bag I was holding. "Depends on what's in there." Her stomach growled just then, my smirk growing into a wide grin as I stepped aside to let her up onto the porch so she could unlock the door.

I wasn't going to let her know what I had brought, just yet. I'd prefer her to let us in before I give up the food. Although if she told us to get the hell off her porch, I'd probably leave it for her anyway. We wanted to ensure her stomach was full and that she felt content in our presence.

"You'll have to let me in so I can serve you what I have, my little ember."

Viv huffed, gripping onto the bag she had slung over her shoulder, while pulling her jacket closer to her body when the wind picked up even further. Her beautiful, otherworldly red hair gracefully whipped around her face, never catching her different colored eyes or her mouth, as if the goddess knew not to disturb her vision or her words.

I was breathless, watching her as those orbs shone in the moonlight.

Then, she didn't make me wait long while she nodded and walked to her door, unlocking and stepping aside. A silent invitation that I was hoping she'd give.

Everything was blanketed in darkness inside, but I could see perfect. Her living room was near the front door, a couch and love seat semi-circled a coffee table, which sat between them and a large TV.

Viv took off her coat and hung it on the rack next to the door, along with her bag. She motioned for me to do the same.

For a brief moment, it felt domesticated. Like we just got home from picking up food to dine alone together in the comfort of our home—her home.

"We'll eat in the kitchen at the island." She said, walking away briskly.

I was left watching her sway her hips toward the kitchen, so enticing and sensual. She didn't understand what she did to me by simply turning her back and granting me a glorious view of her ass.

The kitchen was darkly pristine, with her witchy vibes mixed in. Herbs and flowers hung from a collapsible rack on one of the long counters. They were in the middle of drying and left a light, pleasant, earthy, outdoors smell. Candles were neatly arranged along the walls and on one of the many shelves. The walls were a darker green, and several areas held macramé hanging planters with vines trailing along intricately placed little hooks.

You'd think it would exacerbate clutter, but it was oddly cozy for a dragon to be in. Of course, it would be. It had my mate's touch and aesthetic that brought it together. Anything she did, I didn't think would bother my dragon and me—aside from trying to run from our fated bond that is.

Placing the large bag of food on the island counter, Viv grabbed two plates and utensils. I started pulling out the food I had ordered, which was a lot. I didn't know precisely what she enjoyed, so I got a bit of everything from the menu.

Several appetizers were lined up first: spinach-and-artichoke dip with toasted bread, a large Bavarian pretzel with beer cheese, and wings rolled in buffalo sauce.

Her eyes widened at the spread of just the first round.

Smirking, I began serving her a little of each. "I wasn't sure what you liked for food, so I chose to get a few different items."

"These are starters?" She asked, licking her lips, which I took notice of right away, and so did the miniature monster inside my pants.

"Yes, there's more in the bag."

Her eyes lit up like diamonds in the sky, beaming her excitement; she rubbed her hands together. "Show me what else you brought while I start on this!"

It made my dragon purr knowing she was already so eager for us to feed her.

So I pulled the main courses; we'd share whatever she wanted, or if she wanted something to herself, I would give it to her.

One container held a large, medium-rare steak, adorned with seasoned asparagus, carrots, and red potatoes. Then there were two quarter-pound cheeseburgers, topped with bacon and ketchup, with a generous portion of fries. The last container of the main course was lobster fettuccine with several breadsticks.

I held back on the dessert for now, placing the two containers in the fridge to keep them cool.

Viv was savoring every bite of her appetizers, moaning each time a new piece was placed on her tongue. I shifted on the stool next to her. My cock was impossibly hard; I would likely have no issues cutting the steak in half with it. However, I'd keep that appendage behind my zipper and not use it to touch our food.

"Want to share the steak?" I asked, already cutting it in half. My mate nodded, grabbing one of the burgers, a handful of fries, and a heaping scoop of fettuccine.

"I don't know if I'll be able to eat all this food, but I'm going to try. This is amazing, Kit."

She was happy, and that made my dragon and me purr in

delight. So, we ate in comfortable silence until Viv surprisingly glanced over at me, shyly smiling. "Thank you for feeding me. I didn't get a chance to grab anything while I was in town."

Smiling back, I winked, "No problem, Neesha. I'll always take care of you." My voice dipped, and I reached over, brushing some of her hair behind her ear while her hands were full of dripping sauces.

She cleared her throat, "While I appreciate the food, I don't think it's a good idea for you to stay much longer. It's getting late."

That made me chuckle; it really wasn't that late, but I knew she didn't want to make things physical. Or at least I didn't think she wanted to, "I'm not asking to take you to bed tonight, Viv. I'd like for us to get to know each other. Talk to one another. Everything else will fall in place, and I'll gladly wait for when you're ready."

She left her seat and started cleaning up some of the empty containers. I rose and helped as well.

"Here, why don't you sit down. I'll get the dessert out, and I can start by telling you a little about myself." Our fingers touched as I took the remaining containers from her hands. It was pinpricks of electricity running through the tips into my arm.

I wanted so badly to grip her wrist, bring it up to my mouth, and kiss her there.

Would she be sensitive here and moan for me to continue?

I'd find out soon enough, I had to tread lightly with her, though. She was like a skittish, feral kitten in the streets, unsure if she should trust me.

Moving around the kitchen, she sat, and I revealed a chocolate cake drizzled with white chocolate and raspberries, and then a caramel cheesecake topped with crushed graham crackers and shaved pieces of the hardened candy.

I slid them both to her with a fork. "Here, eat."

Vero woke up just then, knowing the road we were about to go down.

ARE YOU SURE YOU WANT TO TELL OUR MATE ABOUT WHAT HAPPENED WITH OUR FAMILY?

I do, Vero. She needs to know why I won't let her go. No matter what.

Viv hadn't touched the dessert yet. I knew she was hesitating because I was still here, and I could tell she wanted me gone, but I wasn't going to go that easy, yet.

Her hands were balled on the counter. I laid mine over top, making her glance at the touch.

Her eyes narrowed at the contact before peering at my face. "I don't think dessert is a good idea anymore. I think you should go; your dragon seems to be close to the surface."

I glanced down and chuckled. My golden scales had started to poke through. "Vero wants you to know us, even if he's hesitant about our story."

She tilted her head, quirking an eyebrow, "What's that supposed to mean, Kit?"

"Well, for starter since I'm giving you information not many others know, Kit is a shortened version of Atticus. My family's name is Hart, and did you know that a dragon's family is everything to them? They consider them a part of their treasure hoard, and to go against your family is to go against everything you are as a dragon? Which is also why I don't go by that name anymore." I started setting up for why I had to do what I did and what brought me here. Which ultimately led to finding her.

"No, I had no idea, it's interesting to be honest. I don't know a whole lot about dragons, though; you guys seem to keep to yourselves in the little corner of the Veil where most of you reside." She said, her hand was still balled into a fist, with mine on top. And thankfully, she hadn't asked me to remove it.

My dragon and I wanted to remain touching her to keep us grounded.

"That's true, we do keep to ourselves. It's difficult for some to let others in. However, that wasn't the case for me when Finn came to the Veil on his eighteenth birthday."

I remember the day vividly. Everyone was talking about the newest member of the royal demon family, who had returned to the Inhuman world. There was talk that he was forced to return to the Veil even though he had found his mate on the other side.

That was a whole other sort of problem. He didn't take well to the transition and had to be locked up for a while.

The king at the time, his grandfather, had scoured for answers. Finding them with my father and mother, who told him the only way to ease the anger was to bring him something from his mate. They knew it intimately as it was how most dragons reacted when separated from their fated.

So they followed their instructions, and when Finn recovered, we were invited to a dinner in honor of my parents.

I hit it off with the future king of the Veil, and we ended up becoming best friends.

"After my parents helped his family with finding something to ground his anger, we became close. My parents didn't care for my involvement, but they couldn't deny the royal demon family the request for me to join them when Finn urged my presence in the Inhuman Special Forces."

I smiled, thinking about the look on my father's face the day we received the letter requesting my participation. I was ecstatic. They were less so.

"It was a fight for years, but I had still gone home and visited often to appease them. That was until one day when

Finn requested that I join the human world and move into the home next to Teagan's."

Sighing, I had held onto those angry words spewed from my father's mouth and would never forget them.

Viv touched my arm, squeezing lightly, "What happened?"

Her touch grounded my racing heart, even if the hurt still surfaced after three years.

"My father disowned me, while my mother cried watching on, wanting to hug me before I left, but she couldn't; she knew not to disobey her mate, my father. To go against your family was the gravest of offenses for dragons. We're territorial, especially to those we love and cherish."

My father's words echoed in my mind from that day.

"Atticus Hart, if you walk out the Veil into the human world, you'd better never return. You'll be dead to us, to me." My father bellowed.

His fury was evident with the bright red scales that appeared along his neck, face, and arms. My father's dragon was close to the surface, and anything I said would cause a shift.

So, I kept my mouth shut, glancing over to my mother whose tears streamed down her face. Her dragon was also on the surface, but in distress, as her beautiful rose pearl scales shone in the lights outside our home.

It was time I had to leave, and I knew nothing I said would appease either one. So, I held my head high, nodded to them both, shifted, and took flight with my bagged items held within my claw.

I hadn't looked back one last time, but I felt and heard the wails from my mother, knowing I could never say or do anything to repair the damage that I had caused.

My mate's hand gripped my arm tighter, her thumb rubbing back and forth while she tilted her head in sympathy. She drew me back to the present, and the regret I had vanished, knowing that my decisions ultimately led me here, to her.

"I'm sorry, Kit. That's awful to have your parents just disown you because you were following orders from our king."

I moved closer to her, palming the side of her neck with my free hand as I breathed her in. "It was all worth it, because I would have remained over there, never knowing you existed on the other side. Never knowing what I would have been missing."

She gasped, "Kit."

"Yes, Neesha?"

"I can't be what you need me to be. I'm not worth fighting for. I don't want to be fought for either."

My hand dropped, and I moved back from her slowly. I wasn't going to give up on her yet, but I knew she needed space. My dragon was pushing to crowd her, and we needed to treat her with respect and remain in control.

"It doesn't matter, little ember. The goddess has spoken; she'll only push you the more you push back. I'm content to wait for you. However long. Now, enough about me, tell me about you and your life."

Giving her the space and the control was the right thing to do as I watched her shift into ease while I eagerly waited for anything she'd give me.

Chapter Twelve

Viv

Now I was truly in a fuckery of a pickle. Damn, Kit, for making me feel sorry for him and for wanting to soothe his soul.

That's not who the hellfire I was. I was a cold bitch, who fucked, kicked the men out of my bed, and went on with my day. Not some woman who wanted to hold hands with this dragon and take all his heartache away.

Empathy wasn't in my vocabulary when it came to men. Not since the bullshit my father had pulled, making me lose all trust in them.

Kit was something else. The way he could crack the walls I kept erecting time and time again. Just when I thought I had a handle on it, he had to go and stand on my porch with a big bag of food.

The smell that wafted when we came into my kitchen's closed quarters alone made my mouth salivate to the point I thought it was going to seep out the side of my lips. It seemed to do that a lot around the dragon.

And now—now he wanted to know about me.

I wasn't in the mindset to tell him things only Teags knew. Tell him the reason why I couldn't allow myself to give in to the mate bond, that would only put him at risk and put my heart on the line, because he would be used against me as a weapon.

My father was and will always be the cruelest bastard I know. He was sadistic in the way he interrogated anyone he deemed a threat to the coven.

If he found out my mate was a dragon shifter, he'd have Kit kidnapped, interrogated, and then he'd either erase his memories or kill him.

Kit wouldn't be in my father's plans for the future; he was attempting to build one for me, and the dragon shifter would need to be disposed of somehow.

"Come on, Neesha, don't be a scared little witchling. Tell me anything—something." Kit purred. His chest was rumbling like a cat, but I knew it was his dragon reacting, trying to entice a reaction from me.

It was nearly working.

I shook my head, "It's not a good idea. You don't want to know the shit storm that was my life before I came back to Hellfire."

He scoffed, scooting the chair over so he was facing me. "Of course I do! I can handle anything you've done in the past. Nothing would bother Vero or me."

I snorted, knowing he wouldn't feel the same if he knew I helped, unwillingly, torture people. After all, he was the closest to our king and part of the ISF.

If anyone, including Finn, most of all, knew the shit my father was doing under his nose, he'd be thrown in the magical prison along with any accomplices, which included me.

"Vero's your dragon's name, right?" I asked, trying to

distract him from what he wanted. I couldn't remember whether he had told me. I'd tried to block out most of what Kit wanted to say to me when we first met.

"Yeah, he's excited to get to know you as well." Kit bit his lip, contemplating something before continuing. "In fact, he'd like to take you to the skies sometime. In the dark or during the day. Whichever you're most comfortable with."

He was like an eager puppy, and it stabbed a bit of guilt into my lungs.

"I—I don't like heights." I lied. I actually had no issue with them, and deep down, if I had to admit, it would be so fucking cool to ride on a dragon's back. To feel the wind whip through my hair, and dive down from the sky while the adrenaline pooled in my stomach.

Kit's face fell for a moment before his lips quirked, "No worries, we can blindfold you, and you can pretend you're floating through water on our back."

He was relentless. I had to get Kit out of the house before I did something stupid, like make out with the man.

Looking over at the clock on my stove, I left my chair and headed for the doorway to my hall.

Turning around, I nearly jumped out of my skin while making a squeak. Kit had followed me. I hadn't even heard him leave his chair.

He was a sneaky fucker.

"It's getting late. I have a busy, long day tomorrow and need to get to bed early." I lied again, biting the inside of my cheek.

Kit tilted his head, eyes roaming over my face before deciding he knew I was lying. He leaned in, placing his forearm on the doorway above my head as his other arm snaked around my waist, pulling me flush to his front.

"I don't think you do, Neesha. I think you're trying to get

rid of us so you don't have to spill your life's secrets." His face moved into my neck as he took a deep breath. Inhaling and exhaling several times, smelling me.

Kit nuzzled my neck and groaned.

"Goddess, you smell delectable." His whispered breaths moved pieces of my hair while tingles raced down my spine, making my core shiver in need.

My breathing grew heavy as my chest rose and fell into his. Every graze was torture, my body wanting to mold itself further into him.

We were playing a dangerous game, and I was pretty sure this cocky bastard was enjoying every minute of it.

Kit moved back slightly, and I tilted my face. We didn't speak, only gazed into each other.

I was in big fucking trouble. I couldn't stop, nor did I want to stop, what happened next.

He moved in fast, as if he were afraid that if he went slow, I would put a halt to his actions, which I certainly would have if not for my libido ramping up around this sexy as hell dragon.

His lips crashed into mine, the kiss a bruising, punishing tangle while his tongue found its way into my mouth.

A moan formed in my throat as our kiss slowed while deepening. Fingers found their way into my hair, gripping at the base to hold me in place, never wavering, never wanting to free me.

I gripped Kit's shirt and brought him further into my body. Feeling the hardened length against my stomach as he ground himself into me. His other hand found its way under my thigh, helping to hitch my leg around his waist. My clit lined up perfectly with his cock as he continued to grind into me, but this time, where I wanted it most.

Goddess, yes, this felt amazing and was what I needed. Just a little more, and I'll fall over the edge this way.

My center pulsed, trying to grasp onto nothing. I wanted it to be something, a huge something that didn't feel quite like a human cock, which didn't bother me one bit. I had always wondered what it would be like to fuck someone with a cock that wasn't like the men on earth.

"Neesha, my sweet little ember," Kit whispered into my neck while lavishing my skin with his tongue.

I remained quiet, enjoying all the touching, grabbing, and grinding.

He started to remove my shirt, moving his face enough to lift it over my head. And that little disconnect broke the blissful lust swirling around us.

What the fuck am I doing? Has my brain turned to mush from just a few touches?

This needed to end, and Kit needed to leave. We couldn't do this; I wouldn't risk him marking me and creating that unbreakable bond.

"Kit, wait—" I croaked out.

But it didn't deter him; I wasn't even sure he'd heard me, or that he understood the turmoil that had formed once again.

His lips fell against my skin between my neck and shoulder, as he started sucking and nibbling. It was the place I knew some species used to mark their mates, and he was focusing all his arousal there.

"Kit, stop!" I finally pushed at his chest.

The momentum stunned him, and he stopped, pulling back to gaze at me with those lust-filled eyes that had turned golden, his dragon near the surface.

"What's wrong, my mate?" He brushed the tangled hair behind my ear. His eyes searched mine in desperation to understand why I wanted him to stop when things were just getting heated.

I must be stupid for not following through and feeling the bliss of an orgasm.

But it couldn't happen, shouldn't happen. It wasn't smart and would only lead to heartache in the long run anyway.

I tried pushing him away again, but it was like moving a brick wall.

"You need to leave, Kit. We can't be doing this." I heaved, preparing myself for hardening my own walls once again against him.

"Okay—it's alright, Neesha, we can slow down and talk. There's plenty of time to explore one another's bodies another time."

I shook my head, "No, you need to leave you overgrown beast." What I needed to do was get a grip on myself and bring out Viv the bitch. "This was a huge mistake letting you into my home and letting you feed me. Of course you'd want to get right to fucking."

Kit held his hands up in surrender, his eyes widening. "Whoa, I think things definitely escalated, and that was my fault, but where is this coming from? One second you're hot, and now you're cold. What happened?"

"What happened was I came to my goddess-damned senses. This can't happen again—ever!"

I tried walking away, tried separating myself from him. He had somehow completely shattered what I had built, and I was feeling things I shouldn't be, wishing for things I shouldn't.

"Wait," He grasped my arm gently to stop me from walking away.

There was no turning back once I did what I set out to do.

"I said, LEAVE!" I shouted.

Wind formed, rustling loose papers on the coffee table as I blew open my front door. My eyes briefly glanced behind him as I saw how much effort it was going to take to push him out the door with my magic.

It wasn't too far.

So, with my anger fueled, it had started to form. I wasn't mad at him, but raged at myself that I let it get that far and enjoyed it, thrived with his touch, and craved it even now.

My water magic shot out, making his grip on my arm loosen as I pushed him out of my home, soaking his clothes and my floor in the process.

This was for the better; it had to be. I couldn't imagine falling for Kit, just to have him ripped from me when my father inevitably came for me again.

Once Kit was out the door, I raised an invisible barrier at the opening. And thank the goddess I foresought to do so as he tried ramming himself back through the entrance.

"Neesha, let's talk about this. What happened?" He pleaded.

It was hard to look him in the eyes, but I had to, so I held my head up high and glared. "What happened was you took the liberty to think you could walk in here, feed me, and then expect us just to be mates and forgo anything I wanted from the beginning. I told you I didn't want a mate, but you kept pushing and insisting until I gave in and let you into my home."

He reared back, like I had slapped him across the face, and maybe if I were closer or didn't have the barrier erected, I would have.

"All I was trying to do was get to know you better. I admit I pushed too far with kissing you before you were ready—"

"You're right, I wasn't ready for that or anything else for that matter. I've told you several times I didn't want a mate." My fury was rising, like a tide crashing against the walls, as my face and chest heated. Why couldn't he just leave already?

And just like that, it was as if he heard me.

I exhaled heavily, running my fingers through my hair. Things had been going so well tonight. I had thought I was getting through to Viv. Melting down her icy walls.

But I was incorrect, and most of all, I miscalculated and overstepped tonight.

"Forgive me, Neesha. I'll leave."

I didn't say anything further to her. She had soaked my clothes, pushing me out of the house with her magic. And while my heart was pounding and Vero was whining in sorrow inside, I couldn't help but love her strength and determination.

We'd give her the space she needed.

It was too much too soon, and I felt foolish for thinking she'd fall into my arms after feeding her.

Dragons could be foolish sometimes when it came to their mates, and I certainly was. We wanted to ease their burdens, feed, and then satiate each other's lust, which most of the time was reciprocated. And I had thought that's where things were leading when she willingly let me consume and drink in her desire. But then something inside her switched, and I was no longer wanted.

Standing on the lawn, I shifted, not bothering to take my clothes off as the seams ripped apart, letting Vero free so we could take to the skies and pour our energy into the flight.

Our mate didn't like our touch. He whimpered.

It was hard for him to understand her reluctance and hesitance. After all, the mate bond made it nearly impossible to ignore. But she wasn't a dragon; she was a witch, and things were different when species mixed.

Don't worry, Vero, we'll give her time and space. The bond will pull her to us, and we can try again.

It will take too long.

I snorted. He sure was an impatient dragon.

That I am, I just want us to have our mate and love her and show her how good we can be to her.

It would be hard on both Vero and me, but we'd have to cope. Maybe I'd see if Finn had any special assignments that would take us away from Mount Hellfire for a few days.

Anything to keep our minds occupied and bodies moving away from The Molten Java and our enticing female with all her fury.

Chapter Thirteen

Viv

I wasn't panicking. That would be absolutely fucking ridiculous. No way was I in shambles and all tied up in knots without Kit being around.

It had been two, nearly three weeks since the night he left my house.

And I was a complete asshole for how I treated him.

Why couldn't I just suck it up and get to know him?

Because you idiot, if we fell in love with him and got ourselves tangled and father found out, he'd use the hellfire out of him.

But, shit, I just wanted—no needed—to see him, just once, and I'd be fine. Had to be, because the crawling under my skin and the squeezing in my heart were nearly suffocating.

It was blissful at first, and then little by little my throat tightened, lungs burned, and stomach turned at his absence. I hadn't slept worth a shit after a few days without seeing Kit.

Was this normal? Couldn't be.

My sister, Liv, was on speed dial, and several times she had to talk me off the ledge of insanity. She helped me scour texts about mates with a dragon, but there wasn't much to go on except one key mention in a super-duper old book about mates.

Dragons were a secretive species, and anything that was out there further than what was found could have been pure lore.

The first night that the pain began, it had been a week after his disappearance, and it was brutal.

Goddess, pick up the fucking phone, Liv!

The ringing continued like a siren. I held the phone away from my ear when each one caused sharp stabs to the inside of my head. Every. Single. One.

I was going to die, like the miserable dry spell bitch I had been the last few months.

Fuck, I should have just jumped Kit's bones and then sent him on his way. But, no, I had to be a stubborn witch who didn't want to risk a bond forming. And now I felt as if I was going to die, and I didn't at least experience it once with him.

"Hello?" Hearing my sister's voice was like eating a bowl of ice cream—soothing after that inevitable breakup when you were a teenager because boys suck ass.

"Thank fuck, you finally answered." I rasped, my mouth going dry and lips chapping against one another.

"Goddess, you sound terrible, Vivvy. Are you sick?"

No shit, I sounded terrible. Something mystical was happening. This wasn't a normal sickness humans would get. There were some other unseen forces, and she was going to be the one to help me. I had no idea how I knew that, but I just did. Liv was always my saving grace.

"I don't know what's wrong, Liv. I need your help. I can't concentrate, and everything aches."

She hummed on the other end, rifling through papers. "Oh! Here, I found a book with magical ailments. What are your symptoms?"

My cheeks heated, embarrassment coursing through my

limbs as I contemplated telling her everything. But she needed to know, because I wasn't sure how much longer I could take feeling this way.

I cleared my throat, phlegm breaking up at the vibrations before I spat it into the wastebasket near me while I lay like a limp noodle on the couch.

"Gross Vivvy—okay, so build up in the throat is one. What else?"

"Uh," I hesitated, "My ears are ringing, and everything loud feels like I'm being stabbed in the head repeatedly. I feel like my heart and lungs are being squeezed and released over and over. My whole body is achy, including my tits and pussy." Mumbling the last part, hoping she wouldn't hear me.

But she did.

"Uh oh."

It was the only thing she muttered, making me sit up.

"Uh oh, what Livvy?" I asked in a panic.

She knew what was going on, and at that point, I had a feeling about the cause when she asked me her next question.

"Wait, let me grab this other book." She rifled through more pages, tsking when she found what she was looking for, "How long has it been since you've seen Kit?" She asked, flipping through more pages in the background. If she weren't careful, her aggressive page turning would tear something.

"I think it's been almost a week."

She sucked in a breath, "Is there a way for you to see him?"

"Why? What does he have to do with feeling like shit?"

"He's the whole reason you are feeling this way." She hummed, "Here, this says that dragon shifters can't go more than a few days to a week without being near their mates before the bond is solidified. That if the bond isn't consummated in the least, both would begin to feel the effects of the separation."

She slapped the book shut, and the sound echoed like a gavel hitting the surface, making me wince and whimper.

"Sorry, Viv. I'd suggest you get in the presence of that dreamy dragon, and poof, you'll be better for a few days. Or you should be."

Liv said it so simply. I wasn't sure it was that easy, though.

"Okay, I'll see if I can track him down. Maybe I'll call Finn. I don't want Teags to know I'm looking for him; she'll just have questions."

The sweet sense of relief washed over me. I had ignored the warning signs the day before, and as the symptoms had worsened, so had my mood. All of that was going to change, though.

I just needed to get the dragon shifter somewhere where I could be near him.

Nearly two more weeks had passed since I spoke with my sister about the sickness I had.

At least right now, it was under control. I called Liv back the next day to let her know that Kit was indisposed and couldn't be reached until he returned Earthside.

Fucking Finn sent him on a mission, knowing that he was my mate. Knowing what it would likely do to both of us. Although, to his defense, grudgingly, Kit should have been back right after the sickness started.

Something kept him from coming back, and I had had enough of waiting.

Finn promised he'd send someone over on the other side of the Veil to find him. But that someone had remained to be seen as well.

I had eventually grown strong enough to work after taking my daily herbs of dandelion root to detox the sickness and chamomile to help boost my magic that would keep most of the other 'symptoms' at bay.

Autopilot kicked in as I swirled the milk in the frother.

Every time that goddess-damned door opened and the chime dinged, my head snapped to the front, only to be disappointed that it wasn't Kit.

Where the hellfire was that dragon?

Just as I placed the freshly frothed milk on the counter, the door jingled its tinkling, annoying fucking chime, only this time I held myself in check and didn't glance over. The temptation nearly did me in.

"Hey, big sis!" Liv's welcome voice called over the entirety of the store, causing patrons to stare. And I couldn't help but whimper in relief that she was finally here and staying this time! Because the only reason she would be here was if she was finished packing and moving her stuff back to Mount Hellfire.

She rushed over to me, wiping my damp cheeks with her fingers. I hadn't realized I was crying at first until she touched my face, and then the floodgates opened. Sobbing into her shoulder, she shushed me like an infant, while threading her fingers through my hair, soothingly.

"Don't worry, baby sis is here to take care of you." She pulled me away from her body to look at my face. When she took in my disheveled appearance, she frowned. "Vivvy, you haven't been taking care of yourself."

It wasn't a question but a statement, making me huff a half-hearted laugh, "The herbs and my magic can only do so much."

Her eyebrow raised, nearly hitting her hairline. "Is Kit still not back from wherever Finn sent him off to?"

I shook my head, unease coursed through me, and I was worried about the man whom I wanted nothing to do with, "No one knows where he is. They sent someone to go find him in the Veil, but that was almost two weeks ago."

She frowned before plastering a smile on her face. "No

worries, I'll just have to spike your next drink as you do with everyone else."

And she did just that when it was time for me to make my drink. The aches had begun to return, and there was no relief until I finished every last drop of the tea.

With the disposable cup I had just emptied, the door chime rang again. A man in a delivery uniform walked in and headed to the counter, clipboard in hand. He didn't even glance up when he approached.

He grunted once he stopped at the register, "I have a delivery for Vivienne Woodward."

I raised my hand and stepped around the counter to his side, "That's me. Are these the books I ordered?"

He shrugged, "No idea, miss, I'm just here to bring a bunch of boxes in."

"Alright, let me open up the bookstore next door. You can unload them all in there since that's where they need to go anyway."

At least with the books finally being delivered, I could concentrate on making sure they were all there instead of staring at the milky froth of a forgotten drink I never did finish making.

Thankfully, I had incredible workers who picked up the slack for the missed drinks without complaint.

Sitting on top of the counter in the bookstore, I watched two delivery workers haul in dollies upon dollies of boxed books. They filled the back hallway first, then littered the store wherever they could find an open spot.

Teags would absolutely have a shit fit right about now. Nothing was organized, and honestly, I didn't have the energy to direct them.

The tea was just starting to kick in when only one worker returned, clipboard in hand again.

"All finished, just need a signature that all the boxes were delivered. If there's an issue with anything inside, you'll have to call the company you ordered the books from and make a complaint."

I took the clipboard and scribbled my name at the bottom, "No worries, all the boxes look undamaged."

He seemed happy with that response as he left quickly, and I stood in the middle of the store, ruffling my fingers through my dull red hair. The shaky digits found themselves digging in my back pocket as I pulled my cell out.

Finn's name popped up, and I immediately answered, "What's the matter?"

He chuckled, "Well, hello to you too, Viv."

I rolled my eyes, even though he couldn't see. I had to know why the king was calling me and not Teags. She had checked in at least once a day since the fire; his call was unusual.

Even though I was just there last night, being lazy in the hot tub to help relieve my tightened muscles and gossip about the latest sexy lingerie styles that Mitsy had shown me the other day.

It was nice that we had gotten closer to Mitsy since she had grown out of that attitude, gotten married, and then found herself widowed early in life. Not that the bastard didn't deserve what he got, but still, for her to walk into that was likely traumatizing. I think what transpired changed her perspective on life.

With the money she got from her husband's insurance and savings, she sold everything they had in 'paradise' and, for some strange reason, she chose to come back to this place.

Although I couldn't fault her, I did the same damn thing.

Now with Finn on the other line, something was off.

"Want to tell me why you're calling me, and it isn't my best friend on the other end, Finn?" I questioned, suspicion edging in my throat.

He huffed, "Yes, I wanted to inform you that while I haven't spoken with Kit or know where he's at, I had someone else track down the person who was supposed to be finding your mate, and let's just say he was tied up to a bedpost, indisposed."

My eyes widened, and I let out a boisterous laugh while pinching the bridge of my nose. "Hellfire, what kind of guy did you hire?"

"Apparently, one who lets women tie him up, take his money, and leave him for a few days without alerting anyone that he needed help."

My laughter died down, and I slouched to the ground near a stack of boxes and leaned back. I took several deep breaths while staring at the ceiling, where faux vines hung from several areas.

Goddess help me.

"So, what now?" I asked, wanting to know the next steps.

"Now, we wait a bit longer. Think you can manage?" Finn was usually stoic, but he softened his voice. "I know it's a lot to ask, Viv, considering everything. I have a good feeling he'll turn up soon."

"Yeah, I suppose I don't really have much of a choice. My sister just got here anyway, so her magic combined with mine should be sufficient."

His silence was deafening on the other end. I was wondering where Teags was and decided to get him to let her out of her cage, aka the mansion, today. Her books had arrived, and I wasn't about to try to put them away myself. She had a method to her madness.

A girl's books were never to be messed with, especially where they were displayed.

"Teags books came in today. Can you let her free for a few hours?" I bit my bottom lip and fidgeted with the fabric of my leggings while I waited for either a denial or approval.

"I don't know, Viv. I don't think that's a great idea with the stalker still not caught."

Bastard.

"Come on, Finn, you know she's going bonkers stuck in that mansion all day, every day. Let a girl breathe non mansionesque air." I waved my hand around, even though he couldn't see me, and giggled to myself.

"I can't take her today, I've got the worst meetings with the government that can't be put off." He was a party pooper, but I wasn't going to give up easily.

"So? Give her a bodyguard or two while she's here. She'll be perfectly fine with two beefy men and me, her witchy best friend. And I could use the eye candy anyway, give me a good distraction from my woes."

He chuckled, "You sure do run a hard bargain. Fine—I'll get two of my best men to accompany her. But, Viv, no funny business. You are both to remain either in the bookstore or the coffee shop. No, trying to sneak her off to the bar again."

Tilting my head back, I laughed, "Can't make any promises."

"Viv." He warned.

"Alright, alright. I'll be on my best behavior and keep her where you have the beefy bodyguards bring her."

He grunted and hung up the phone. Finn wasn't one for goodbyes, and I was okay with that.

Now, I just needed to keep myself busy until Teags showed up.

And what better way than to get to work, helping my baby sister with some more protective spells.

Nothing would be solidified until we performed several

enchantments, but I wasn't worried about it. The stalker hadn't shown his face in several weeks. I wasn't sure whether he'd moved on from all the heat he was taking, or if he was lying in wait for an opportunity to get Teags alone.

I snorted. That definitely wouldn't be happening with all the guarding Finn did, and she'd have two chaperones to keep her safe while she was with me. Plus, I'd just fry his ass. I was in the mood for a good sizzling of someone's balls.

Chapter Fourteen

Viv

I'd spent time staring into the recesses of my mind, eyes glued to the brown cardboard box that sat in front of me after hanging up with Finn.

He was finally seeing reason, letting Teags out of the mansion to help with her bookstore. I knew that I'd never get it all done myself. Having Kit gone and knowing that I was suffering from the stupid mate sickness left me weak and irritable.

"Knock, knock." Liv's meager voice strayed in from the partition.

I had left it mostly closed while the delivery driver and his partner hauled in the boxes. There were nosy patrons on the other side who would likely gawk, trying to see what was coming in. They knew, though, that the bookstore Bound in Fire was set to open soon. Or at least Teags and I had hoped it would, seeing as the bastard stalker had yet to be caught.

But, no matter, I knew if Teags had it her way, she'd open with or without him being in jail.

She was my tough cookie, and I loved that she came into herself as an adult.

Frankly, I was a fucking proud bitch watching her blossom, especially with Finn at her side now.

"Viv? Where in the Veil are you?" Liv called out louder, her footsteps clicking against the hard floors as she moved further into the bookstore.

I was still sitting on the floor with boxes surrounding me like a makeshift fort, hidden from anyone who had looked in from the windows or partition.

Clearing my throat, I answered so she'd know where I was, "I'm over here."

She rounded the boxes, her eyes softening when she saw where I was. There was no hesitation as she joined me. Her shoulder rubbed against mine, and she took my hand with hers.

"You doing okay, Vivvy?"

"Define okay." I quipped on the verge of frustrated tears. No one still knew where Kit was, and I was suffering because of it.

Is he suffering just as much as me? I thought angrily.

She huffed, "Stupid question, I know. I'm just worried about you, and I guess I need verbal reassurance." She squeezed my hand gently, a delicate buzz seeped in between our palms, and my frustrations eased.

Liv wasn't just good at putting physical things back together and restoring order. She was also an expert at pulling emotions, righting them with a single touch when they were elevated. And while her tea had helped earlier, this was what I had needed, and she knew it.

"Thanks," My throat clogged again, her presence soothed me. And even though I was the big sister, there were moments in time where she had to act as the eldest, especially when it came to our parents. They treated her vastly differently from how they treated me.

She was their 'golden' child, and I was the black sheep.

Thank the goddess we never let that come between us. I couldn't stand it if I didn't have her in my corner. She was my world for most of my life until Teags came in. And then everything good I wanted to do and be, I did for them both.

I glanced over at her, our fingers entwined, "What took you so long to get here?" I hadn't had the foresight to ask earlier. Too many things were happening, and while I usually kept my cool during distress, everything was currently a jumbled pile of Legos waiting for some unsuspecting person to step on a dislodged piece with the arch of their foot.

Liv rolled her eyes, "Mom and Dad are what took so long to get here."

"They tried convincing you to stay, didn't they?"

"Sure did." She exhaled heavily. "Mom put on the water works while dad bore his classic scowl and disapproving grunts. I told them it wasn't going to work, that I needed a new change of scenery for awhile."

I could see it now. Dad acting as a caveman just grunting around the room as if he owned it and gurgling, 'You no leave, daughter. You stay. You follow rules set by me. You servant like sister was.'

The imaginary scene played in my mind, and I couldn't help but chuckle.

"What's so funny?" Liv asked, curious about the sudden shift in my mood.

"Just thinking about dad acting primitive, is all." I waved my hand and changed the subject, "Anyway, do they know you're here?"

She bit her lip, and I groaned.

"Vivvy, I couldn't help it. Mom was tugging something

fierce on the ol' emotions. You know how I get, I'm so sensitive to people's feelings."

I sighed, knowing that it was inevitable they'd find out where Liv went anyway.

Let's just hope they didn't want to come for a visit and try to talk to me. It had been a few years since I left. And when I had departed, it wasn't on good terms at all.

The door slammed behind me as my father's latest prisoner's wails echoed in the chamber. Every painful scream dug further into my heart and lungs, nearly suffocating me.

While I wasn't the one to dole out the final blows before most of their lives were snuffed out into the void, every single one of them still resonated in my soul.

My father was heartless, and he didn't abide by the coven's or even the supernatural laws set in place by the Demon King. Most didn't know what he was up to, and I was forbidden from speaking about what happened in this desolate area, where seemingly crumbling buildings from the outside concealed reinforced prisons within. It wasn't like I could tell anyone anyway, as my father had a spell placed on anyone who entered. It would make them forget what happened the moment they left.

That was until one day when I was at home, playing with a new Sodalite crystal someone had placed by my door. It was a beautiful, vibrant blue tower with golden fissures, and while my fingers rubbed along its flat surfaces, pieces of my memory flashed before my eyes.

The pain was immediate, making me drop the crystal on the comforter I had over my legs.

Sucking in air that didn't seem to fill my lungs was futile as black spots edged my vision before Liv had entered unannounced into my room.

And thank the goddess for that, because any longer without proper oxygen, I would have passed out.

"Goddess Viv!" Her hands lay on either side of my face as she poured her magic from her palm into my skin.

My hands gripped hers once I took that first deep breath, "I'm fine." I coughed, taking a few more deep inhales, allowing my speeding heart to slow.

"What happened?" She demanded.

I was unsure whether I should tell her what I saw. It terrified me. And even though I didn't see everything I had been forced to do, I knew there was more. However, the one face that kept replaying in my mind was our father's menacing smile.

But before I could make something up, she sighed, and I knew what that sound meant. I couldn't keep anything from her; she was too good at reading people. There were times I thought she could read minds, but she had sworn she couldn't.

"What did he make you do?" I reeled back, my eyes widening, and the panic swarmed once again around my lungs. "Shh, it's okay, Viv. You don't have to talk about it right now. Just," She bit her lip, tears formed in the corners of her eyes, on the verge of rolling down her cheeks. "Don't hide what he's made you do when you're ready, okay? I'll be here, and there'll be no judgment from me, I swear it by the goddess."

I nodded as she rocked us while holding me as I let the sobs roll past my lips.

Eventually, days later, I spilled all the things the crystal had helped me see, and in return, she helped me escape our father.

I had no idea who left me the Sodalite, but I was meant to have it and be shown the truth about what had been happening.

Father, of course, was furious about me leaving. He punished Liv when he figured out she was the one who gave me a sleeping powder to knock out the guard. Thankfully, her punishment was light because she was his favorite. And I got away from it all after she promised to keep track of me for him.

He had no idea that Liv and I knew what he made me forget.

We had all his dirty little secrets he kept locked in my head, waiting to be used if necessary. Even if it meant I was imprisoned alongside him.

Liv had pulled me into a tight hug; she didn't let go either as she spoke into my hair while we remained on the floor. "I promise I won't let him take you. You'll never have to be alone with him, okay?"

I nodded as she let go while smiling brightly at me. "Okay! Enough of the heavy shit. Let's have some fun and protect this paradise you've built yourself."

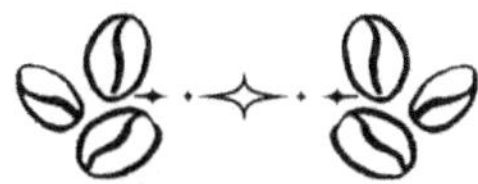

Another protection spell was completed, and Liv left to rest.

Teags had finally shown up, and I couldn't help but drool over the two green beefcakes that were her guards. Of course, I wouldn't touch, but that didn't mean I couldn't look. After all, Kit wasn't here, and even if he claimed I was his mate, I didn't claim him back. I wouldn't be forced to be tied down like when my father had forced me to do his bidding.

Finn had assigned two Orc brothers, and boy, were they big, with scowling faces that didn't deter me one bit.

I'd fuck with them a little. Had to, because I enjoyed eliciting reactions from the men in our paranormal world. It was easy to rile these fuckers up, and it gave me immense pleasure to do it.

We gathered the drinks I had made and walked over to the partition where we'd left the two enormous bodyguards.

We were giggling as we put books away, and I felt a lightness in my heart having Teags here.

"So what's up with those two?" I asked, pointing my thumb behind me, where the two Orc bodyguards had their backs to us.

"Finn almost didn't let me out of the house today. I told him I would become resentful if I didn't have some semblance of a life. Or something like that. He only agreed to letting me leave if I remained in sight of those—what did you call them? Oh yes, the two beefcakes."

I turned, smirking, knowing they'd hear me while I assessed them, "They are indeed beefcakes. I could nibble on their chiseled jaws and climb them like a jungle gym."

Hawk, or maybe it was Jorrik, chuckled. Honestly, I couldn't remember who was who since they were twins and looked identical to me. The other brother grunted in annoyance and huffed.

At least I got some sort of reaction from them. They sure didn't get riled up easily, though. But that was okay. It made my heart lighter anyway, making me feel more like myself than the mate-starved woman I had become.

My mind wandered back to Kit while we dug through boxes.

I had thought long and hard about it and decided it wasn't like I hadn't wanted a mate, just that I couldn't.

Until my father was either dead or behind bars, it wasn't safe. Maybe one day, but even then, I likely wouldn't have that opportunity, as I might go down burning with him. And I was a goddess-damned coward for not turning him in years ago because of it.

My heart and body slightly ached. I just wanted to know if Kit was okay. And if I was bound to feel this mate sickness forever, I hoped he didn't feel it as acutely as I did. That was a prayer I had sent up to the goddess many times over the last few weeks.

Even if I was a bitch, I still cared about his well-being.

"I want romance next." Teags had stated. Unfortunately, I missed some of what she said, but I plastered on a smile and told her they were in the back hallway and that I'd get them next.

Weaving through the boxes, I made my way down the narrow hall, glancing at each one and the label slapped on the side.

When I reached the romance ones, a breeze blew strands of my hair into my eyes, and my brows furrowed as I glanced up. The back door was cracked open, a sizable rock wedged between the door and the doorway to keep it propped open.

"What the hellfire?" I questioned, then walked over and kicked the rock aside.

As soon as I had it moved, a hand wrapped around my face, covering my mouth and muting the cry that didn't make it anywhere.

Then a man's voice whispered angrily in my ear, "Don't even think about using your witchy magic on me, or I'll blow the whole place up and slit your throat."

I whimpered, terrified and unsure if he was telling the truth. I wasn't going to risk our lives or those of the people still in my coffee shop, so I complied.

If he hadn't threatened others' lives, I would have retaliated right away with a blast of water to his fucking face and been done with it, but here we sat.

He held a knife to my throat and was breathing heavily as if this took all his energy and courage to pull off the attack.

"I'm going to tie your hands now. You make even a peep, and I'll push the button, exploding everything and everyone in the building. Nod if you understand." The unknown assailant said. I was unsure what he wanted. If it were money, he was barking up the wrong tree, as the bookstore hadn't been open yet.

He tied my hands and put his sweaty palm back over my mouth with the knife lodged against my skin. "Good, now remember, when we go out, don't make a peep. I don't need those two green bastards to come barging in."

He shuffled us around the boxes, and Teags noticed us. She gasped when she saw he had ahold of me.

"Don't hurt her. Please, what do you want?" She pleaded. Her eyes widened as the asshole pushed the knife further into my neck.

I briefly closed my eyes, hoping that if he did slit my throat, it would end quickly.

Dickface whispered next to my ear, "I'm going to remove my hand from your mouth. Keep it shut. Understand?"

I barely nodded, afraid of the knife going further into my skin, and his hand left my lips.

Once he had his free hand, he removed something from his head. If I had to guess, he was wearing a mask.

As he revealed his face, Teags gasped and stiffened. Everything was at a standstill, and the world slowed. I immediately knew who had me.

It was Teags' stalker, Vincent.

The bastard somehow broke into our building. Even with the minimal protection spells, it should have stopped anyone from entering with evil intentions. Or so I had thought.

Once we got out of this pickle, I'd have to talk with my baby sis.

For now, I had to think quickly about how I could subdue him without him blowing everyone up.

Teags and Vincent were talking, and that's when I heard her tell him she'd go with him.

"No—Teagan, don't do it. We can figure this out." I urged. She couldn't go with him. I'd rather die than let him have her.

"Shut up, you stupid bitch!" he hissed in my ear, pushing the knife further into my throat, and I knew he was furious.

I sucked in air between my teeth as the burning pain began. A trickle of blood rolled down my neck, and as Teags slowly walked toward us, tears pricked at the edges of my vision.

And when she was close enough, Vincent let go of me.

Only, he didn't let me go far when a blinding pain struck the side of my head.

I fell, my eyes briefly closed, all I could do was lie there, my hands tied behind my back, and when I reopened them, there was nothing I could do as I watched him take Teags' limp body through the back door.

I had failed to protect her.

There was nothing I could do as my eyes fluttered while I struggled to remain awake.

So, with agonizing hopelessness, the darkness consumed my consciousness and all sense of time.

Chapter Fifteen

Kit

YOU ARE A FOOLISH MALE.

I internally scoffed at Vero.

Tell me something I don't already know, dragon. But our mate needs space, and once the bond sickness hits, she'll call with questions, which we will gladly answer for her, but it will be on her terms.

He grumbled, huffing and turning his back to me. Obviously, he couldn't go far since he was in the depths of my mind, but his dismissal stung anyway.

Even though I loathed the thought of our mate aching, I couldn't impede on her stubbornness. She'd just have to learn the hard way. We would suffer alongside her as well, but that didn't matter. I'd suffer tenfold if it meant giving our mate what she wanted.

Now here I was on my way to head back through the Veil to contain a new vampire whose mate was currently locked up at the Inhuman Special Forces building.

News was traveling as the fae's magic waned with her persistent breakouts. She had gotten herself lost several times.

Luckily, there was a tracking spell coursing through her freshly turned blood, and each time she was apprehended, the spell lessened.

First, though, I needed to speak with her mate, Cadence, and get a bit of a background on his feisty mate.

The large building that housed the ISF loomed in darkness on the corner across from a quiet University. It was nearly two in the morning on a weekday, and there wasn't a soul to be seen.

That was until you entered the paranormal policed building.

Here, it was bustling, with a variety of species roaming. The building not only served as the headquarters for our division but also housed businesses of all sizes. Mostly fast-food slots, but here and there were a florist, an artist, a hairdresser, and a tailor.

Then there was the specialized wall of cells that faced the bustling open space. Finn had designed it that way to show those who had to be imprisoned what freedom and happiness looked like if they followed his rule and law.

Most of the time, it worked.

Then there was the special case of Cade, his unauthorized turning of a human, whether or not she was his mate.

Cade's clan was a constant bother as they petitioned for his release, but he didn't want to go with them.

While he wasn't my biggest fan, at least not since we had imprisoned him, he was currently the only paranormal locked up. Most of the Inhuman community had been on their best behavior to avoid such predicaments—well, as far as we knew.

I entered and set my sights on the wall of cells. The only one lit up was Cades, and he was pacing from one side to the other until he stopped. He glanced over, his brows turned down, and he bore his fangs.

Ah, yes, those must be for me.

I chuckled to myself. Dandy as could be, regardless of whether I had volunteered myself to help the fae with a baby vamp problem, his reaction was what I was looking for.

Hands in my pocket, I strolled to his enclosure.

"Evening, Cade."

He grunted, running his claws through his thick, dark, textured shag.

I eyed those very claws and quirked my brow. Vampires usually didn't have them protruding except when they were stressed or on the verge of defending themselves or their mates.

"What do you want, dragon filth?" He spat, his 'r's' rolling heavily while he was pissed.

I couldn't blame him. After all, if someone were to keep me from Viv, I would go feral, like he was now.

"Oh come now, Cade, bud. Don't act like that, man. I'm just here to get a little bit of information about your mate so that I may be of help."

He eyed me wearily, his claws still out, and returned to pacing while remaining silent.

"What's her name, first of all. No one knows except the fae who are helping her adjust."

"Brooke."

"Perfect, anything I should know once I get to wherever the hell they have her?" I questioned. Did I know where she was? Nope. But it wouldn't be hard to find her if she were with the fae. The only thing that would be challenging was them letting me help.

"No. Nothing, I want you to know. I barely know her myself. Remember? You and our *King* took her from me shortly after she changed." When he spoke of Finn, it was with vehemence.

He was pissed, and I didn't blame him. Poor sucker. Literally.

"Look, Cade, I'm just trying to help. Finn—our King," I corrected, remembering most paranormals weren't on a first-name basis like I was. "He's asked me to ensure her safety and assess if we need to release you soon. I'm going to advocate that we do so. I couldn't imagine being locked up away from mine."

He stopped pacing, his eyes flashed red, his rage at the forefront. "You know nothing about being away from a mate."

I held up a finger, "I beg to differ."

He hummed, "So, you are leaving your mate to ensure mine doesn't go feral on every living thing in this world and the next?"

Nodding, I took a step closer, "That I am."

His posture relaxed, and he finally sat on the edge of his bed. "I can't help you, Atticus. No vampire has ever been separated from their fated. All I know is that time is running out. I can feel her ire through my veins, regardless of how far apart we are. She's continuously fighting a war with herself that only I can quell."

"Then, I shouldn't wait much longer to find her." I straightened my coat, preparing to enter the cold drafts of the fae lands. Their little corner of the Veil was close in seasonal weather to Hellfire, and with it being late fall, nearly winter, it was going to be chilly.

I sure missed the warmth of my home in the Veil. There wouldn't be any time to visit, as this needed to be done as quickly as possible to return to my mate before we both fell under the bond sickness that only happened to particular species, dragons being one.

"Can you do me one thing, Dragon?"

"Of course, anything for a friend."

"I wouldn't call us friends." He paused, his fingers brushed through his hair, his red eyes focused on me. "Tell Brooke to close her eyes and feel me within her veins. Reassure her we won't be apart for long. And tell her she is my light to my wretched, damned soul."

I stepped back further, glancing around to ensure no one was listening.

"As soon as I find her, I'll have someone come and free you. Finn will have to understand. Once you get to her, you both need to hide for awhile."

Cade quirked a brow, peered around, likely to gauge if this was a trap, and when he found no one was around, he nodded.

Now I just needed to keep my word.

I left quickly, the ISF building getting smaller as I watched it briefly in the rearview of my truck as I made my way to one of the portals near the Mount Hellfire Park. It was one of many that Finn had allowed open.

No one knew where they were or what to look for except the supernaturals, and even if a human were to stumble into one, they'd have to have some kind of tie to the inhuman world.

Finn thought no humans should enter, partially because he didn't know what the atmosphere of the Veil would do, but also because he didn't trust the humans. They were known for destroying their world along with their own people.

Ancient texts back home at the Kreli Isles showed that long ago, dragons had found their way to another world where there were people who couldn't shapeshift. The people were known as humans, and while they never hunted us down, as the stories say. Most of our people had mates among them, and those who mated came back to the Isles and made homes with their dragon companions.

It was a long-kept secret that I wasn't even allowed to spill to my king and best friend.

I pulled into the lot near the large entertainment gazebo,

where many events were held in warmer weather, and put my truck in park at the closest available space.

I'd have to go on foot from here; it would be a long trek through the woods, but it was ideal so that no one could stumble into it.

I was barely through the first treeline when a sensation ran up my spine, putting my dragon and me at attention.

SOMETHING IS AMISS.

I feel it too. Can you tell what it is?

The unease dug deeper under my skin, and my golden scales began popping to the surface. Vero was close to the edge, ready to shift if needed.

Scanning our surroundings, I found nothing wrong in the sense that there was no movement anywhere. And maybe that was the problem, since it was silent except for my breathing.

Vero was suddenly quiet as well and didn't answer my question. I could still sense his presence in the back of my mind, but he had retreated.

Vero, what is it?

Still nothing from him, and then it was as if I could see him as he curled in on himself and fell asleep.

Pinching the bridge of my nose, I resumed my walk but stopped abruptly.

Right there in front of me was an entrance to the Veil.

It was entirely in the wrong spot. It made me wonder if they could be moved easily and, if so, who would move this particular one?

Cautiously, I approached the electrically charged translucent gateway, peering around as I walked toward it.

No one had popped out, and I couldn't sense anyone else among the pines.

So, I quickly entered, and when I exited on the other side in the Veil, I wasn't alone and was greeted by the fae that I had been tasked with finding.

"Evening, Atticus. What a pleasure to have you finally join us." A tall, eloquent woman spoke. Her long lavender hair was intricately braided, cascading down to her waist like a waterfall. She wore a glittering dress that complemented her shimmering skin.

She was young-looking; however, something told me she was much older than she appeared.

"My name is Lula, I am the Clan Mother of the Fae." She chuckled, "You must have some questions about how I know who you are?"

"I do, among other things," I responded, glancing around at the men who accompanied her on either side. They watched me closely and without so much as an inkling if they'd draw their weapons that were slung on their backs.

Lula nodded, moved aside, and gestured behind her, "Please let me take you into the village where I'll show you where you'll be staying."

All I could do was follow. To resist was disrespectful among the fae, especially if shown towards the Clan Mother or Father.

As we passed through the village, several children darted in front of us, their squeals of delight echoing through the dense forest that surrounded the homes and buildings.

My gaze followed their retreating forms, and when I lost sight, I glanced back at the village.

It was evening in the Veil. Instead of the street lights on Earth, the trees intertwined among the landscape, homes, and buildings came to life the farther we walked.

I had heard of the phenomenon and natural lighting before, but never witnessed them with my own eyes, since I had spent most of my time either in the isles or on Earth.

Each tree was lit with a luminescent blue glow under the

bark, creating unique patterns, like snowflakes when viewed under a microscope. They slowly pulsed in time; the rhythm was hypnotic and eased worries I hadn't realized were seeping into my dragon and me.

Lula leaned over, whispering so as not to disturb the sequence of light, "It's magnificent, isn't it, the trees?"

I remained quiet but nodded as we walked through more trees and stopped in front of an ancient cobblestone home. Vines grew from the base, reaching toward the sky, running along some of the slightly protruding stones. Off to the side was a small patio that held several chairs made from branches.

It was small, cozy, and a place where someone could sleep for a few nights.

Which is precisely how long I planned to stay. The urge to return to Viv strengthened as the day wore on.

She was livid with me last night, and I couldn't help but enjoy her wrath because any little emotion that was dug into me meant she felt something aside from indifference.

But I wanted her love most of all, and I was a patient enough dragon to wait for her to change her mind. Even if the mate sickness pushed her to be in my presence, it was still her choice whether she wanted to complete the bond or break what had developed.

I was hesitant about letting her know about that yet. Not until she got to know us better.

Lula guided us into the house, leaving her guards outside as she took me on a tour of the small home.

"I hope you find the dwelling adequate while you are with us. Feel free to explore the village, you'll more than likely run into Brooke while out and about." She clasped her hands in front and exhaled slowly, "I do have to warn you, though, she doesn't fully have herself under control yet. It doesn't help that Cadence isn't here to help her along."

I knew full well she could be unpredictable without her mate by her side. If someone had separated Viv and me, I would burn every single building and dwelling until I found her.

"Understood, however, I did speak with Cade before I came here. I have a message for her from her mate that I think will help. And I plan to help release him when I return so that she won't be without him for much longer."

Lula quirked her brow, "And our King has agreed to this already? It hasn't been very long since he changed her."

Shrugging, I let a mischievous smile cross my face, "He'll find out when the time comes. I'll deal with the consequences when that happens."

"You play a dangerous game, dragon." She chuckled, "Nevertheless, having him here would be beneficial for them. He will be welcomed with open arms as well; it's not safe currently with who's in charge of the vampires."

Interesting.

Each species within the Veil had its own leaders and its own laws. Ultimately, though, everyone followed the law of Finn, the Demon King. His family was the oldest inhumans there was, and it was said that each supernatural was born from different parts of their blood, bones, and skin.

But that was a story for another time.

"Anything I need to relay back to our king?" I asked.

"Not at this time. We are monitoring, with the gargoyles leading that front as they are extremely stealthy."

"Well, just let us know, and we'll be there to help as well. We don't need anyone to get out of line, and if and when humans are allowed to travel to the Veil, we'll need to quell any dangers before they rise."

Lula nodded. She glided to the front door, her hand hovering over the handle before she turned back, "Have a pleasant evening, Atticus, and get some rest, you're going to need it."

"Thank you, good night to you as well."

As she opened the door, the illumination from the trees poured in. I caught the tail end of one of the fae guards staring with his jaw clenched briefly before he dropped any kind of expression that was forming, and it was as if it was never there when he smiled at the Clan Mother when she exited.

I'd have to keep a close eye on that one while I was here. He was up to something, and I wasn't sure if Lula knew or not. Only time would tell if his actions betrayed his duties.

Chapter Sixteen
Kit

Agitation rose as I flew through the air in my dragon form, scouring yet again for the baby vamp, Brooke, who had escaped for the tenth time in the last few weeks.

I had planned on leaving after only a few days, but that was impossible with her constant attempts at reaching her mate on the other side of the Veil.

It didn't help that the fae kept magically moving their location. Every morning, we'd wake up, and it would be in a different part of their woods, making it tempting for Brooke to take off yet again, thinking she could find a portal back to Earth and to her mate, who was currently in a heavily guarded supernatural jail cell.

According to Lula, the change in locations was a precaution, as the vampires desperately searched for Brooke and had nearly succeeded a few times when they'd broken through the barrier the fae had erected, which hid their village from anyone aside from their own people.

That also meant the portal I had used had moved. And every time I set out to search for it, the baby vamp would take that opportunity to dodge her guards and disappear. I'd have to track her down and bring her back kicking and screaming.

She hadn't yet figured out how to use her powers of persuasion or her inhuman speed, thankfully, but that didn't make it any easier when it was nearly a daily occasion. And my strength had waned since being here and away from my mate longer than I wanted.

Brooke had refused to speak with me at first, knowing that I was close to the king and he was the reason her mate wasn't with her. And when I finally did give her the message from her mate, it only made her more prone to fleeing.

Do you sense the female, Vero? I said to my dragon as we flew over the tops of trees, our eyes constantly scanning for any movement.

SHE'S CLOSE.

His response was brief and lacked the information I wanted, so I tried again.

Which direction, dragon?

STRAIGHT AHEAD, SHE'S SLOWING DOWN.

Vero huffed, smoke billowing from our nostrils as his growls grew. He was as agitated with the woman as I had been.

The baby vamp prevented us from returning to Earth and to our mate, who was likely now suffering from the mate sickness as we were.

Luckily, it wasn't nearly as bad as others had talked about, although it had been horrendous for a few days. In those early days, I couldn't even leave the bed they had provided me with. And during that time, Brooke hadn't left her home either, which I found odd.

But then, like a spell, the shivers, sweating, and aching dulled to an annoying light pounding, and I was able to function and attempt to speak with the vampire, which turned out to be a colossal mistake since she was yet again running for what felt like the millionth time.

An exaggeration, I know, but you would be the same if someone prevented you from returning home and wooing your woman.

We cleared the dense forest into a large open field, where, in the Veil's moonlight, like a beacon, Brooke stood, watching as we flew through the air towards her, unmoving.

My scales stood on end, or at least they felt that way as tingling ricocheted at the back of our mind that this was wrong and that she usually didn't give up so easily. However, there she was waiting for us to land.

Vero dove through the air, landing away from where the baby vamp was so as not to jostle the ground too much from impact and knock her over.

Her stance was all wrong, and her hands clenched and unclenched in terror while her breathing became labored.

"You need to shift back to human so we can talk." She said, her voice trembling. Her shaky hands dug through the bag she had slung over her body as she pulled a thin blanket and tossed it at us.

Brooke turned without another word, giving us her back as I shifted quickly, grabbing the fabric and wrapping it around my waist.

"Thanks," I said, tucking one edge in so I didn't have to hold onto it. "What made you stop?"

She turned when I spoke, and her eyes sparkled; red tinged the edges, her chest rose and fell rapidly before she swallowed.

"Something's wrong."

"What do you—"

"What do I mean? Just as I said. I can feel it through my veins—through my mate." The wind picked up, swirling around between us, and on the cusp, whispers echoed. "Lula and the rest of the fae are on their way."

Tilting my head, I wearily eyed Brooke. She was different tonight than she had been on any of the other attempts to escape. Something stopped her from advancing, which allowed Vero and me to catch up.

"Is this one of your tricks?" I asked. She had a knack for tricking the fae, but I was never one to fall for her acts to enact sympathy and was harder on her than most in the village.

Brooke's eyes flashed a deeper red, her jaw clenching, "No. This isn't a trick. If my mate is panicking through my veins and calling out to me, there's something wrong. It's like I can hear him and he's telling me to stay put, there's someone who needed me to stop running so he could find me and then get to you to send you a message."

"But, why all the running the last few weeks?" I asked, still perturbed by being this woman's babysitter, even if I was the one who asked Finn for a mission to keep my mind off my mate.

"You would too, wouldn't you? For your mate? I have no reason to run now, especially if what Cade is trying to say adamantly through my veins is true."

"She's right, Atticus." The Clan Mother, Lula said beside me.

I nearly jumped out of the blanket, grabbing hold of the edge before it began to fall and expose my birthday suit. "For the love of the Veil, you can't sneak up on a dragon like that!"

"Oh, calm yourself, Vero knew I was here. The mate sickness clouds your human mind." Lula pointed out, which I, of course, knew: she didn't need to be Captain Obvious.

"Is that so?" I questioned anyway, looking inward at Vero, who nodded in my mind and tucked himself into a round lump of scales. I scowled at my dragon, who decided to ignore me as I turned back to the Clan Mother.

He was sulking without Viv.

"See," Lula said, her face unreadable as I narrowed my eyes at her. She nodded to several guards and turned to Brooke. "Your mate will be here soon."

The baby vamp sucked in a breath as she brought her hands to her chest, "How do you know?"

Lula smiled, waving someone forward from the back of the crowd she had brought.

A male began moving through. I couldn't tell at first who it was, but as I slowly peeked through bodies, I saw red skin and black hair.

A fire sprite.

However, it wasn't just any fire sprite but that of Jeron, Arlo's best friend and business partner at the Charred Peaks.

What was he doing here?

That question wouldn't remain unanswered for long.

"Hey, Kit," Jeron called out, "I tried getting here sooner, but needed to reach Cade before I could travel here. There's not much time, and we need to make our way back to the village. A portal has popped up just outside of it."

What is going on, and how in the world did he know where we were?

"In simple terms, I'm psychic, and I don't really have it down to a science because it comes and goes, but when it comes, it's pretty adamant. And right now it needs you to come with me."

I reared back, glancing around at the fae who didn't seem bothered by the news or that Jeron basically read my mind.

Lula grabbed some items from one of her guards and thrust them into my chest.

"Put these on, you don't want your mate shrieking once she wakes up in your arms. You'll have enough to deal with as it is with that one." She said, as if she knew my mate herself and what was going to transpire.

"Wait, what the hell is going on?" I growled, my anger rising as no one was speaking plainly to me, only in vague comments. My mate was mentioned, and that she'd be waking up in my arms, but how did she get there, and was she alright?

No one was severely panicking, so I wasn't too concerned, but I'd keep my weariness in the back of my mind until I learned more. After all, I was a more logical dragon and asked questions first before taking action.

Or I thought I was pretty good at that, which had been why Finn appointed me as his second.

Jeron stepped forward, placing his hand on my shoulder as if to calm me or keep me grounded, "I'll explain on the way, but your mate is going to need you to keep her calm when she wakes."

"And why is my mate not awake?" I asked as I put on the clothes Lula had given me.

"I'm not sure, that part is blurry. As I said, I don't have it down to a science. I can thank my mother for that." When I stood staring at him, he continued, "She's not a fire sprite, my father is, but no one is able to tell me my mother's origins, and my father won't open up about her."

When I finished dressing, we all began moving back to the village, which turned out to be closer than it had been when I left to find the woman.

I glanced back toward Brooke, the baby vamp I had been tasked with keeping an eye on, and she was walking with us without a fight; she no longer had the desire to continue her escapades, as evidenced by Lula whispering in her ear and Brooke nodding. Her first smile shone brightly since I had arrived. It was as if her spirits had been lifted by whatever the Clan Mother had uttered.

When we approached the edges of the village, the fae and Brooke broke off while Jeron, Lula, and I kept walking, passing by the familiar homes and businesses of the fae.

We reached the other side, and just past the last building, there was a portal, shimmering like it had been there all along.

I quirked my brow and glanced at the Clan Mother, "Is there a rhyme or reason to the portals appearing?"

She shrugged, "For us, they show when they are needed. We don't go looking for them like you have been. Now, go and take care of your mate. We will handle Brooke from here on out; she won't be a problem. But, don't break your promises to Cade, and as soon as you can, release him or she'll try to escape again." She glared at me and, like it was a threat, said, "You and I both know it would be disastrous if she were left to her own devices or if the vampires in the Veil got their hands on her."

"Of course, I won't go back on my word. I don't know what's going on over on Earth, but I'll make sure Brooke has her mate again soon."

With that, Lula turned from both of us and walked away. Jeron didn't hesitate and approached the portal. "See you on the other side."

He disappeared, and I followed.

When I exited the other side, my truck was right there in front of us, with snow piled on the roof and hood, while fresh powder covered the ground.

Winter was upon us.

And when I glanced behind me, the portal disintegrated as if it had never been there to begin with.

I would never understand the logic of magic, but maybe my mate would teach me a few things since she was a witch. I could only hope she'd want to see me after being gone for weeks. But she didn't have a choice, and neither did I, as an invisible thread pulled me.

My mate. She needed me, but I didn't know where she was.

"She's at the bookstore, and right about now is unconscious. You need to hurry, she's going to lose her mind when she wakes, and that will be soon." Jeron ushered me into the truck and took the driver's seat, leaving me as the passenger princess.

I wasn't going to challenge him for driving, but I had more questions than I had answers.

Like, for instance, why the hell was my mate unconscious? Who could have made her that way? Or was that her own doing? And why wasn't this more urgent?

As Jeron sped towards town, my dragon had awoken, and we were both filled with anger, and whoever had touched our mate would pay with their life because Jeron's speeding left something unsettled inside.

It was indeed a good thing he drove because my mind began to spiral as the flashing blue and red lights appeared in front of the bookstore. This was more serious than he had led on, and I wasn't sure whether he did so to keep me calm or if he genuinely didn't know the magnitude of the situation.

I didn't wait for Jeron to stop completely as I lurched my door open and ran past detectives and EMTs, the same supernaturals I worked with.

"WHERE IS SHE?" I bellowed as I entered.

Everyone shrank back except for Jorrik, who stepped forward. "This way, Kit." He grunted, picking up and forcibly moving those who were in the way out of it.

We made it to the back hallway, where stacks of boxes littered the area, and Vizek was lifting Viv's lid and examining her pupils with a flashlight.

A growl built in the back of my throat as I approached. We didn't fancy another man touching our mate while she lay unconscious, and when Vizek glanced back, he had the foresight to move away quickly.

Viv was on the floor, a jacket rolled up and placed under her neck, propping her head up slightly. She looked like she was asleep, but she was too still for our liking.

I gathered her in my arms, careful not to jostle her too much, and glanced around, trying to locate Vizek. "What happened?" I croaked, my throat clogging with uncontrollable emotions of anguish and anger.

"We don't know yet, but Teagan is missing, and it looks like there was a tiny struggle near where Viv was lying before we moved her out of the hallway," Vizek said. He started packing his medical bag and moving away to give me room to be with my mate.

Jorrik and Hawk joined the conversation, standing back to give Viv and me room when a low growl rumbled in the back of my throat when they initially approached.

Vero and I were eager for our mate to wake, and any men that came near, regardless of whether we knew them or not, were unwanted and perceived as a threat.

Jorrik spoke while his brother remained quiet, watching and observing all the inhumans roaming the bookstore looking for evidence, "Hawk and I were tasked with watching over the Queen, and the females made us stand outside of the partition while they had 'girl talk' and while every so often we could hear their laughter nothing seemed amiss, but after awhile it grew quiet. When neither one of them answered when we called out, we chose to investigate. That's when we found the back door cracked, and Viv lying on the floor, knocked out."

Anger grew beneath my chest, my scales made their appearance along my arms as I felt them emerge, and then they covered my chest and neck. Vero was on the verge of showing himself, but I talked him down when we both realized it would ruin our mates' building and make her angry at us, which we wanted to avoid.

I wanted to be furious at the two orcs, but I couldn't bring myself to chide them as I held my mate in my arms. Her weight was a constant reminder that I was here, and even with the mate sickness still lingering, it began to lessen the longer I had her next to my heart.

Ignoring the men and chaos swirling around the bookstore, I glanced down at her. At the woman whom I couldn't and wouldn't live without. Her flame-red hair dangled past my forearm, and my fingers itched to thread themselves in those locks and brush the stray strands away from her forehead.

My heart lurched, gazing down at her serene face while she had her eyes closed. And even though she was in a motionless state, she looked at peace, not warring with me or fighting our bond.

Others were trying to speak with me, but I ignored them as I felt Viv's body jerk. And then she bolted upright, sucking in a breath as she gripped my arm so tight her nails dug into my flesh, and the tinge of copper floated in the air as her grip tightened further.

She glanced around briefly, taking in all the chaos, before her head snapped toward the hall. "Where the fuck is she?"

With my free hand, I cupped her chin, gently bringing her face toward mine so she was looking at me when I told her the news. "Teags is missing, and they're doing everything they can to find her."

It took Viv a moment to clear whatever fog was still hazed over her, and she began to push at my chest while I held her tight. "Don't fucking touch me, asshole. You are the last person I want to see. Let one of your other dickface co-workers look me over."

A smile spread on my face as I was relieved to be at the end of my mate's ire. She was my fire, the flames that rose from my dragon's throat, and her temper was the best thing to be at the end of, after missing her for weeks.

Chapter Seventeen

Viv

One moment, I was being bashed over the head with a gun by a crazed stalker, and the next, I was waking up in the arms of the asshole whom I wanted nothing to do with.

That same dick-face who left me for weeks without a single word to anyone.

Who, as it seemed, smelled divine and whose hands currently felt like bliss after being without him around for what felt like eternity.

Fuck, I was kidding myself if I denied that I didn't miss him and his persistence.

Even if my mouth was saying one thing, my mind and body didn't really want him to let go of us. So I didn't struggle too much in his hold.

"I can't do that, Neesha; it is my duty as your mate to take care of you." Kit purred, his hand slid to my waist while I was still cradled against his body.

And then I stiffened again because my foggy mind was finally clearing, and the world around us that had been silent slammed into me with all the moving bodies.

Teags was missing. My best friend had been taken by her stalker, and I couldn't comprehend why no one was out there looking for her.

Why were there so many men standing around the store?

Jorrik came into view, followed by Hawk.

And fury surfaced at the sight of those two green bastards.

They were supposed to protect Teags.

They were supposed to have superior hearing.

They were supposed to stop anything from happening to her.

I glared at the two orcs, and my fiery disposition flamed to life. "You two beefcakes had one fucking job. And that was to protect Teags. Where the hell were you?"

Hawk scoffed, "Did you forget, female? You were the one to suggest we stay out so you both could have your 'girl talk,' so we listened at the behest of you and our queen."

It was a slap in the face because he was right, but he didn't have to throw it like a damn baseball square to the nose. I just wanted Teags to have some semblance of normalcy with her stalker still on the loose.

Kit growled, his chest vibrating against my arm while he glared at the green hulking male. "You will watch your tone with my mate Hawk, or it'll be the last thing you do."

And...suddenly I wanted to jump Kit's bones. His threat was intoxicating and revved up my engine. I shifted in his arms, tightening my legs together and praying to the goddess no one could smell my desire for the dragon shifter, even if it were wishful thinking in a room filled with supernaturals of all kinds.

But as it was, Kit was too close; I saw the moment his nostrils flared. His head snapped over, and his eyes found mine. They burned with lust, his pupils shifted to the slits of a dragon, and scales surfaced along his neck and arms that I was touching.

He cleared his throat, and I knew I was busted with the way his eyes roamed my body, making my cheeks heat.

Why was I embarrassed by my reactions? It shouldn't have, it had been forever since I was thrown around, and a big dick was pounding into me. Maybe I needed to ride him and get it out of my system.

I still had no craving for a mate, but I did need a good dickens, and he was looking mighty fine right about now.

First things first.

My best friend.

"Why the hellfire is everyone standing around the store and not out looking for Teags?" I questioned, glaring at Jorrik and Hawk.

Rayth walked over just then, "We have others roaming around the city looking for her, Vivienne. Have no fear, the Queen will be found soon enough. Especially with the King scouring for her now as well."

I slumped further into Kit's hold.

If I knew anything, it was that Finn would go to the ends of the world and beyond for my best friend.

Guilt crept in as I thought about our evening. Had it truly been my fault that the creep was able to get past my wards?

And that perked me up because how in the goddess did he get past my wards in the first place?

I was desperate for answers as I felt myself for my phone.

"Where's my phone? I need to call my sister."

But as soon as I said the words, Liv's voice shrieked from the doorway. "Viv! Oh, thank goddess!"

She rushed over and knelt in front of Kit and me, pulling me into her arms and out of Kit's.

And while I didn't mind the reprieve from his touch, I longed to return anyway.

Liv pulled back, and while I thought she was going to pull me into another hug, her arm pulled back before making contact with my shoulder, punching me.

Grabbing ahold of the spot she hit, I glared at my baby sister, "What the fuck, Liv? Why would you do that?"

She sniffled, wiping her nose with the back of her hand and grasping my upper arm. *Gross.*

"You bitch. You had me fucking worried sick. Jeron called and told me to get over here pronto. He said Teags is missing, too?"

Jeron—who the hell was that?

Before I could open my mouth to ask, she lifted her hand to silence me. "I already know you're going to ask. He owns Charred Peaks with Arlo. I just met him the other night. He's really nice and stuff." She shrugged, trying to be nonchalant, but I knew better.

My eyebrow raised as suspicion took root. My baby sister was talking to a boy, okay, man—whatever. To me, she was still that little girl that I protected, even though I was the one who really needed the protection from life and our father, most of all.

"Have they found her yet?" Liv asked no one in particular.

"Not yet, that I know of. I just kind of woke up from getting whacked in the noggin." I lifted my hand subconsciously and touched the spot where I had been punched with a gun, only to hiss when I felt the open wound sting.

It wasn't bleeding, but it hurt like hellfire.

"Neesha," Kit gently pulled my hand away, kissing my knuckles and helping me to my feet after Liv finally let go of me long enough for him to sneak in between us. "They got the bleeding to stop while you were unconscious. Don't disturb it, or it could start again."

I nodded, swaying on my feet for a moment as my vision blurred. His strong hands gripped my waist as he brought me into that warm, hard body.

"Thanks," I muttered, unwilling to fight him for touching me, before turning to Liv. "The wards—" I cleared the lump that formed in my throat, thinking we could have prevented him from entering, and thought we had been in the clear. "What happened to the wards? Why didn't they work, Liv?"

My baby sister shook her head, "I have no clue, Vivvy. They should have prevented anyone with malicious intent from entering any part of the property, not just the building."

She was silent momentarily as she scrolled through her phone. And then it was like a light bulb went off. "The only way our wards would have failed was if someone tampered with them, and the only person that could do that would be another witch or warlock."

"You're telling me that creep was able to have someone in our community help him kidnap their soon-to-be queen?" I asked, more to myself than actually expecting someone to answer me.

Who could it have been? And why would they do this?

There had been no word of resistance from the supernaturals; most, if not everyone, was ecstatic to join the humans out in the open on Earth.

Unless they were hiding and secretly helping the disgruntled humans who wanted us to go back into the Veil and close up shop, that is.

I wasn't privy to the inner workings of Finn's deal with the government, but I was sure Teags knew a little bit about what was going on. He wouldn't hide that from her, and that put her at risk as it was.

"Don't worry, Viv—Liv, we'll find out who could be behind taking down your wards. Can you tell if they're still active or completely taken out?" Rayth asked, clicking his pen as he flickered between a solid body and a translucent one.

I didn't have the strength to focus, but Liv did, and she went silent, closing her eyes and humming in the back of her throat.

She opened them and frowned. "They're completely gone."

I gasped. The only way that could be possible was if it were a powerful witch or warlock, or if there were multiple people.

"You don't think?" I left the question vague; only Liv would understand who I was talking about.

"No, he wouldn't risk his reputation by helping a human, and he despises them. It had to have been several of our people. The question is, are they people that we know?" Liv's response sent shivers down my spine.

Kit's arm tightened around my waist, and I found comfort in his touch.

"There's nothing more we can do right now. Kit, why don't you take the girl home and stay with Viv? I'll call if anything changes and we find Teagan." Rayth said, his body flickering in and out as the high stakes of the future queen's well-being hung in the balance.

"Sounds good, thanks for being diligent, Rayth," Kit called out.

The ghostly detective vanished, and the once-bustling bookstore grew quiet as investigators began packing up. Nothing more could be done here.

Liv turned to us, grinning at where Kit had his hand gripping my side. "I drove here, so I'm gonna take myself back to my place. Kit, why don't you take my sister home and stay with her tonight? I have things I need to take care of once I leave here."

"By things, do you mean Jeron?" I asked. My protective big sister senses were activated.

She shook her head, denying talking about the man she met. "I'll talk to you later. Take care of her for me." Liv winked before turning and zipping out of the building before I could call her back.

I had so many questions about this, Jeron, and whether they were involved, because if that was the case, I'd have to put on my big-sister pants and have 'the talk' with him. AKA threatening his balls with a knife if he hurt her. There were plenty to choose from if I went to the restaurant to do it.

And then there was the question of whether my father was involved in our wards being taken down. Liv seemed to think he wouldn't dare, but I had other suspicions.

It could be his way of trying to get me to come back home, especially with Liv moving back to Hellfire now to be near me.

Our parents knew about the fire in the bookstore weeks ago, but how much of that was orchestrated by my father as well?

He had to have a hand in what was going on. There was no other explanation.

Kit's thumb rubbed circles on my lower back, soothing my worries and bringing me back to being in his arms again.

And while it felt absolutely orgasmic just having his fingers tighten and loosen against my back without him actually touching the goods, I was still pissed.

Beyond a doubt, peeved.

No longer watching my sister vacate the store, I turned in Kit's arms and pushed at his chest. The desperate need for space consumed my thoughts, while I chewed him a new one. The space would serve my purpose since I couldn't think straight while he continued his soothing touch.

"Where the hellfire have you been dickface?"

His brow rose while the left side of his lip twitched.

"Dickface, huh?"

"Yup. Seriously, where have you been? Do you even know what I have been dealing with?" I questioned, my fury growing as his smile grew, making him look delighted with what was occurring.

"Oh, I believe I know very intimately what you have been dealing with and going through, my Neesha." He purred, slowly moving forward while I countered, taking steps backward.

It was no longer crowded in the bookstore. In fact, everyone had vacated rapidly, leaving Kit and I alone when I glanced around.

"Is that so?" I said breathlessly, swallowing the spit pooling in my throat at the sight of how his eyes devoured me.

"Yes, my mate. Every part of you aches, wishing to be touched, consumed—worshipped."

Oh boy, yes, it was indeed craving all that and more.

"The only relief you beg for is my fingertips grazing along your soft thighs as they part for me, inviting me in for a taste between them, in heaven."

Good gravy, who in the world was this man, and what happened to the dragon shifter who tried to go slow, like I was a scared kitten that would run at any sudden movement?

This man in front of me, right now, didn't care if I'd run because he'd likely find joy in chasing me.

He was the predator, and I was his prey.

And I was thoroughly enjoying this as well. I shouldn't be. I should push him away as I have been, but I was too exhausted from fighting him for weeks before he left.

My back hit a wall, and I could no longer escape his advances.

Kit's arms caged on either side of my head. Fleeing was no longer an option, not that I wanted to anyway at this moment.

My breathing picked up as his face inched closer until his lips brushed against mine in an almost kiss, but not quite enough to satisfy me. But I wasn't going to be the one making the first move; I was still pissed at him for leaving me.

"I'm taking you home with me. It's up to you whether you want me to ease your aches or if you plan to be stubborn. You can continue being angry with me either way, but wouldn't it be more satisfying if it were soothed?"

He waited for my answer while his body shifted closer to mine. The hard length of him pressed into my stomach, and I couldn't take it any longer.

I know I said I wouldn't make the first move—but fuck it.

Threading my fingers into the nape of his neck, I pulled him in as our lips crashed together, moving against one another and dulling the ache even further.

His throaty growl turned into the most sexy moan I had ever heard come from a man as our lips parted and tongues flicked against one another. Electric shocks prickled down my spine, and heat pooled in my core.

I wanted him badly. Wanted his mouth, hands, and body to encompass mine. Needed it.

Kit pulled away, panting before placing his forehead against mine in a sweet gesture.

"Don't deny what we have together, Viv. I won't take what you don't want to give. I need to hear the words. Need you to tell me that I can touch you the way I want."

I didn't—no couldn't make him wait any longer, it was agonizing being this close and not getting the relief I so desperately needed and wanted.

"Yes, I want you to touch me in every way possible." Swallowing around my dry throat, I bit my lip and gazed at him through my lashes, "Take me home, Dragon."

Chapter Eighteen

Viv

The door slammed against the wall with the jingle of keys still in the deadbolt, rapping against the wood. The aftermath of Kit's carelessness left a doorknob-sized dent behind it as we fumbled through the entrance.

Our mouths never leaving one another as desperation swirled with our tongues. Kit's hand worked wonders as he meticulously extracted his keys while shutting the door, all while the other held me against his warm, hard body and delicately pushed me further into his house.

Once it was closed, he wasted no time as his hands gripped the back of my thighs, and he lifted me, wrapping my legs around his waist. I crossed my ankles behind him to keep from slipping, all while we ignored everything around us as he walked to a bedroom, which I had to guess was his, before he threw me onto the bed. My body bounced a few times while a giggle left my throat.

I liked this side of him, the side that let go and didn't worry about what I thought, just what we were about to do in the throes of passion.

The cold from the silky soft sheets seeped through my clothes while I shifted on his mattress. When I glanced around, the bedding was rumpled like he didn't care to straighten it after waking up. His bed was large; one of his pillows remained perfectly straight while the other was slightly turned, telling me that this was the one he laid his head on.

My gaze landed back on Kit as he watched me examine his space. His eyes flickered back and forth from golden dragon slits to his human ones, like he was vying for control over himself.

But, I didn't want him controlled, I wanted him feral, to devour me and give my body what it was craving all these days and weeks without him. To sate the lust coursing through my veins, when every night he had been gone. Over the course of that time, I'd overuse my vibrator just to get myself to pass out.

Kit stripped his shirt, a trail of gold scales led down to the edge of his pants, and I could only imagine what lay just beyond the waistband. The anticipation left my mouth to water as I watched his fingers slowly unbutton his pants, leaving them open at the top, and all while his eyes never left mine.

I loved seeing him so unhinged and frantic to join me on the bed as he prowled forward like the predator he was.

The cords of his muscles shifted seductively as he moved over me. His body pressed against mine in a delicious, warm cage that I never wanted out of.

His fingers traced delicate lines along my cheeks down to my lips, like he was memorizing every part of me before his head lowered.

Kit's lips grazed over mine lightly, like butterfly wings, while he spoke, "You haven't changed your mind, have you, Neesha?"

His question made me giggle, as I bit my bottom lip. It was a silly question at that, one he shouldn't have to ask, so I tilted my head, staring into his eyes, daring him to look away while I slowly dragged my tongue over his bottom lip. He groaned, his fists tightening in the sheets on either side of my head.

"Does that answer your question?" I whispered, pulling back slightly to gaze into those eyes that kept flickering from human to his beast.

He smirked and nodded. "Yeah, I suppose that does."

I was tired of waiting for him to continue; my impatience won out, and I threaded my fingers in his hair, making a fist and pulling him into me. Our lips met with fevered frenzy. Taking his bottom lip in between my teeth, I lightly bit down before soothing it with my tongue.

He groaned, panting into my mouth, never protesting the pain mixed with pleasure. The control was heady and addicting, ramping up my already heightened desire.

"Take my clothes off," I demanded, pulling away, my hair spreading across his pillow while I lay back.

The dragon shifter did as I commanded, his hands roamed across my stomach while he pushed my shirt up and off. The once frenzy slowed down while he undressed me bit by bit, taking his sweet time grazing his fingers along my heated skin with each piece of clothing he took off.

It was maddening, but it would make the release that much sweeter.

Everything I wore was discarded on the floor, besides the black lace panties that he left on. And he left me that way while he slowly slipped off his pants to reveal an already rock-hard cock that sprang free, bobbing at my perusal.

No boxers. Fucking hot.

Licking my lips, I couldn't keep my eyes from trailing his body. More golden scales dotted along his frame, like the dragon was fighting to be let free. And when my gaze trailed along the scales that had sunk below his waistband on his stomach, reaching his dick, my mouth watered. It was the most glorious one I had ever laid my eyes on. Thick, as if I reached out and encompassed the base, there would be at least an inch separation between my fingers. He was long but not overly so that it would bruise my cervix—too much at least. And veiny, oh those veins. I had never been one to examine a cock at great length, but this one was perfection. And most of all, he had ridges unlike a human man; they ran along the top of the entirety of his cock.

I could only imagine how those would feel rubbing inside me, and the thought made me whimper, shivering in delight.

"Shh—I'll go slow, my mate." He whispered soothingly.

Kit's concern was adorable, but those noises were for something else entirely different.

"I'm not worried, I want you inside me. Now. Fuck me like you mean it."

He chuckled, crawling back over the bed and hovering over me, our bodies barely touching.

"Patience, woman. Let me enjoy you first."

I opened my mouth to object, but what came out instead was a gasp when his lips found their way to my neck. He sucked, bit, and licked his way down over my collarbone, trailing wet kisses before he reached between my breasts.

His hand reached up, cupping one while his mouth closed over the other, sucking lightly—the perfect pressure and attention to each one. My toes curled, and I found myself trying to grind into his stomach. I needed to relieve the pressure and ache that had been building for what felt like hours.

And Kit knew what I needed as he continued his descent, kissing and licking his way down my stomach in agonizing slowness, nipping at my hip before settling his shoulders between my legs.

Anticipation was a bitch right about now because it made

me needy and extra sensitive to his hot breath over my damp panties.

I wanted to growl at him in frustration.

Then, he threw my legs over his shoulders, grinning as he closed his eyes, taking a deep inhale at my center. His nose rubbed teasingly along my clothed pussy, and I finally growled, "Take them off or push them to the side already!"

"Patience, Neesha," he snickered.

I blew out a huff of annoyance.

Patience, my ass. If he didn't start doing something, I was going to push him to the side and take matters into my own hands soon.

There had never been a man who had taken his sweet time with me. I wasn't built for this slow-teasing bullshit. I liked it fast and rough; no one had ever 'savored' and lingered. It just wasn't in my vocabulary before him.

Kit finally began rolling my panties over my hips, down my thighs. And then I heard the rip before he flung the tattered material across the room.

"Those were my favorite—Oh!" I cooed, silenced when his mouth closed over my pussy.

His fingers parted my lips, and the tip of his tongue swirled around my clit, shooting electric ecstasy through my body. My hips bucked against his mouth while my head thrashed wildly. It was what I had been missing. Being touched by a man reverently. It was intoxicating, and I wanted more. Wanted to feel Kit's body pressed into mine while we moved as one.

"More," I moaned greedily.

Kit chuckled against my pussy, tasting me like he was a starved man while he ignored my demands. His fingers found my entrance, and slowly he pushed in two, pumping until his fingers were coated, and then he added a third.

The stretch was exquisite, and I keened at the feeling of being so full.

Kit's eyes never wavered from my face. His lips closed over my clit, and he sucked. I was seeing stars in the back of my head. Crying out, I reached the height of pleasure when my climax slammed into me; I was finally being rewarded after so many weeks in an involuntary dry spell, and it was earth-shattering.

My body shook while he tenderly licked up my release, groaning when I tightened around his fingers that were still slowly pumping in and out before he pulled them from my warmth. He brought those pleasuring digits to his mouth and sucked the wetness from them for one last taste.

I loved it; his need to savor my flavor was such a turn on, and it made me greedy because now I wanted his cock inside my body, rearranging my insides if possible.

"Fuck that was amazing, I want more." I panted, reaching for his arms to pull him over me so we could continue.

"Neesha, don't you want to give yourself time to breathe?" Kit was too sweet in this moment, considerate of my feelings, but I was a sexual person, and when I got it once, I wanted it a few more times before I'd tire, especially if it was out of this world orgastic.

"Fuck breathing, let me make you and me feel good together. Lay down." I urged. My body heated with the intensity of his gaze when he finally lay on his back.

I climbed over his legs, putting my pussy over his thick, hard cock, and when our skin touched, he twitched, and I had the instinct to start rocking over the length, coating him with my recent release.

Kit's hands roamed over my thighs up to my hips, every touch tingling and sending renewed heat to my core.

His grip tighten helping me move back and forth. But I was

done playing because I wanted to feel every ridge inside while I rode him.

Lining up his cock to my entrance, I slowly sank, rising briefly only to lower further to the base.

"Gods, Viv. Your cunt is so tight, you're sucking me in. This is everything I have dreamed of and more."

I continued moving up and down, watching the muscles along his neck, chest, and arms tighten as I moved.

A gasp left my throat as the ridges rubbed inside like the best kind of sex toy a girl could have in a drawer, only this was Kit, *my* dragon shifter.

Mine?

There was no time to think about that, only time to feel because I wasn't going to waste our night together overanalyzing the instinctive thought.

Kit shifted, and I was being lifted off his dick, "Hey!" I protested before he flipped me onto my stomach and then lifted my ass to the air while he settled behind me.

Okay, this I could deal with, I loved this position—

The crack of a hand landed on my ass cheek; the sting was a sweet release as much as it had shocked me. I didn't take Kit to be that kind of man, and it only made me more excited because it was what I craved.

"Oh, goddess yes!" I cried out as he reentered swiftly, and my second orgasm caught me by surprise.

"Shit, Viv. Did you come again for me, sweets?" He asked, and all I could offer was a nod while I caught my breath.

His hand landed a few more stinging slaps to my ass without reprieve, which I went wild for as I bucked back against him. His taking over control of our pleasure drove me to nearly climax again, but he stopped as my pussy began fluttering around his cock.

Kit's breathing picked up; the wisps of hot air on my back

made me arch. And then hands wound their way into my hair. He gripped tightly and turned my head so I was looking at him over my shoulder.

"You're so beautiful with my cock buried deep in this cunt." He grunted, slamming in harder, and another sting landed on my backside.

It was too much but not enough at the same time, making me want so much more.

Kit's fingers left my hair and reached around my waist while his cock pistoned in and out from behind. He thrummed my clit in circles, picking up as I tightened around him, already feeling another climax on the edge.

"Let go for me, Neesha. Let me feel this pussy tighten and take all of my seed."

I threw my head back and screamed his name as my release took over with his command. Kit followed, gripping tightly to my hips that would surely have bruises in the morning. My name rolled off his tongue in a moan as he kept slapping his thighs against mine.

Soon his thrusts slowed, his lips finding my salty, wet skin as he pressed gentle kisses to my back, worshipping me before pulling out. He truly did make me feel like a goddess.

He withdrew slowly, and I collapsed, absolutely boneless, onto my stomach.

More kisses littered my back, and I couldn't help the smile that spread on my face while his fingers trailed after each one.

A shiver rolled through, bumps rose on my arms, and I squirmed when those fingers roamed over my heated ass cheek.

"Was I too rough?" He asked, voice rough from some unnamed emotion.

I smiled again, my cheeks aching from their disuse except when I was around Kit.

"No, it was perfect," I said. Sleep was already starting to

pull me under from the stress of being knocked out earlier and then thoroughly fucked by this man. But before I could fully let myself indulge in slumber, I turned to face the dragon shifter.

"Have you heard from anyone?" I asked, biting my lip, worried for my best friend even if I had been preoccupied just moments ago.

Kit pulled the thin covers over my body before he reached for his phone on the wooden nightstand. The room was lit by his phone while he opened it to the messages, quickly scrolling through whatever was on there.

His lips pierced, and then he nodded. "She's safe, a little bruised, but she fought her way out of the stalker's hold. I'm sure she's going to want to see you tomorrow."

I sighed, relieved she was found, but guilt crept in.

While I was safe, warm, and getting fucked into oblivion, she was out there in the cold, fighting for her life to reach her mate again.

Mate.

Fuck, I couldn't think about the implications of what we just did. I wanted to savor the post-glow bliss for awhile longer before reality kicked in and I needed to distance myself from Kit again. At least until the mate sickness came crawling back, and then I'd need to be close to him to appease the pain.

Kit put his phone down and wrapped his arms around me. He pulled me close, adjusting himself so my head lay in the crook of his arm. He pulled my thigh over his waist and kept his hand possessively attached to the backside of my leg. It was oddly comforting, the possessiveness in his touch, yet it was tender.

I breathed him in, the familiar campfire aroma filled my nose along with cinnamon and something uniquely Kit. I wanted to brand this moment in my mind forever because I couldn't allow it to happen again, no matter how much our bond insisted.

His fingers played in the strands of my hair; it was soothing and just plain ol' nice. To feel wanted by someone.

However short this time would be, I'd savor the closeness and normalcy of this moment. That was until I woke the next morning, then I'd need to set a few things straight in my head.

For now, I'd let myself sink into this feeling of rightness and let the day wash away in Kit's warmth and my dreams.

Chapter Nineteen

Viv

Warmth encompassed my entire body. I was wrapped in it like the best heated blanket on a winter night while sitting in front of a roaring fire. It was the sort of comfort you could only long for after a tireless day of slinging double shots and dodging conversations with certain patrons.

I nuzzled into what was supposed to be my cushioned pillow on my bed, but instead, my nostrils flared, filling with the aroma of campfire smoke and cinnamon, making my eyes snap open.

Quickly glancing around without moving an inch of my body, I deduced I indeed was not in the comfort of my bed, nor was I alone.

Something very hard, thick, and long was poking my ass cheek while that possessive hand I had enjoyed the night before was gripped tightly onto my hip. That hand held me like I was a lifeline, and if I moved the thin barriers between us, it would slip through the cracks, and everything would crumble to pieces.

I bit my lip, closing my eyes, breathing in and out deeply to slow my heart that was pounding with wild abandonment, all while the pulse in my neck throbbed so harshly my head moved to the rhythm, while I lay against a very large, tempting bicep.

I glanced around the floor and spotted a few pieces of my clothing, though I already knew I would be without underwear; at least my pants and shirt had remained undamaged. The only piece of clothing I couldn't immediately spot was my bra, which, if I had to go without, I would.

I had to get out of Kit's house and fast.

There was no way I could face him in the light of day and watch his hopeful expressions while he tried being domestic with breakfast.

No fucking thanks.

Ever so gently, I pried his fingers from my hip and slipped from the bed when all was clear, and he didn't stir from the removal.

Turning around silently, I continued watching to ensure Kit remained asleep now that I wasn't against his body. His breathing remained the same, and his lids stayed closed. My eyes traveled down to the thin blanket barely covering his lower half, and I had to admit the view was glorious. He truly was perfection wrapped in muscle, skin, and scales, which, if he weren't so keen on making me his mate, I'd wake him with my mouth.

But with that naughty thought, I had to shake my head to clear those dangerous wishes of remaining by his side because I couldn't be here when he woke up. It would only fester false hope that I wasn't ready to give, not now and possibly not even in the future.

Just because I gave my body over to his didn't mean I wanted to release my heart to him. So, the only thing that would work was to slip out before his eyes set on mine.

It was still fairly dark outside, but the horizon showed signs of the suns emanate arrival. Quickly, I grabbed my clothes, which were scattered across the floor. I glanced around for my keys and phone, only finding them outside the bedroom in the hallway, like he had dropped them without thought before entering.

My feet ever so lightly crept along the hallway, only pausing when a creak in the wood echoed from the pressure of my body. When it remained silent, and Kit stayed asleep, I diligently tiptoed naked down the stairs with my items gripped tightly in my arms. And only when I reached the landing did I scramble to get dressed.

Remembering I had left my car at the coffee shop, I decided I would call my sister as soon as I left the house and start walking. There was no way I was going to sit here and wait for her when Kit could wake at any moment.

Taking one last longing look up the stairs, my hand poised on the handle, I hesitated.

What would it be like if I could be with Kit freely? To be his in all ways, to love him how he deserved, to give all of myself over to him?

Oh, what a dream it would be, and so much simpler as well.

But that wouldn't happen. Not as long as my father was still head of our coven, having power and control over the witches and warlocks, procuring anything to blackmail, and twisting his manipulation into what he needed and wanted done.

So, while I wished to linger, I didn't.

I hastened my walk until I turned the corner, only slowing to bring my sister's name up on my phone and waiting until the dial tone on the other end was answered.

A groan protested on the third ring before I distinguished my sister's frustrated sigh.

"Do you have any idea what time it is, woman?"

I snorted. Obviously, Liv wasn't a morning person, but I didn't want to walk all the way to the coffee shop.

"I sure do, it's time to come get me o'clock. I'm a block past Teagan's and need a ride to the store to get my car."

Sheets ruffled, and a thump sounded before Liv swore. "On my way, but what in goddess' name are you doing at Teag's?"

"I wasn't at Teag's house, I was at Kit's," I said, simply. There was no use in hiding anything; it would all just come out anyway.

"Oh, thank goddess, you've come to your senses and are finally seeing the light of day where it comes to Kit."

"What? No, Liv. I just spent the night."

She snickered over the phone while her keys jingled in the background, "Right—right, just spent the night. Nothing funny or sexy happened at all."

"Liv," I warned. I didn't want to get into the fact that yes, I banged him, and it was the most amazing and breathtaking night of my life. She didn't need to know that little detail, though.

"Don't you 'Liv' me, that man has it bad for you. Everyone in the coffee shop sees it every single time he sits in there while you work. He is down bad, like super bad for you."

You don't have to tell me three times; I already knew that. For fucks sake he was my mate, but no one knew. Or at least I didn't think anyone else knew but Kit, me, my sister, Dom, and, of course, the king. I hadn't even told Teags yet.

Fuck, I'd have to do that. But, what was I going to say, 'Oh, hey yeah your mate's best friend is my mate, and I just fucked his brains out while you were in danger.'

Nope, now was not the time to bring that to her plate. She needed to recover just as much as me if not more. Her stalker put her through the wringer, mentally. I couldn't imagine what he did to her physically while I was knocked unconscious.

"Are you on your way?" I asked, changing the subject, because we were going down a path I didn't want to travel.

"Turning the corner...right...about...now."

Liv's car comes into view, and I hung up. No sense in remaining on the line when she's right there.

She crawled to a stop, rolling down the window and whistling, "Hey, pretty witch, need a ride?"

I giggled because she's obviously in a decent mood, considering I woke her up at the ass crack of dawn.

So I curtsied, holding out a nonexistent dress, then yanked the door open and plopped into the front seat.

Rolling my neck, I rested my head back and closed my eyes when she whipped a shitty to turn around.

"So, want to tell me why you are having me pick you up on your walk of shame and why you couldn't have just stayed until the dragon woke up?"

"No, not particularly," I grumbled, gazing out the window as snow started to flutter like glitter from the sky. The sun, finally peeking over the horizon, shone as Liv turned down the road to the Molten Java.

She sighed, putting the car in park, turning to face me. "Look, I might not know what's going on, Vivvy, but you can always tell me about it. As always, there's no judgment."

That was it, wasn't it? Judgment. Like anything I do could fuck someone's life up in the drop of a hat. And that someone being Kit. Because surely being involved with a Woodward witch would get his life snuffed out.

I knew I wouldn't receive it from my baby sister, but I would from our other family members—one in particular who was the sole reason I was trying to protect the dragon shifter in my own fucked up way.

Liv bit her lip, grabbed my hand, and intertwined our fingers together. "You need to know Mom and Dad called last night when we were at the bookstore. I hadn't realized they were calling until I left, and it was persistent."

She grew quiet, contemplating before I urged her on, "What is it, Liv?"

She groaned, "They know what happened last night at the bookstore."

"Shit," I swore, closing my eyes to brace for what was next.

"They were adamant about coming to check up on you. I think I got them to stay home, but I needed to warn you in case they show up."

I huffed, tilting my head back and gazing at the ceiling of her car while I spoke, "Great, just what I need. I hope for everyone's sake they don't." Gritting my teeth, I blew out a heavy breath.

"I know," She whispered. I could tell she held guilt that she couldn't keep them at bay this time around, because their arrival was inevitable. And as the older sister, my duties shouldn't burden her.

I was supposed to protect her, not the other way around.

Squeezing her hand, I plastered the best smile I could muster, "No worries, baby sis. We'll deal with it if it comes. I doubt Father would deign to come here anyway. He didn't care for the city other than what it offered in terms of business benefits for him in the past."

"True, but I wanted to warn you. Just in case."

"Well, I appreciate your efforts, Liv. I really do." I guess time would only tell whether our parents showed their faces in Mount Hellfire again. For now, I wouldn't worry about it; I'd just have to worry about what I could handle and take care of right now. "Want a drink and a pastry before you go back home to bed?"

"Obviously!"

Walking into the coffee store, several patrons were around,

either chatting to one another or engrossed in some sort of solo endeavor.

Strolling behind the counter, I made both Liv and me drinks when Saige walked in.

"Hey, Liv—Viv." She smiled brightly, throwing a sack of flour on the counter where her preparation area was set up. The customers loved watching her work, so we ensured she had ample room and clear safety glass to prevent contamination while they could still see what she was doing.

"I made blueberry muffins this morning," Saige said, pulling on gloves before grabbing two out of the display case. "You both look hungry."

I snorted, "Thanks, Saige. You've been at it early. I'm glad you're here. I wanted to talk to you about the grand opening. I still have to talk with Teags about when we're going to do it, but I wanted to finalize everything so she didn't have to."

Saige hummed, "Yes, of course! Tell me what you want and how many people we anticipate, and I'll handle how much I make."

I smiled, even though it didn't reach my eyes. I wanted so badly to talk about anything to keep my mind off of a certain dragon shifter, but I knew that was fruitless, seeing as I was currently thinking about him, anyway.

It made me wonder if he had woken up and discovered I was gone.

I shook my head; those thoughts were plaguing, and being with him dulled the mate sickness further than what I had done. I just hadn't planned further ahead if it returned and what I would do when it did because I wasn't going to complete that bond.

Not ever.

I was doing it to save him.

"I think that muffins, cookies, and maybe a big cake for

Teags would be fantastic. A small variety without being too boring." I said, handing my sister her coffee while Saige brought us the mouthwatering muffins.

"I like that idea, I just need an idea of when the opening will be so I can make sure everything is baked the night before." She pointed out.

"Good idea, we don't have an exact number, but I would assume that at least thirty to forty would attend. Friends and family, and of course, some potential customers as well. It's only a bookstore opening and not the Winter Festival or anything."

Saige pointed a whisk at me, "True, I just want to make sure we have more than enough. Can never be too careful."

"Well, then it's set." I rubbed my hands together, licking my lips as I brought the blueberry muffin to my face, speaking to it as if it was going to hear me, "Oh, sweet, lovely muffin, how I'm going to devour your soft, sweet goodness, and you'll fill my stomach allowing me to forget all the fuckery the last few days."

"Might take a few of them if you want to get full enough to forget all that." Liv butted in.

I smirked, "Never said this would be the only muffin I stuff in my face, just that it'll fill my belly."

"You're ridiculous."

"And you love me for it."

Liv rolled her eyes, sipping the coffee I had made for her.

Saige was diligently working on batter, flour smudged across her cheek while she smiled brightly. Having the baker here felt right, even if she did tell us she was just traveling through town. I was slowly working on her; I'd get her to be here longer than just the few weeks she claimed she would stay.

There was something unique about her. I couldn't put my finger on it, but I knew she had a place in Mount Hellfire and our ever-growing paranormal, human mixed community.

"So about this Winter Festival, what's it like?" Saige inquired.

The festival was a few short weeks away, and I knew that the only way to drag out Saige staying here longer would be if we planned the opening after the Winter Festival was all said and done.

I was ecstatic about the thought.

"You're just going to have to see for yourself. After all, I think holding the grand opening after the festival would be the most logical idea. Don't you think?"

She pierced her lips, "You're scheming, Viv."

"Who me?" I feigned innocence, but deep down, there was a tingle that told me that there would be an event significant enough that it would keep her here permanently. We just had to bide our time and find things to keep her busy.

Chapter Twenty

Viv

A few weeks later...

I stood outside the entrance to the Winter Festival, breathing in the crisp air as it stung my lungs with just that single inhale.

It was freezing on this side of the shimmering, magical bubble that Liv, myself and a few other witches had erected for the event. This year was by far the most different from the others, since it was the first with the paranormal and inhuman community out in the open, mingling with humans.

And most of all, it was my best friend Teag's wedding and coronation, dubbing her our official Queen to our King, Finn.

Vendors hustled in and out of the bubble as they set up for the day. Light snowflakes started falling from the grey skies while the wind picked up, sending a shiver up my spine and making the hairs on my neck and arms rise. I steeled myself to face everyone. Most of all, I strengthened myself to face the one man I had been deliberately avoiding since the night Teag's had been taken, and I was knocked unconscious.

That night, we had been more intimate than I thought possible. Something shifted between us, and it scared the living daylights out of me. So I did what I do best. I ran.

Ran from the swirling feelings that enveloped my heart and mind. I was already terrified that not if but when I saw Kit, I'd fall all over myself and into his arms again. I'd try my damndest not to make a fool of myself, but it wouldn't surprise me at all if I did. I was falling for the dragon shifter, even if I was stubborn and still refused to admit it out loud. I could barely believe I even thought it to myself.

Leaving Kit alone the next morning was certainly a choice, but one I needed to make in order to realize what stood before me. Now, though, I guess I'd just have to see which fire would brew when I was forced in the same proximity as the dragon shifter and what I would see swirl in those golden globes. Would it be desire, pity, and indifference, or worse, hatred?

I'd like to think maybe it'd be easier if he did hate me, but the thought alone sent pangs of heartache through my soul.

I was terrified, all these feelings shifting like the sands of time, and I knew my time was running out when I'd inevitably give in and accept his love and everything that came along with being a shifter's mate.

I straightened my jacket that covered the fancy dress Teags insisted I wear for her big day, shifting the body backpack to the front and waltzing through the bubble.

All had been silent on the other side, and it was as if I had walked into a completely different world. Which, I suppose, was the concept of the bubble. It was still cold, but not freeze-your-lungs-into-a-popsicle kind of cold in here, more bearable.

Making my way through the already gathering crowds and vendors still setting up, I made my way to the falls where Teags and Finn would say their otherworldly vows, which would connect them not only as husband and wife but as King and

Queen. Their combined event would echo through the inhuman world and, hopefully, lay the foundations for unity between humans and paranormals.

"Viv! There you are, Teags is beside herself that you haven't shown up yet." Saige had sought me out, entangling her arm with mine as she led me the rest of the way to a tent that had been erected just for my best friend.

There were still a few hours left before the ceremony started, so I was unsure why there was such a big rush. But when she brought me to Teags, my best friend had been pacing back and forth, and I knew immediately she needed me.

"Oh, thank goddess!" Teags rushed over when I entered, wrapping her arms around my neck, squeezing while I patted her back, trying to soothe whatever anxieties she was currently facing.

"Almost can't breathe there, Teags," I choked, tapping her arm when it tightened further before she released me.

"Sorry, sorry! I just—I'm so happy you're finally here." My best friend started pacing again. "Do you think the paranormals are going to be okay with a human as their Queen? What if I can't do the job? What if I fail and they tell me I can't be with Finn and they find a different Queen to fill my shoes?"

She rattled the questions off in rapid succession. I chuckled because there was no way anyone would ever come between the King and his fated mate. She'd be a natural ruler by his side, and I knew one thing: Finn would burn the world before anyone told him she couldn't be their Queen.

And no one in their right mind would question the fates. She had absolutely nothing to worry about, but then again, she didn't understand that, so I'd have to make her grasp that her role was much greater than she knew, and no one would come between her and Finn, ever.

"Teags," I stepped in front of her, taking her cheeks

beneath my fingers so she could focus on my face. "You have nothing to worry about. No one and nothing is going to stand in the way of today. Well, I take that back, only you stand in the way of completing the ceremony and the bond. But, I know you won't do that because you, my sister from another mister, love Finn with everything that you have, and he sure as fuck loves you back, unconditionally."

She sniffled, nodding as her eyes filled with unshed droplets. "He does love me, doesn't he?"

I rolled my eyes, "Duh, silly. He did reveal the supernatural world to the humans, didn't he?" She nodded, while I could see Saige beside me moving her head up and down as well in agreement. So, I continued because I was calming her nerves the more I spoke, "And he was determined to come back to you, come hell or high water. It might have taken thirteen years, but that demon did it all for you."

Teags took a deep breath, and when she let it out, all the tension and worry drained. "You're right. I'm just being ridiculous. I didn't want to disappoint anyone, especially not Finn, but I know I'd never let him down."

Seeing my best friend so beside herself with love twisted my heart with a longing that kept building the longer I was away from Kit. Only this time it wasn't the mate sickness, which I had to assume was cured when we had sex, since I hadn't felt that bone-crushing ache since then. But the need to be near someone you like or maybe even love was still there, lingering just beneath my skin.

For me, it was only a matter of time before everything came to a head, because for inhumans and supernaturals alike, when we fell in love, we fell fast and hard.

Did Kit love me already? And would he forgive me for walking out the morning after we had shared our bodies?

I felt like a completely different woman after the night we shared, as if he were more intertwined with my soul.

I'd just have to ask Kit myself when I saw him. He'd be here today, I knew he would, since Finn was his best friend, and he wouldn't miss this day for anything other than to be next to the King's side.

There was scratching at the entrance to the tent we were in, and a moment later, Mitsy popped her head through the opening. Her eyes lit up seeing us, and she entered quickly before closing the flap behind her.

"Oh my goodness, Teagan, you are a vision. I knew my designer friend would make you the best gown fit for a Queen." Mitsy squealed, pulling Teags into an embrace, which was returned without hesitation.

"Thanks, Mits, she really did an amazing job. I can't wait for her to come to the city soon!"

Mitsy pulled back, glancing at us all before a grin spread wildly, "Ready to make this official?"

"Absolutely." Teags nodded, sucking in a breath and straightening her spine.

We all helped our Queen out the door, ensuring every stray strand was put back in place, and her dress remained undisturbed.

Mitsy, Saige, and I walked toward the front, where Teags had demanded we stand, and joined my baby sis, Liv, who was already waiting for us. And then, with blurry eyes, we watched our beautiful friend walk toward Finn, who stood out against the bright blue hue of the frozen falls that fell in droves behind him.

His eyes remained fixed on Teags the entire time, from the moment he saw her until it was pronounced that they were man and wife, King and Queen. And only then did he take his eyes from hers as they closed while their lips sealed the human side of the ceremony.

The entire grandeur passed quickly, while I didn't pay a lick of attention to it. I was too busy trying not to meet Kit's gaze, zoning out until the very end when cheers and clapping erupted. Only then did I briefly meet his eyes before everyone began moving up the wooden steps to make our wishes to the frozen falls and enjoy some hot cocoa to counter the chill that still lingered even in the magical bubble.

With a styrofoam cup in my left hand, I gripped the railing with my other, staring idly at the back side of the iced falls.

Back here, you were meant to make a wish, and if you did so with the one you loved, it would last an eternity.

I snorted at the absurd myth as I thought about it.

"What's so funny, Neesha?" Kit chuckled, the snow crunching beneath his boots at his approach.

I glanced over once he was up against the railing next to me. "Just about the silly childish tradition people seem to think is real, being behind the falls, making equally foolish wishes."

He glanced over, a sparkle in his eye as his grin widened. "You don't think they're true?"

I shook my head, "No. I think they are made-up fairy tales for little girls and boys to believe that true love exists when all it does is crash and burn, eventually hurting one or both parties."

He hummed a rumble deep in his throat, not saying anything else as we stared into the frozen wall of water.

It was a companionable silence that felt easy, unstrained, but with the edge of something else entirely that was only Kit.

I hadn't seen him in a few weeks, and being near him again reminded me that I could indeed have that fairy tale ending. If only I were brave enough to confess to him why I was so apprehensive about solidifying our bond.

That I was keeping him at a distance to save him from being used by my father.

Exhaling heavily, Kit's head turned, giving me all his attention.

"You look breathtaking today, well, every day you do. But, like an emerald shimmering just beneath the surface as the late-day sunlight reflects off it."

Flattery would get him many places, especially since I had been missing him, even though I was still hesitant to admit it out loud.

"You've been missing from my coffee shop the last few weeks and in my front yard prowling in your dragon form, you know."

"Ah, yes, well, I figured I'd stay away since you seemed keen on sneaking out before I woke up. And Vero didn't much feel like being rejected again."

Wincing, I went to open my mouth to tell him why, but closed it. Glancing back to the ice and the symbols one of the local artists had sculpted before the Winter Festival, my brows furrowed. He had every right to be upset, but it hurt regardless, even if I did it to myself.

What could I say to him? Everything I thought of sounded pathetic and were poor excuses for how I treated him.

So, without glancing at him, I mustered enough of myself to apologize. "I'm sorry, Kit. You have to understand it's not you, it's me."

He burst into laughter; the sound was loud and drew a few people's attention to us. "Really, Neesha? The whole it's not you, it's me bit? I respect that you have your reasons, but don't fill me with that bullshit."

He confirmed he was upset and rightfully so. We had shared an amazing night, and I mucked it up by being my usual hit it and quit it self.

Crossing my arms, I turned to face him, irritation blooming because he didn't understand that it was indeed me and not him. I was the whole fucking reason for this mess.

"It really is me, Kit. You have to believe that. You're amazing and seem to have your life figured out without complications arising to fuck it all up and collapse any semblance of normalcy that you try to find." I was rambling, but goddess did it feel good to do so. "You have no idea what I've been put through, what I've dragged myself out of before moving back here years ago. I'm no good. Not for you, nor anyone else, regardless of whether you were my mate or not. I can't risk you."

There, I said it. Well, without actually saying anything, but fuck it was wonderful all the same.

Something deep within had begun crumbling the moment Kit had thrown me over his shoulder the night of the fire, and those walls I had erected were scattered, like dust in the wind.

I looked up and gasped when I saw what swirled in his eyes. They were his dragon's golden slits, staring incredulously before he took a hesitant step in my direction, closing the gap that had been between us.

Kit's fingers threaded through the strands of my red hair while he brought his forehead to mine.

"Neesha," He whispered, "You think pushing me away is the answer, but it isn't. We are mates, and anything that is troubling you troubles me. Anything you have to deal with, I will be right beside you, dealing with it as well."

He gently shook his head, his chest rising and falling slowly while he kept his gaze glued to mine.

"Whatever battles you think you have to fight alone, you no longer have to. Let me fight beside you, let me take some of those burdens and lessen them for you."

Sighing, I knew this was a fight I was slowly losing, and

there was so much I still wanted to protect him from, "I want you too, Kit, I do. But you don't know what you're asking for. What's in the past and the kind of danger I put you in just by being your mate."

"Then tell me so I'm prepared and can help keep you safe. Vero demands it, and I do too."

I giggled, lightness filling my chest at the sound of those words Kit uttered, "Vero does now, huh?"

"Yes, he's very insistent." Kit's smile brightened, allowing those last bits of apprehension to fall away, and I found myself gripping onto him, ready to spill everything and anything.

"Kit, my parents—"

I started but didn't get to finish as my sister's frantic calls echoed in the tunnel of the back side of the falls. Liv spotted me above a group of people and hurried over to where Kit and I stood close together.

When she reached us, my heart was thudding wildly in my chest, making its way up my throat, "Liv, what's the matter? What's happened?"

I looked within myself, checking the wards we'd erected back up at the bookstore and coffee shop, along with those at my home. But, there was nothing amiss, so I searched her face for anything that would give away what was going on. And slowly the ebbs of dread tightened across her face.

"It's our parents." She hastily spat out, breathing heavily from jogging over.

"What about them?" I questioned, queasiness hit me as my mouth watered at just the thought of our parents being mentioned.

"I'm so sorry, Viv, they're here."

I stared at her because I could have sworn she said they were here. "What do you mean they are here?"

“I meant what I said; they are here at the festival, and they brought Kash.”

Like a record screeching, I became frozen. This wasn’t happening right now. Not when I was close to revealing to Kit that the people who posed a threat were my parents and that they were now here and could very well find out who he was to me.

“The fuck?”

“Yeah.”

“Who’s Kash?” Kit asked, glancing between Liv and me.

Shit, I had almost forgotten I was still holding onto him. It was like everything in my life suddenly came to a halt. So I let go of his arm but remained by his side.

I was about to answer, but Liv waved him off, ignoring his question. “You need to make yourself scarce before they make their way up here.”

And I was certainly about to do just that when I heard my father’s voice. Deep, booming, commanding, and utterly terrifying.

“There are my two girls.”

Instinctively, I stepped away from Kit, putting as much distance between us as I possibly could. Not that I wanted to, but I was still trying to protect him regardless of what he just said.

When I moved away, the air rushed between us, making a shiver run up my spine as my father approached with my mother hanging on his arm and the man he had argued was my fiancé and ex, Kash, trailing close behind.

“Liv, my most beautiful youngest, come here. It’s been too long.”

As our father wrapped my sister in his arms, she chuckled; it was strained but practiced nonetheless to fool anyone into thinking she was at ease. “It hasn’t been that long dad.”

"Regardless, it is good to see you." He turned to me, the smile he held for my sister fading slowly as he perused me with a slight disdain, a grimace on his lips. "As for you, my eldest daughter, I'm disappointed you haven't tried reaching out to your mother or me. It is such a shame your talents are being wasted in this city."

I bared a forced smile, pretending those words didn't work. The little daggers cut like paper slits against my skin.

"Hello to you, too, Horace," I said, with a careful clench to my jaw.

He waved in dismissal, "I'm your father, young lady. You will address me as such."

I huffed, "Of course, where are my manners?" I curtsied in mock, bowing my head before lifting it back up and smirking. "So good to see you, Dad. It's been too long, how silly of me to let it get that way."

My father's face didn't show an ounce of anything but anger, before my mother had the foresight to distract him when she spoke up, "Well, we've traveled far to ensure you are well and even brought Kash. He's been so worried about you, Vivienne."

I glanced at the warlock and turned back to my mother. "Thank you for being concerned, but I'm alright. Nothing I can't handle."

Kash moved forward, while I could just pick up Kit's growl at his approach. And Kit, not understanding the dynamic and my panic at his presence, stepped closer, crowding my back.

"Vivienne," Kash quickly gripped my hand with his, bringing it up to his lips to kiss my knuckles. "You are even lovelier as the years pass." A small smile tugged at the corners of his lips. I wanted to gag.

Kash was nice enough, but there was always something that I disliked. Maybe that's why I had decided to make him my ex and call off the wedding, which neither my father nor Kash had taken into account.

Kit reached out, offering his hand to my warlock ex, "I'm Kit. It's nice to meet some of Viv's family."

Kash chuckled, taking Kit's hand in return, dropping it after shaking it. "Oh, I'm not Vivienne's family, yet at least." He glanced down at me, "Though, I hope to be soon, once Vivienne has solidified all the wedding preparations."

Goddess almighty, take me out now before I combust.

I held up a finger about to protest when my father annoyingly cut in, glaring at Kit, who was glowering at Kash.

"And who might you be, young man?"

"Oh, I'm nobody. Just a friend."

Kit's answer seemed to placate my father for the moment, and I couldn't help but stare in shock at the dragon shifter. Something lurched at his wording, 'just a friend.'

Was he saying all this because he could sense my panic, or did he see it that way because Kash decided to open his big fat mouth and declare that there was something more there?

I needed to tell him that this warlock was mistaken and that I didn't plan to have a wedding with this man. But every second that passed, those fleeting moments when I thought I could overcome my fear, felt weighed down and chained, locked in place.

"You know, I should actually get going. There's lots to see, and our King and Queen's wedding and coronation reception will be starting soon." Kit didn't glance at me as he walked away. Didn't utter another word, not even a see you later.

"Kit, wait!" I yelled, but that didn't stop him as I continued watching him retreat and slowly disappear into the crowd, my heart shattered with every step he took. Was this goodbye? Did he just realize who the kind of people I called my family were, and bow out?

Shit. Shit. Shit.

Now, I was the one desperate for him to return. My chest tightened, my breathing picked up, and all I could think was that I completely fucked this up.

This was the exact scenario I wanted to protect him from.

I was fucked, every which way but in the fun kind, where my hair was pulled, and my ass cheeks were getting clapped.

Stupid father. Stupid Kash. Stupid everything!

"Viv? Do you need a moment?" Liv asked, gently rubbing my arm while everyone was staring at me.

I needed to leave. I had to get out of here. I'd just have to apologize to Teags later. I didn't want to cause a scene or worry her on her big day.

So, I nodded, "Yeah, I'll just go freshen up a bit."

But that's not what I was going to do as I turned and headed for the stairs, making my way down toward the parking lot.

My eyes kept scanning the crowd, looking for any signs of Kit, but he was absent, sending my head into a spiral and my heart panging with mounds of guilt.

I hadn't spoken up, hadn't been brave enough to stick up for myself, and I was afraid that I'd never get a chance to tell Kit I wanted to be his mate badly, but that I couldn't because of Horace Woodward, my father, the destroyer of everything I have good in my life. And this was just another thing he'd obliterate, turning to ash before I could save it myself.

Chapter Twenty-One

Viv

After leaving the Winter Festival, I'd locked myself in my house and bedroom, ignoring everyone who knocked on my door or tried calling my phone.

That irritating buzzing was ingrained in my head, vibrating for the hundredth time. I still didn't bother to check who it was.

The sheets beneath my head were soaked from the endless stream of tears that rolled over the bridge of my nose and down my temple as I lay on my side. I didn't bother with a pillow since I had thrown it across the room in a fit of rage sometime during the night.

I stared at the wall across from my bed; it was a good vantage point to lie and wallow in self-pity.

Because that's what this was, pity for myself. I had fucked up the one thing I had started to come to terms with, and even though I was still leery about letting Kit in, I knew it was inevitable.

Avoiding my parents and Kash was easy enough the last few days, but I couldn't go much longer without contacting Teags. She and my sister Liv were the only two with whom I had any sort of contact, and even that was limited to texts here and there.

Liv threatened to drag me out of the house, and that was why I had decided this morning, after a good cry, I'd muppet myself from the sheets, and it would suffice.

So, with more effort than I wanted to admit, I rolled through the motions of all the basic hygienic necessities I had been neglecting.

When I finished dressing and dabbing a little mascara on, I felt lighter but still weighted down by the fact that Kit hadn't tried reaching out to get some kind of explanation. And I think that hurt me the most. I was too scared and stubborn to do it myself, so I sat in this limbo of a plague.

I could deal with my asshole father and my meek mother's insistence, but the absence of Kit was a hollow hole. One that kept getting larger and deeper, just waiting for my body to plunge from the edge, just to be buried alive.

Walking down my steps toward the front entrance, I could see someone trying to peek in through the thin glass window next to the door. The sun was shining bright today, so it was hard to see who it was right away until they spoke.

"Knock, knock, big sister. Time to rise and shine." She smooshed her face against the glass, making a small giggle bubble from my throat.

That small sound alone caught her attention, and her gaze found mine, smile widening, and her excitement flew out in different directions. "I see you! Little witch, little witch, let me in. Or I'll huff, and I'll puff, or I'll blow something that you probably don't want to hear about."

Liv really was trying to make me feel better. And okay, it might be working. So, I unlocked the two deadbolts and flung the door wide open.

The cusp of a fresh winter breeze blew in, reviving the stale air of my home along with my sister's lilac perfume as she waltzed in.

She hugged me tightly without saying a word. The comfort of having someone else around was something I hadn't realized I needed. And the overwhelming emotions blubbered out, making me hiccup and fresh tears to stream down my face.

I was sure that my newly done-up mascara was running, making me look like a raccoon when I swiped at my eyes.

Liv pulled back, holding my upper arms, "Look, I know that you kept in touch with me and all that, even if it was through text, but this isn't good for you, Vivvy."

I nodded; she was absolutely correct, but I was hesitant to face our family and even more terrified to see Kit. So I took up making myself count Dracula and avoided anything to do with daylight and the outside world for the time being.

"Enough, hiding yourself away. We're getting out today, going to the coffee shop, and you're going to make a drink for you and me, and then we'll figure it out from there." She clicked her tongue, gathering my jacket and purse shoving them in my hands. "I'm driving. Kay? No more wallowing."

She sniffed in my direction, nodding to herself, "At least you smell good. So that's a plus."

Indeed, it was.

I barely spoke two words as she drove us to my store. The only thing playing was a metal ensemble, with a saxophone lulling everything and defying the song's rockiness. It was a welcome distraction from everything that was crumbling.

I wanted to ask if she'd seen or spoken to Kit, but I had kept those questions to myself. I didn't know if I even really wanted to know that answer because knowing could crush my soul even more than it already was.

We walked into the store, and Saige was near the front. She peered over briefly before going back to her kneading and then doing a double-take. She squealed, and with flour caked to her fingers, she ran over, embracing me while keeping her hands poised away from my clothes.

"You are a sight for sore eyes, Viv. We've been missing you, girl!" Saige said excitedly. Her smile was infectious, and it took little effort to return it.

"Missed you too, Saige. Sorry, I didn't say bye at the Festival."

She waved me off, walking back to her prep area. "Eh, it's so alright. It had gotten so busy that no one knew who was where or if up was down. No matter, you're here." She lowered her voice to a hushed whisper, "I heard your parents are here, yeesh, sorry to hear that. They've been by the store a few times, but I think they gave up the day before because they weren't here yesterday, and so far not today either."

That was good. I didn't want to see them, let alone speak with them. I had already made it abundantly clear a while back that I was not going to marry Kash under any circumstances. But my father must have failed to let the warlock know that detail since he had traveled to Mount Hellfire with them, expecting a more warm welcome than this cold bitch attitude.

After a few more pleasantries with my favorite baker, I slung some drinks for customers to help out my baristas before making Liv's and my drink.

I was humming along to a tune when the doorbell chimed at the front. I was too engrossed in finishing up the drinks to notice that someone was standing directly in front of me on the other side of the espresso machine until they cleared their throat.

Glancing up, my eyes locked with Kash's. He was smiling, it was warm with a hint of charm, and there was something else I couldn't name. And if I were a superhero with arachnid abilities, my senses would be going haywire. But as it were, I couldn't comprehend what it was, so I tried to mask it with an equally pleasant smile.

Fake it till you make it, they say.

"Vivienne, it's good to see you." He purred. That alone made unpleasant jitters scatter across my shoulders and up my neck.

"Hello, Kash. What can I help you with?"

He grinned, that sly gleam in his eye which gave me the heebie jeebies, "Nothing much really. I just wanted to stop by and see if you'd be at work today or if I'd have to wait longer to see that beautiful face of yours."

Oh, gross, that alone made me snort because that was the cheesiest thing a man could spew from his mouth. "Well, I'm here, and you saw me. Now, if you don't mind, I have things to do."

Turning, I put my back to him when the door chimed again, and my parents walked in. I halted my retreat, panic exploded inside me, and I frantically peered around to see where Liv was.

But I didn't have to search for long when she stood from one of the love seats and approached, standing by my side in solidarity.

"Mom, Dad, what a pleasant surprise. I didn't realize you were still in town." I said, Liv glanced at me and then did a double-take with Kash, like she hadn't paid attention that he had walked in before them.

But I was fully aware. Their presence and Kash's was an ambush.

"Enough. We've been patient and have waited for your little rebellion to run its course. You've been hurt and put in danger one too many times. It's time you forget this silly little endeavor and come home where we can protect you." My father adjusted his designer coat, glancing around at all I had built with a sneer on his face. "We'll handle everything and hire someone to oversee your project so it doesn't fully go to waste, but we're taking you home. It's for your own good."

His false promises of protection vaulted me back to the past when I was a meek young woman who did anything and everything to please her father and squeak out any semblance of affection. Of course, all of that was a lie, and he just wanted to control and manipulate me into doing his evil bidding.

"Again, Vivienne, he knows more than what his tongues spew," Father said in the dark corner of his torture chamber.

I was in the center with someone who could have been innocent or not; I'd honestly never actually known when I was called to help my father in this room. Each person who was strapped to this chair was someone who had crossed my father in one way or another, and their standing with society never mattered.

Today, my father had us in a new section, away from the bar, where the moon's blue light rained down on us through an opening in the ceiling. It was the only illumination I had aside from a few lit candles near the exit, but I couldn't see where my father prowled. He always terrified me while we were confined to this room, because I was afraid one day he'd turn on me, and I'd be the one strapped here while someone else used their magic to drive me slowly to insanity.

I eyed the mysterious man with a cloth bag over his head as I tried to figure out who he was. Still, it was useless without angering my father, who always ensured that whoever he brought in here had their identity concealed.

"Vivienne."

My name alone was a warning; I was taking too long to start my spell that would conjure water and pour continuously over the man.

Pinching my fingers together, I flicked my wrist, drawing up water from the dirt ground and forming a halo of liquid above the stranger. At first, light trickling drops began to fall silently, until it became a deluge, drenching the man and rising back to its beginning.

Over and over I splashed, splattered, and sprayed him, twisting the water to my will and hurling it at his body, and each time he gasped for some semblance of air before coughing from inhaling moisture, my heart tore little by little. No one deserved this sort of torture, no matter if they were a good person or a bad one.

I didn't know how much more I could take of this. The longer I complied, the closer I was to going to hell for my sins. I was probably already there, but I had to hope there was some kind of redemption if I could get out of this. It was all because my father had forced me to do this. At first, I had helped with less dangerous tasks and had thrilled in the one time he had praised me.

It felt like I was finally gaining his approval and possibly the same love he'd shown Liv.

However, that was a significant moment and a change in course for what I did for him today. That, and he threatened to use my baby sister for his depravity.

So, I took the brunt of the misdeeds so she would never know this kind of pain and ache.

"Alright," the man gurgled, "I'll tell you where the shipment went and who did it."

I dropped the floating liquid, breathing heavily as it soaked back into the dirt beneath the chair.

My magic's exertion was waning, and this small reprieve was what I needed to ensure I wouldn't face my father's wrath if he demanded I continue with this poor, wretched souls' torture.

Father clapped his hands, chuckling darkly as he slowly approached the chair.

Stepping back, I made my retreat as this was the part he

never permitted I stick around for. Because once he retrieved that information, he'd cut that man's life short regardless of his promises for freedom. However, today was much different, and I froze at the call of my name just as I reached the doorway between the burning candles.

"Vivienne, you'll stay this day. You need to see what comes next." He waited until I stood beside him as he adjusted his designer coat, flicking an invisible piece of lint from one shoulder.

"You have the information I need, speak then, and I'll set you free."

Lies. The silver tongue of my father twisted in my gut. My hands balled into fists, jaw clenching as I watched him stalk around the tied-up stranger.

"Ye-es, Master Woodward, the shipment was intercepted by the Inhuman Special Forces. They seized everything and made us swear not to speak of their interception. Th-they promised us protection."

My father burst into laughter; it echoed in the chamber, making me flinch.

"Protection? Silly warlock, you think they can protect you from me? How do you think you got here? I have eyes and ears everywhere."

My father unsheathed an emerald-bladed dagger. It was spelled; I knew that much from the texts of our grimoires that were forced upon us to study. This one would hold the soul of anyone whose flesh it pierced, trapping them for eternity. Or until the wielder decided to set them free.

He had to have countless souls trapped.

I bit my lip to silence the sob that wanted to escape as he plunged that dagger into the man's chest. Tears rolled down my cheeks, dripping to the ground and joining the rest of the damp earth as I slowly watched the life seep from the stranger's still body.

My father turned to me, dagger still held in his grip as he perused my reactions to his doing.

"Very good, Vivienne. Even if you did shed tears for someone not worthy of them, you remained quiet. Tomorrow I'll have you do the honors, but for now, you will be rewarded with a stroll in the gardens. I'll fetch a guard and have him meet you at your room." He waved his hand, "You're dismissed."

And that was the thing. I shouldn't have had a guard, but I had tried to run too many times, and my father no longer trusted me. Not since I broke his spell.

He had continued making me forget everything I did, but the last few times I did his bidding, I remembered, and his spell no longer controlled my memory.

Quickly walking away from the gruesome scene I just witnessed, I knew one thing: with this newfound slice of freedom, I needed to sneak to Liv's room, tell her it was time, and escape. I had played my father's puppet long enough, and I drew the line at taking life.

It was the one thing I didn't want on my hands, regardless of the horrible acts I was forced to endure. It would shatter my soul and will to live, and I needed to be here for my baby sister. Once I found a safe place away from this hellhole, I'd send for her, and she'd be free of him, too.

For now, though, she was my saving grace since my father favored her and gave her anything and everything she desired.

She saw what he was doing to me, and so she concocted a plan that if my escape had ever arisen, I'd take it. No matter the consequence of leaving her or my forced fiancée, Kash, whom I had once liked, but when I realized my father threw him in my path, and it wasn't an organic relationship, I had made her a promise in a blood oath. Now was the time she'd call in that oath, and I had to obey it.

So, with tears streaming down my face, I barreled into her bedroom, waking her, telling her everything that happened and what our father wanted me to do the next day. We hugged, said our temporary goodbyes, and I was sent on my way.

The guard who came to retrieve me was one of my sister's closest friends' brothers. He knew what needed to be done and ensured that my escape wouldn't fall on my sister or her friend.

He handed me a vial, "Your sister said you'd know what to do with this when the time came."

And I did. The guard thought it was for me to consume, but in reality, it was sleeping dust; when shaken, it would slosh the liquid around until it solidified into dust. So, I did just that, and when we were on the edge of the garden, I uncorked the top, pouring a heaping pile into my palm, blowing the dust into his face.

He dropped, and I ran.

Ran like it was my sister's lifeline. And it certainly was because if I didn't fulfill my end of the bargain, her life was forfeit until she uttered the words that would unlink us.

When I was far enough, I darted into the woods, where a tree was etched with a 'W' around an 'O', mine and my sister's secret symbol. On the ground was a backpack with enough money to restart somewhere and a few changes of clothes.

And so under that same moonlight, I turned my face up to it, closing my eyes and praying to the Goddess, "If you can hear me, Goddess, guard my sister where I can't. She doesn't deserve to witness what I have. Keep her safe until I can return for her and make things right."

Whether or not she heard me, I wouldn't know because once that backpack was secured, I never looked back.

I stared at the man who had once controlled me in my

adolescence, when my magic was squeezed like a vice by him. The background noise of customers talking, the whirr of the espresso machine working, and my own heavy breathing faded as I glared at Horace.

My father thought he could continue his tirade from my younger years, but I was older and wiser, and my magic stronger.

"I'm not going anywhere with you." The quiet vehemence left my throat; we had an audience, and I was trying to remain calm for my customers' comfort.

"Oh, don't be naive, Vivienne. We can protect you better from the comfort of the mansion than in this city. Our flight leaves in a few hours." My father was persistent, but I wasn't going anywhere.

I had a mate I needed to make up with because no matter how far I dragged myself away from Horace Woodward, he'd find some way to control me. I was done living in fear of what he'd do to Kit because I would protect him myself. And not speaking to him was sending me into a spiral.

"That doesn't matter to me, because I won't be on that flight, and neither will Liv. We are done being your puppets, Father." I spat in disdain. Liv gripped my hand in comfort and support. She was like Switzerland in our family, but she'd always said she would be on my side when the time came.

Father's neck grew red as it spread up to the top of his forehead, "Listen here, little witchling of mine. My blood runs in your veins; you will obey me. You'll marry Kash, bear his children, and resume your duties as eldest daughter in the sanctity of the coven."

I spit out a singular laugh, "There will be no marrying Kash, the fates have already decided what I shall do." And that was to mate Kit, not this warlock.

"Fates? There is nothing the fates can determine that isn't

already in place. We have an agreement with the Harding family that will need to be upheld."

"A vow, I'm assuming?" I asked, not knowing what he would say next.

"No, a signed contract, one that was made when you were a child. And the only way to void such a contract would be if you had a fated mate. But, those are rare as they are, so you will make good on my word."

It was a good thing I could void the contract.

I turned to Kash, addressing him directly, "The contract is voided."

He folded his arms, furrowing his brows, "How so?"

"Because as fates would have it, I do have a mate."

"What?" My father seethed, while Kash's shoulders sagged. The young warlock already knew he was defeated when his eyes met mine, and a silent understanding passed between us. Which was surprising in itself, for how much he had tried pursuing me over the years.

"The dragon?" Kash questioned, and I nodded.

He must've seen how close we had been at the falls before my parents arrived; it was the only explanation as to how he knew. I wasn't going to question it, though, because he seemed not to be putting up a fight for my hand any longer.

Liv squealed next to me. "I fucking knew you'd come to your senses!"

"Olivia!" Father's raised voice drew a few patrons' attention to our direction, but she waved him off.

"Oh, please, I'm an adult. Get used to it." Liv spouted. Our father retched back, like he was kicked and punched by his favorite child. And I had started to laugh because he was losing his grip on us, and had been for years.

Kash bowed his head, turned, and left without another word or glance at our father.

My eyes found my mother, and she had tears nearly on the verge of falling in the rims of her lids, and a small smile pulled at her lips. My father, on the other hand, had a sour look on his face before he glanced around and noticed we had everyone's attention.

He grunted, shifting and adjusting his coat, "Iridia, let's go, my dear. We have a flight to catch, and it seems the Harding's to meet and straighten things out with."

My father had seemed defeated, but only time would tell if he was up to scheming again. No longer would he control either Liv or me.

The goddess answered my prayers, even if it took years for it to stick, but she answered them nonetheless.

I glanced around, and several people, human and inhuman alike, had their heads together.

Shit, I hadn't even told Teags yet, and she would be furious if she found out other than by me. I had to do something about it and stat.

Clapping my hands together once I got everyone's undivided attention again.

"Listen here, gossip queens, if anyone goes spouting to anyone outside of this coffee shop about what you heard, and Teagan finds out, there's going to be hellfire to pay. So, to sweeten the deal, everyone gets one, and I mean only one free cup of whatever the hell you want."

Cheers roared, and someone whistled at the offer.

I just had to hope it would hold until things settled, so I could tell Teags, then find my mate and speak with him.

Chapter Twenty-Two

Kit

Folding my hands behind my back, I strained to stand tall in the face of the people I assumed were my mate's parents and apparently her fiancé.

Vero was prowling, ready to strike at the male who dared to try to take Viv's hand in marriage or matehood. I had to placate him, telling him we'd bide our time and use our investigative skills, because none of this made any sense.

It was like pulling a gopher from a hole with the stubborn witch. She had been adamant that she didn't want a mate, let alone any kind of relationship. So, when her parents showed up to the King and Queen's wedding and coronation with a male claiming to be her fiancé, it didn't add up.

Before Vero could take over my body and crush the man, Kash, into the ice, I decided retreating was for the best.

"You know, I should actually get going. There's lots to see, and our King and Queen's wedding and coronation reception will be starting soon."

Placing my hands behind my back, I gripped my fist, grounding myself and pushing past the ache of leaving my mate with those who she seemed uneasy around. At least Liv was with her, which was enough for me to walk away.

I didn't actually join the celebrations. Instead, I made a wide berth in the crowd, keeping Viv in my peripheral until I saw her make her departure.

So, I followed, prowled was more like it, keeping her in my line of sight while she hastily left, glancing over her shoulder several times to ensure no one had followed her outside of the magical bubble barrier. However, she was looking in the wrong direction as I continued following from the side, ducking behind a tree when she finally glanced where I was lurking.

When she reached her car, she struggled to turn the key, heaving sobs left her as her chest rose and fell rapidly. I wanted to go to her, but I needed time to watch, observe, and understand what the fuck just happened.

Vero was insistent that we shift and keep guard over her home once she reached her driveway, and I agreed.

OUR FEMALE NEEDS US.

I know she does, Vero. But things are complicated, and until we know what exactly is going on, we need to keep out of sight.

WHY CAN'T WE JUST APPROACH HER AND DEMAND THAT SHE TELL US?

I snorted.

That's not how it works with females who are not dragons. Especially our mate, she is stubborn.

And so during the day, we kept watch over our mate and her homestead. Her parents showed up once with the warlock at the house, but Viv neither opened the door nor spoke with them. Then, another day, just her mother showed up, and once again, there was no answer.

She was inside, I knew it. Her sobs shot guilt through me, and Vero had almost succeeded in barging into her home to comfort her, but by the stroke of luck, Rayth had called, informing me he had information that I would be interested in.

And now, I was standing in his office, facing the empty jail cells of the ISF building. Smirking, my eyes found their way to what had been Cade's cell. He was no longer in custody and had been let free to tend to his mate in the Veil, pardoned of his 'crimes' in changing the human.

Rayth appeared suddenly in front of me on the other side of his windows. His stoic face was unreadable as he entered his office.

"I told you to be here a few days ago." He chided.

"Yes, well, I was busy."

"No matter," He waved his hand at me, and began flipping through pages of a report he had shown up with. "It seems that your mate's family has been at the center of an extensive ongoing investigation. She is only listed as one of two children to a Horace Woodward, their coven's leader."

Well, I had suspected that my mate's father was someone important, with the way he carried himself and spoke. Like someone who had immense power, someone who knew how to bend them to his will.

As it seemed, my spitfire mate was the daughter of an influential man. The relationship between Viv and Horace seemed strained at the Winter Festival, and I had to wonder if she knew what his dealings were.

And if she did, did that put her in harm's way?

Rayth continued, his body flickering the further he skimmed the pages. He summarized what they said, "Mr. Woodward is at the center of some questionable practices with the coven's laws and is believed to be involved in a few disappearances of informants with the ISF. And it looks like he is in business with another magical family, the Hardings. Kash Harding, to be specific. He is the eldest son of Gregory Harding, who is a very wealthy politician in the human government."

I grunted. No wonder her father was so keen on his daughter marrying Kash. With that sort of connection and power, they'd be unstoppable. And depending on whether they were for or against the paranormal community revealing ourselves, it would alter the safety of our King and Queen.

"Do you know if they are for or against our cause for unity?" I had to ask. It was gnawing at me, an inkling at the back of my mind told me they were against, but I had to be sure.

"There's no mention of their stance, so I haven't a clue."

"Interesting, do you think my mate is in danger?"

Rayth glanced up from the paperwork, his brow furrowing. "Why would you ask?"

"It seems her father isn't taking no to Kash's union and may be intent on taking her from Hellfire. So I need to know what I'm up against. To protect what is mine. Because she is my mate, the fates have deemed it, that bond is unbreakable."

He nodded, seeming to understand where I was coming from. "What I can tell, no, but I'm only basing that judgment on knowing she's his daughter and he needs her for whatever deal he had with the Harding family. Only she can stop whatever has transpired."

He closed the folder, dropping it on his desk and taking a seat, "From my understanding, she hasn't claimed you as her mate in public, has she?"

I shook my head, "No, and only a very limited number of people know that information, by the way."

"I see. Well, it's in her hands, I'm afraid. You can be there to ensure she's not hurt, but ultimately, no one can step in but her. It's not against the laws of our people to make arrangements. Only if she deems it, she still does have choices, and we'll step in if we have to enforce her rights to walk away."

My shoulders sagged in relief. I was grateful to Rayth for looking into both the Woodwards and Hardings; however, many questions remained.

Specifically, was she unwillingly involved in her father's investments and potential illegal dealings? Did she know about them? Was her reluctance to complete our bond due to her father?

I would protect her from her father, as would Vero. And we'd see to it that if her father were indeed found guilty in any dealings, we'd ensure he was put away for life so she might have some semblance of peace.

There was something about the whole ordeal that sent a ripple of caution through my scales beneath my skin.

"Thanks for the information, Rayth. I truly appreciate you looking into this for me."

"Of course, Atticus. You are, after all, the right-hand man of our King."

I smirked, knowing this may very well get under his skin, "And your friend, right?"

He pursed his lips, nose flaring slightly while his corporal self flickered in what I assumed was irritation, "Not sure I'd say that, but you're not terrible to be around like some others."

I clamped my hand on his shoulder, "Ah, shucks, Rayth. I'm honored."

He quirked a brow, rose from his chair, brushed past, opened his office door, and stood aside. "That is all I have for now. I'll be in touch if anything else is uncovered."

"Thanks again." Turning, I exited his office and kept walking until I was outside the ISF. The sky was clear today, making way for the startling warmth of the winter sun. Soon, the chill in the air would cease, flowers would begin to bloom, and the desolate trees would once again fill with leaves.

I imagined myself taking Viv to Hellfire Falls Park in the summer. Being lazy on the beach, watching while she donned a bathing suit, soaking in the rays. Side by side, we'd fall into a rhythm of being one another's best friend, where we shared our thoughts and feelings and held one another.

Clearing my throat, I shook my head to clear it from those possibilities. In truth, I didn't know if she'd like to lie on the beach and tan. She had yet to give me a chance to get to know her better.

But I'd change all that soon. I'd stay away until the grand opening of the bookstore.

There I would corner her; it was wrong of me to want to do so, but I'd do it anyway and get answers from her.

Beg if I must.

I'd do anything just to get her to accept this bond and give us a chance. She'd be treated like a queen, my whole world, my Neesha.

Chapter Twenty-Three

Viv

Holding empty metal trays, I booty bumped the back door open and walked across the drive to where Saige had her bakery food truck parked. Cables were strewn across the lot, tying her truck to the power of my building.

I was still unsure why she insisted on prepping and baking in her truck when we had done some minor renovating and had everything set up inside. I had made the arrangements over the last few weeks, dipping into my savings so I could give her her own space and hopefully convince her to stay.

My gut feeling told me to keep her here as long as I could until the right time when all would right itself, and she'd stay permanently.

But, she had insisted she didn't want to make a mess and didn't want to overcook anyone since there was already a long line waiting out front, and the building would heat up with the bodies of people anyway.

There were a hell of a lot more people, humans, and inhumans waiting to get a glimpse inside and speak with our King and Queen than anticipated when I had quickly peeked through the windows before coming out here.

It would be the grandest opening I could have hoped for, for my best friend.

Balancing the tray in one arm, holding the edge with my fist, I knocked with my other.

Saige opened the door and hurriedly grabbed for the tray. I glanced around, and several more of those baking trays were full of goodies. She had already made an array of delicious sweets that had my mouth watering.

I wanted to sink my teeth into the blueberry muffin that was steaming next to me, but I had to hold off because it was almost time to open the doors, have Teags make her speech, and then cut the ribbon.

"Oh my goddess, these look and smell divine, Saige." I bit my lip, fidgeting with my fingers to keep from snatching something up.

"Thanks, Viv!" She brushed a stray hair from her face with her forearm, taking out a piping hot tray from one of the four stoves she had built in near the front of her truck. "This is the last one, and then we'll be ready. Are you able to handle two that are already cooled down?"

"Of course, girly pop. You just tell me what to do, and I'll do it like a good girl." I wiggled my brows at her, which made her snort in laughter.

"You're so bad, Viv." She gripped two trays of her own and followed me out and to the back entrance that I had propped open of my coffee shop.

We walked through the tables and chairs until we reached the front, where a large buffet was set up, with nearly everything already displayed: cookies, muffins, cinnamon rolls, and some cupcakes.

A large cake had been baked and frosted yesterday, stored

in the back fridge, and was already on display. It was glorious, and I couldn't wait to see the look on Teag's face when she saw everything Saige, Li,v and I had helped put together for today's celebrations.

"This is amazing, you should see the line outside! Do you think this will be enough? I think there are more people than we had anticipated." I asked, already trying to calculate the probability that we could stretch this out.

However, Saige walked over to the entrance of the coffee shop, glancing out the door, and then gasped, "Oh shit."

I was momentarily stunned. I didn't recall her using profanity very much, if ever, and the word tumbled from her mouth.

She turned around, her eyes wide, "I think I need to make more goodies, Viv. Holy hockey sticks, there are so many people."

Nodding, I finished unloading the metal trays onto the waiting tables. "What do you need me to do?"

She waved me off, "Nothing you haven't already done. I actually need to drive to the store and get more ingredients. I ran out of flour, sugar, and vanilla. I have everything else, but I'm going to have to miss the ribbon cutting if I want to ensure we have enough for everyone."

She was gathering the metal trays, stacking them one on top of the other, when she turned her head to look at the display case where the other baked goods were stored.

"If we run out before I'm done baking, just grab stuff from the case, and there should be some in the cooler as well, just to sublimate until I bring out more. It shouldn't take me too long to get the rest plus some made up. The cake can be divided as well. Crackers, I hadn't realized the magnitude of the opening." Saige was biting the tip of her thumb as she mentally ticked off how much more she needed to make. "No worries, we'll get it together!"

She was suddenly even more excited.

Teags squeezed around the partition we had temporarily put back up. She glanced at the table and then at us, her smile widening.

"The treats look yummy, Saige! You did an amazing job, I can't wait to dig into that cake too!" Teags licked her lips as she eyed the pastries.

"Thanks your highness, I hope they are to your liking when you taste them." She curtseyed, and I burst into laughter.

"Saige, girly, you don't have to do that. She's only been Queen for like what, a week and a half?" I bantered. It made my new baker friend relax, and Teags rolled her eyes.

"Viv is right, you don't need to do that with me. We're going to be fast friends. Now that things are settling down, I do hope we can get together more often and do some girls' nights. Finn is finally letting me out of the mansion, with an escort, of course, but freedom all the same."

"Well, I won't keep you both. I do have to leave and get those ingredients. I'll be back shortly. I'm just going to temporarily unhook the power cords. I have a parking cone I'm going to stick where my truck goes back if that's okay?" Saige asked.

"Of course, remember, anything you need, just let me know," I said, hugging Saige, followed by Teags.

Saige grabbed the trays and walked toward the back, muttering cheerfully to herself.

I smiled widely at my new friend and knew that things were coming along perfectly to keep her here in Mount Hellfire. Now I just needed to find a way to talk to Kit and figure everything out between us.

It was scary, but I knew time was not on my side, and I

would have to tell Teags and come clean to Kit on why I was so apprehensive.

"Hey, girly pop, you ready?" I asked, wrapping my arm around Teags waist as we glanced outside. She nodded, and we squeezed through the partition, where several volunteers who had signed up to help with the grand opening were waiting, including Finn.

I squeezed Teags side one more time, "Let's get out there and cut that ribbon, give the people what they want. Books and crafts!" I sang as I approached the door and opened it, letting the crisp winter air into the bookstore.

A ribbon was tied on either side of the doorway, waiting to be cut, and to mark the beginning of a new start for my best friend.

Teags made a short but heartfelt speech, and once everyone was finished clapping, the ribbon was cut, and we moved aside so the customers could start waltzing in and browsing the new bookstore.

Everything was going well, and several people had exclaimed their excitement for craft night. It seemed Teags idea to host those nights was going to be a big hit, especially for the enthusiastic old biddies whose eyes shone with new fervor and youth.

I stood to the side watching as Teags mingled, charming her way through humans and the paranormal community who had already loved her from the beginning. Not just because she was the King's fated mate, but because she had that approachable aura.

Teags was given only a moment of interlude, and she took that time to walk over and pull me into a hug. We silently looked over the bookstore as it filled with people.

We'd definitely have to open the partition to the coffee shop as overflow, since not even a fourth of the line had moved into the space.

"Hey, I'm going to open up the coffee shop as well, so we have both places for people to mingle. It seems we underestimated the power of the Inhuman community and those humans who openly accept us. We're already packed." I squeezed her arm and walked away.

Keeping the partition cracked until I was ready to open it fully, I stepped through and ensured the treat table was fully stocked. We were going to wait a bit before opening this side, but it seemed we needed to do so right away.

I'd ensure that if someone wanted a drink, we could accommodate that as well.

When all felt as if it was ready, I headed for the partition only to stop when a clang came from the back stock room.

Odd, I didn't think any of my workers were here.

I'd closed the coffee shop today for Teag's opening to avoid any hindrances and to keep the attention solely on her. So, it was unnecessary to have anyone working today who wasn't already in the bookstore.

"Hello?" I called out as I walked to the back.

No one answered, and when I entered, no one was there either. A metal frother pitcher lay on the ground. I cocked my head, glancing around before picking it up and tossing it into the sink.

I'd just have to clean that after the grand opening was finished. I thought, quickly washing my hands and walking back out to the front with a towel in my hand.

Suddenly, a hand covered my mouth as an arm wrapped around my waist, pulling me into a hard chest.

I struggled at first, dropping the towel I had been drying my hands with, pissed I hadn't sensed danger and that my wards were once again useless.

Was this the work of my father? Had he come back to kidnap me?

As far as I knew, my parents had left Mount Hellfire since they hadn't been back to pester me, but that could have been a ploy to weaken my sense of safety.

I didn't have to wonder long when the scent of campfire reached my nose, and a rumble began against my back.

Kit.

He was here after being absent for so long.

My body melted against his, giving myself over in his presence.

His one hand remained over my mouth as the other spread low on my stomach, inching closer to where I wanted him to dip his fingers beneath my waistband and touch me between my thighs.

I whimpered when he stopped. He inhaled the side of my head, and when he spoke, his voice was deep and gravelly, like he hadn't used it in days.

"I've been watching you, little ember, trying to figure out if there was something else amiss." He lifted his hand from my mouth, lightly gripping my chin while he turned my entire body around, backing me into the closest wall.

Fuck, it was hot, and I wanted nothing more than to pull him into my office, lock the door, pull out his cock, and taste him.

He made me into a wanton woman when he was around, and when he wasn't, I was as dry as the Sahara Desert.

I tried swallowing, my mouth parched from gazing at him because all that moisture was going straight to my pussy. "You haven't been around to watch me, Kit." I pointed out, rolling my eyes.

He chuckled; it was low, heady, absolutely sultry. "Just because you didn't see me doesn't mean I wasn't around. Especially when your parents showed up at your home with that warlock, your fiancé, what was his name again? Oh yeah, Kash."

It was as if he doused me in cold water. My fiance? Was he serious? He had left me at the Winter Festival and didn't give me a chance whatsoever to explain anything to him. And even after the festival, he had vanished.

Poof. Gone. No trace of him. Nada.

Just when I was starting to think I could give this bond a shot, he had to throw Kash in my face when the whole situation wasn't even my fault to begin with. It was my father's doing.

"Kash isn't my fiancé. And you'd know that if you hadn't walked away and just let me tell you what was going on. But you did, you walked away from me." My voice raised, the hurt hurdling forward. I felt abandoned, left on my own yet again to deal with my father.

I had Liv, of course, but it was different with Kit. I had wondered if he would be by my side and stick up for me without any explanations. But, instead, he walked away, as if I didn't matter.

Kit hummed, stepping closer, pushing me further against the wall so I could feel all of his hard muscles and the thick bulge between his legs.

He was hard, and even if I was pissed, it made me want him.

"Be that as it may, you never spoke up and said he wasn't your fiancé."

"Because you didn't give me a chance. My father is a fickle man, and if you say or do the wrong thing, it could backfire. And at that moment, I only wanted to protect you from him." I spat, breathing heavily from the exertion of anger that kept building.

He was infuriating, and I just wanted to push him away so I

could think clearly. Tonight was not the night to hash this out. It was Teags' night, and we were about to ruin it by being loud.

Well, I take that back, I was the one yelling.

With all the gentleness Kit possessed, he lowered his voice, changing whatever tactic he was trying to pull, "Neesha, I don't need protection from anyone. I'm the one who is supposed to protect my mate. I admit I shouldn't have walked away, but I knew there was something else going on with your father."

"Oh, good, you knew there was more, but still chose to walk away." I was stubborn and wouldn't let this go easily because his decision left my heart aching for days.

"I'm sorry, Neesha." He said breathlessly, threading his fingers in my hair to hold me where he wanted. His eyes glistened as they searched my face. "It's my job to investigate those in the inhuman community, and it was a natural reaction." He drew closer, and the breath from his mouth grazed my face and my lips.

I wanted him to press those lips to mine. Devour me, kiss me, take me away from here, and forget that my father was likely planning something devious now that he knew fates had bestowed me a mate.

He was still in danger, and I knew he said he would protect me; he didn't know my father, though, and the wicked things he had done behind closed doors and in front of my eyes.

So, I needed to distance myself before anyone came looking for me, like my best friend who was currently mingling on the other side of the building.

"You know what, I can't do this with you. You've already broken my heart once; I won't allow you to do it again. Leave." I demanded, attempting to move, but he kept me against the wall as he towered over me.

He was hurt, as much as I was, but that wouldn't change my mind; he had fucked that all up himself.

"Why won't you leave me alone, you prick?" I sneered, my hands found his chest, and I tried but failed to push him away.

"You're my mate, Vivienne, my sweet princess. My dragon refuses to allow you just to slip through the cracks of his clawed talons." Kit responded.

A gasp left my throat at the intensity in his gaze as his dragon, Vero, surfaced.

Then, someone cleared their throat, and Finn's voice cut through the tension. "Is everything alright in here?"

Fuck. Shit. Goddess damn it.

If Finn was in here, Teags was likely with him, and she probably heard Kit announce he was my mate.

So, I answered my King while glaring at Kit. "Fucking peachy."

Kit's eyes narrowed, and he lingered for a moment before letting me go abruptly, turning and walking out the unlocked door of the coffee shop.

I was stunned, shivering from his hot body leaving mine as I watched him disappear past the window.

Looking over at Teags, I quickly wiped a stray tear that had escaped and then closed them.

Her footsteps were nearly silent, but I heard them and felt the wind from her movements.

"Viv?" She questioned, and I knew she wanted to know what the hellfire just happened.

"I don't want to fucking talk about it right now. Cat's out of the damn bag, but I'm not ready."

She nodded, understanding that I needed time. "I'm here when you are."

And then she wrapped me in her arms, and all the strength I had carried fled as I wept into her shoulder. The deluge of emotions caught up to me. And while I tried to put on a farce, she could always see through it, yet she still gave me the grace and patience of a saint until I was ready to spill it all.

A few moments passed, and I lifted my head, wiped my nose against my sleeve, trying but failing to smile at her.

"Why don't you go home? We've got it here. I have Finn to wrangle anyone, and the other's helping. Come over when you're ready. Okay? That's an order from your Queen."

Teagan was the kindest soul and was already making a wonderful Queen for our people. She'd have no troubles if I left and took care of myself. So I didn't push back against her advice; instead, I listened.

Leaving the coffee shop, I saw Saige hadn't returned yet, and I was worried something had happened, but right now—right now, I was ordered to take care of myself.

If Saige didn't return, I knew that Teags and Finn had it under control.

My mind was a mess, and my eyes were blurry.

The time passed as I drove home and locked myself inside once again, picking up the opened, nearly full bottle of Serpent's Wine I drank straight from the neck. No point in dirtying up a clean glass when I was in need of drowning my sorrows and forgetting Kit.

So, I did just that, and while I went off to never-ever la te da land, I didn't have a care in the world for anything that had to do with Atticus Hart, or my never-ending misfortune in life as a Woodward witchling.

Chapter Twenty-Four

Viv

Waking up the next morning after having drunk the rest of the Serpent's wine was always pure annihilating hellfire. I don't know why I kept doing it to myself because it wasn't a first for me, either, or even a second.

Lifting my hand, I pushed my palms into my eyes, giving in to the pressure I created. It was a sweet brief relief until I groaned, and then the pounding started at my temple, radiating to the tippy top of my skull.

I felt like someone was fucking into my head and not in the pleasant way where their cock went into my throat.

Shouldn't have drunk all that wine; I knew I'd pay the price this morning.

No matter, it was too late to turn back time and upchuck the paranormal version of alcohol that was intertwined in my bloodstream.

My phone buzzed on the nightstand; I opted to ignore it for now. Answering the phone as a hungover witch was not something anyone wanted because I usually turned into a bitch. The inconveniences I put myself through were taken out on anyone who dared disturb me before I had an inkling of caffeine.

So, I gripped the still buzzing phone in my hand and zombie walked my way to the bathroom, pissed like I was a water tower emptying, and shuffled my way to the kitchen, where my trusty coffee machine had a pot of light roast coffee just waiting for me to ruin it with sugar and creamer.

I loved coffee, and despised it at the same time. The taste of pure black coffee was like shoving a burnt piece of chocolate down my throat, but when adding sugary goodness, it made it bearable, just to have that kick that light roast would give. Not that it made a huge difference between light and dark, but at least the latter was less burnt ass tasting.

With the pleasant warmth of sweet coffee and a touch of rejuvenation from my magic, I finally lifted my phone to check who had been blowing it up earlier.

Taking a sip from my cup, I smiled as Teag's name popped up on my screen for the twelfth time.

"Hello, your majesty." I purred, finally starting to feel the effects and jump the coffee gave.

"Viv," Teags warned, it only made me laugh. "You know I don't want you calling me that."

"You say that, your highness, but it's not going to stop me from time to time," I teased.

She gave an annoyed grunt at yet another honorific.

"Whatever, anyway, I'm calling to make sure you're still alive since you drunkenly sent a voice note slurring your way through whatever it was you were muttering. And to offer meaningful girl time, which includes and is not limited to pool time, snacks, and gossip."

Usually, I'd opt for alone time a few days after something major, like, oh, I don't know, my mate announcing to my best friend before I could that I did indeed have a mate.

She didn't seem perturbed in the slightest that she found out the way she did. Regardless, it still made me feel like utter shit, with anyone else that was supposed to be a huge deal, where celebrations were planned.

As it were, that wasn't my case with a dickhead father who I still had a fear would use my mate somehow.

I had had enough wallowing for a lifetime; I needed to see my best friend. We hadn't had time since her wedding and coronation. I missed her fiercely.

"I'd love to come over, give me a couple hours to eat something, and let my magical coffee work to expel the hangover I gave myself."

Teags chuckled, "Alright, you heathen." She cleared her throat, and prickles of unease shot down to my toes.

"What is it?" I asked, demanded more like it.

"There's something we need to talk about when you get here."

I quickly glanced at the clock, determining how fast I could shovel food into my face while simultaneously picking up the pace of curing my hangover. Guess I'd just have to make another cup of coffee and add something extra because I wasn't going to wait a few hours to make it to Teags.

Something serious happened, and it was enough to make her want to tell me in person.

"Give me fifteen minutes, I'm on my way." I urged, already taking the phone from my ear.

Teags distant voice came through the small speaker, but I didn't hear anything further than "Wait."

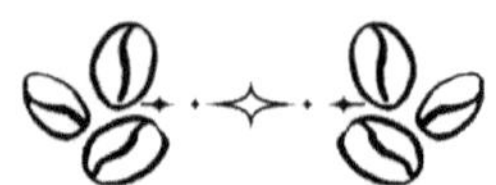

The food I had hoovered into my face was still settling at the pit of my churning stomach as my tires squealed to a stop at the front entrance of Finn's mansion.

Finn was already waiting at the door, holding it wide open. "She's in the pool lounge," he said as he closed the door once I was through the threshold.

I power-walked my now mostly recovered ass through the doors and found Teags sitting crossed-legged on one of the lounge chairs, fiddling with one of the many crochet projects she liked to occupy her time with.

She was nervous crocheting, and when I hastily threw open the doors, she squeaked, throwing the start of what looked like a derpy lizard onto the table.

"Gods, Viv, you scared the ever-loving shit out of me making that kind of entrance, I almost thought it was an intruder." Her hand gripped her chest before she met me halfway and pulled me into a hug.

I needed this. Needed one of her hugs that felt like it could cure any heartache. Pulling back, I peered into her eyes, worry pulling at the corners like she hadn't slept all night.

"What happened—what is it?" I questioned, ready to get into whatever it was that she didn't tell me over the phone.

"It's Saige."

"Did she finally come back to the building?"

Teag shook her head, "No, I'm afraid not. I didn't have time to tell you before you left. With everything that transpired between you and Kit, I didn't want to worry you further. Plus, it was my duty to take on this responsibility." She rambled, fidgeting with her fingers.

"It's alright, T, I'm here now, what's going on?"

"She's lost."

Wait what?

"Define lost? Like, she forgot how to get back to the building or something else?"

"Something else." Teags took a deep breath before releasing it. "We got news that she somehow drove with her bakery truck into the Veil and hasn't been seen since. The only reason we know she's over there is that someone reported seeing a human drive through it on our side. Finn has his men scouring the Veil for her."

It took me a moment for the information to catch up, but then I realized something: "Isn't Saige fully human?"

"Yeah, that's what has us worried. No human has been allowed or has ever even attempted to go to the Veil. There's no record of entrance from anyone who doesn't have some kind of magic in their veins."

I contemplated what this could have meant. Saige had never expressed any magical lineage during the time we worked together. Did she have someone in her family who hid something from her, or did she keep it from us?

But that wasn't right either because Liv would have felt anything otherworldly with her; it was part of her many gifts, even if it wasn't a strong suit for her.

"Goddess, what a fucking mess."

"You're telling me. I haven't even been Queen for a month, and we already have a crisis."

I gripped her arm, giving a strained smile, "It will all work out, and they'll find her. I'm sure of it. Anyway, Finn has the best men in the ISF who will find her in a jiffy."

She sighed heavily, walking over to the lounge chairs, where I followed, plopping my ass down.

"Well, not much we can do for now until we get more information. Rayth should have that soon. So, tell me." She typed something into her phone before placing it on the table, turning her full attention to me. "Kit."

I knew she'd ask fairly quickly about the huge elephant in the room. Afterall I did tell her I'd explain later. And the cat was certainly out of the bag. My phone had blown up with Mitsy texts, and even some from Teags therapist-turned-friend, Millie, wanting to know the gossip. I'd explained that I would tell them more once I spoke with Teags.

So, here we were now. She was waiting for me to spill the beans on all things Kit. My mate and the most frustrating man in my world, aside from my father, of course.

"Well, he's my mate."

She gave me a look that spoke of 'duh, I knew that already.'

"Yeah, stupid way to start that. I don't know what to say. I've been fighting the bond, got mate sickness because, did you know that was a thing with dragon shifters? I certainly didn't and suffered when he went off to do goddess only knows what that time I told you he wasn't answering me."

Teags interrupted, "He was helping with Cade's mate."

I glanced at her, "Who the hell is Cade?"

"Oh, right, you probably don't know him. He's sort of a friend of Kit and Finn. He's a vampire and turned his mate without permission, and was imprisoned while she spent some time with the Fae. She kept trying to escape, and they needed his help to track her down and convince her to stay. I'm sure there was more to it, but that's what I know."

Well, that explained why he hadn't been around and why that mate sickness took hold until we fucked the first and only time. I hadn't felt that kind of agony since then. I did, however, once in awhile feel his desperation, anguish, and determination through our very fragile bond.

It wasn't fully solidified yet, and wouldn't be until he bit me, but that was something for another time.

"Anyway, back to you fighting your bond with Kit. Why?"

She asked, and even though she didn't fully know about my father, she knew enough.

"I was afraid my father would use him against me to come back to the coven to work for him."

She whistled, "Yeah, I can see how that would hinder things, but Viv, you know that you have me as your best friend and I'm your Queen now. Anything Finn or I say is law. If your dad tried anything funny, he'd have the ISF so far down his throat he would think they were fucking it."

My eyes widened because what the hellfire happened to my best friend, and who was this sassy, outspoken woman?

"Guess I know not to get on your bad side," I muttered, only making her burst into laughter.

"You've never been on my bad side, and that's so hard for you to do. But, tell me, take your dad out of the equation, what else is stopping you?"

I glanced up, tears glazing on the edges of my vision as emotion welled quickly within me. The answer was there and rolled from my tongue easily.

"I'm scared he'll turn into my father," I whispered, because that's what it was. My mother and father were fated, but it didn't stop him from being a shitty person and doing bad things or treating his own spawn as pawns. I didn't want to risk finding a man like that, and I certainly didn't want kids, or thought I didn't.

"I also don't know if I even want kids. Aren't shifters supposed to be possessive and like demand to breed their mates until they are barefoot and pregnant all the time?"

She snickered, "That's most shifters, but not all. Dragons are complex creatures; they are possessive, which means they don't like to share their horde, aka you. And as far as that translates to me, it means they want their mate to themselves for a very long time before they think about making a family. That's something you and Kit need to talk about, though."

She shrugged, glancing at the entrance when a figure appeared in the doorway.

"Sorry for the intrusion, but I have your food, my queen." Said one of the guards who lurked around the mansion. Finn was still very cautious, even with Vincent behind high security bars. There were other dangers to consider, like the fact that her stalker had apparently been working for someone high up in government.

"No worries, and Claus, you already know not to use honorifics with me. Just Teags or Teagan, please."

He strode over, placing the tray the chef had piled food onto, and bowed, "Yes, ma'am."

Claus turned and hurried out the door before she could chide him further. And I couldn't help but smile. She couldn't get away from the titles, "You'll just have to get used to it." I pointed out.

She waved a hand, "No diverting." She gripped the grilled cheese sandwich, took a huge bite, and pulled it away. A long strand of gooey cheese kept the food that was in her mouth, and the sandwich connected until she cut it with her fingernail. "Mhm, this is delicious. So, aside from your father and the kid thing, is there anything else?"

I thought long and hard, and I couldn't come up with any other excuses. That's when I knew she had me beat. So, I shook my head, "No."

"Well, I see no other reason than to go for it. Come on, Viv, you deserve to love and be loved in return. Stop fighting it. And wouldn't it be nice to be able to have sex anytime you want? I know you were struggling for awhile without having that intimacy. And having a mate, you get that and more."

She knew me all too well. We had lots of late-night calls

after some trysts or if I just needed to use her as an excuse to leave some poor schmuck after riding them like a very enthusiastic cowgirl.

I closed my eyes, "You're right." I opened them to peer at her with new determination. "I'll give him a shot. "

"That's my girl! That was surprisingly easier to convince you than I thought." She crawled onto the lounge I was sitting on and hugged me tightly. "Here. Text him and tell him to meet you at your place. If he shows, which I know he will. Lay everything out. And if he doesn't, just let me know and I'll send Finn to punish his ass."

Smiling at Teags, I couldn't think of a better person than her to convince me I was being a dunce and that giving love a shot was something worth risking.

So I sent off a text in hopes that he would either answer or show up later this evening.

Me: Hey, I know I was harsh on you last night, but we need to talk. Come to my place later, say nine?

My finger hovered over the send button, and I finally took a chance on myself. On love and on Kit.

He texted back a few short moments later.

Kit: I'd love to talk. Are you sure? Do you want me to bring dinner?

Me: Yes to both questions, I'm not picky, get whatever you are craving.

Kit: Alright, it's a date.

Just as I was about to slide my phone into my pocket, it vibrated again.

Kit: Oh, and Neesha? I can't wait to see you later.

A stupid smile spread on my face. Teags squealed, clapping and making it echo in the pool room.

"This is fantastic, okay, so let's make a plan on how you're going to seduce the dragon shifter."

I snorted, "I don't need to seduce him, Teags. All I need to do is strip my clothes, and he'll be speechless."

She frowned, crossing her arms in an adorable Teags-sized pout. "That's no fun."

"I'll put on something sexy underneath from Mitsy's store, then only wear that when he shows up. How's that sound?"

She rubbed her hands together, like she was an accomplice in a successful heist. "Perfect. Okay, let's finish this food and then get our swimsuits on and take a dip. I need to float in relaxation."

So, we ate all the food, talked some more, and once our stomachs had enough time to settle, we headed for the pool, where I cannonballed into the water just as Finn walked in, soaking him from head to toe, making Teags and me burst into giggles that ricocheted off the walls. We filled the space with happiness and the beginning of something good.

I could just feel it.

Chapter Twenty-Five

Viv

I had arrived at Mitsy's lingerie shop, Embers Lace, and was scouring through the racks. Nothing was catching my eye for what I wanted to wear for Kit. Nothing seemed right or called out to me like it normally did.

Then, Mitsy came out holding a gold set. It was a g-string, the bra was lacy, its design was an intricate see-through swirl, the bottom lace had the same spiral twists, and on the back, where it would lie just above my ass crack, was an amber gem.

"It's perfect," I whispered, the gem shimmering in the sensual lights above, making my stomach giddy.

Mitsy smiled, "Kit's going to love this one. I had specially shipped it here for you to show off to your mate when you were ready. Which seems like it's happening sooner than I expected."

I glanced at her, surprised she would do such a gesture. "Why would you do that?"

She shrugged, "I love, love, and well, if someone can have it when I can't, I want to make sure that person has something sexy to wear for any magical night you spend with your mate."

Mitsy sighed, a wishful smile crossing her face, tinged with sadness.

My heart ached for her. She definitely deserved to be loved, and I had a feeling she'd find it, but I think that trust would need to be built again. What she went through could cause some emotional trauma in a girl, that was for sure.

I reached for her arm, placing my hand on her to get her to look at me. "You'll find that someone, or multiple someones, who will be nothing but doting and never let you leave their sight. We have all kinds of monsters who'd love nothing more than to spoil you rotten."

"You're too kind, Viv. I'm afraid that might not be in the works for me. I have a hard time trusting after everything that's happened. Thanks for giving me another chance at friendship after the way I treated you and Teags."

I waved her off, "All in the past, Mits. We don't live there anymore. We live in the here and now."

Her eyes watered, and I pulled her in for a hug, "Gosh, look at me being a sob. Okay, do you want to wear these out, or do you want me to wrap them?" She sniffled, pulling back and going about business as usual.

I grinned, knowing what I wanted and the whole reason I was here in the first place, "I'll wear them out. Kit is supposed to meet me at my place in like twenty minutes."

"Perfect, let's hurry this so you can get busy! Oh, and here's something you can place your other items in to make it easier to carry."

I thanked her again, walking through the red hanging beads that clinked delicately together, to the changing rooms, and quickly slipped into the beautiful gold lingerie. Glancing into the mirror that was provided in the private room, I admired myself. Smiling and knowing he'd love undressing the sexy clothing from my body. And I dreamed of the way his hands would roam over the material before stripping me bare or tearing it apart.

I'd just have to make sure that didn't happen, and he didn't rip these, because I liked them too much already.

With the new, magnificent, lacy piece beneath my clothing, I went to the front to handle my purchase, and as I handed Mitsy my card, the unmistakable unease of my wards flared.

The wrongness settled in my bones, and I had an urge to drop what I was doing and run down the half block to my store.

Mitsy glanced up with a smile on her face that quickly faded. She was quite perceptive for a human and immediately sensed that something was amiss.

"You okay, Viv?"

I nodded, "There's something that's set my wards off. It's not urgent, but it is at the same time. It's hard to explain. I need to head over, so I can't chit-chat any longer. I'm sorry."

"No worries," She paused, handing me the card back, "Do you want me to come with you?"

I shook my head. I didn't want her anywhere near the building if something was actually wrong or if there was danger. I could handle my own, but Mitsy was a human, and I didn't want her getting hurt and have that be on my conscience.

"It's alright, Mits, I'm sure it's nothing. I'll see you later."

"Alright, Viv. But, offer stands if you need help or anything, I'll be around for awhile."

"Thanks, see you later, girly pop," I said cheerily to lessen anything she could read on my face.

It worked when she smiled and waved me goodbye.

Even though my building was only a half block away, I didn't want to leave my car in front of Embers Lace in case I needed to make a quick getaway.

Keeping my car running, I shot a quick text to Kit. It was

nearing the time he'd be waiting for me at my place, and I didn't want to worry him.

Me: Hey, I'm going to be a bit late. Something is off at the Molten; my wards are going haywire.

Placing my phone in the cup holder, I left before he could respond. The magic from my wards was throwing out level ten intruder alerts, and it was blaring like the dickens in my ears. The phone I had left behind began ringing, but I ignored it.

Entering the front showed nothing was wrong. I double checked the back doors of both my shop and Teags, and everything was locked up tight. Nothing and no one were moving inside, and the back lot was empty except for the cone Saige had left. No one wanted to touch it in case she showed up with her bakery truck.

Locking the back door again, I closed my eyes, humming quietly under my breath to feel out if all was clear. There had been a lingering warning; however, it didn't seem like a cause for concern. An animal could have triggered it.

The pressing urgency finally lifted, and I took a deep breath, slowing my heart that had been racing inside.

How irritating, I thought.

I could have been making up with Kit right about now, but oh no, my stupid magic was being weird. I'd have to talk with Liv tomorrow and see if we could make the wards ignore any little critters, unless they were shifters, of course.

Taking one last look around, I left, locking the door, and before I could turn back around to walk the few feet to my car, I was hit in the back of the head with something incredibly hard.

And it wasn't the kind of hard I'd prefer to be smacked with either.

The sting pulsed when I gently put my fingers to my head.

They came away with blood, and I stumbled to get myself upright.

Dizziness consumed my vision, but my hearing was still spectacular, as I made out two sets of feet shuffling, then, frantic, hushed murmurs that slowly formed into words.

Okay, maybe my hearing was off slightly from the blow.

"You fucking moron, we need her unharmed. She won't be able to perform any kind of spells if she can't think straight. And the boss needs her to do many." One voice said harshly.

"Sorry, dude. I panicked, she could probably use her magic to hurt us, and I didn't want that to happen." The other voice said, a bit louder. There were only two of them, and they were men. And they wanted me because, as far as I knew, I was the only witch around.

Who the fuck sent them, and what did they want with me?

Words were hard to form. I slowly began crawling toward where I knew my car was parked, still running. If only I could reach it and somehow drive away, even if I ran into a few things, I'd have Liv fix anything that needed it.

But, just as I reached the cold curb, rough calloused hands gripped my arms. Something was blown into my face, and I could feel my powers slipping from my fingers before I could do anything if my mind would only clear enough for me to think.

I began thrashing around, finally finding my voice. Pure rage at whoever these guys thought they were, trying to take on a witch.

"Let me go, you pieces of shit." I spat, liquid landing in one guy's eyes. They had black ski masks covering their heads, and all I could see were their nearly hidden globes. They were clearly human; mirth and hatred seeped from their pores. It made me shudder, and pain shot through the back of my head.

"Hold her arms, I've got her legs." One of them said.

I was weak from the head injury, so my efforts to escape were thwarted.

Then, I saw where they were taking me. Back doors to a windowless van that was parked across the road were open.

How had I not seen the van before?

My efforts doubled because all those late nights watching homicide and police shows taught me one thing. Never, ever let them take you to another location. When they got you elsewhere, that would be the absolute end, whether I was killed or trafficked, it was a big fuck no.

I wrenched my arm from the first guy's grip and swung it as hard as I could backward. The tip of my elbow landed on the guy's side, and he dropped me to hold himself.

My already throbbing head pulsated harder after smacking the concrete of the road hard from him dropping me like I was a hot potato.

"Motherfucker," I muttered, since the one guy had let go, the other one struggled to hold onto my feet, and I kicked him square in the chin. "Take that asshole." I groggily chuckled.

And just when I was about to stand, a grotesque roar echoed in the distance, followed by fire lighting up the sky.

Kit.

I cried out, sobs left my throat as the relief coursed through me, knowing my mate was on his way to keep me safe and take care of these two. Right now, I was in no shape to do anything as my vision continued to blur, and every time I went to use my magic to conjure water to hold them, nothing happened.

The two men who had hauled me to this kidnapper van froze; from what I could tell, their eyes were the size of saucers. They glanced at one another and then down at me, where I was still lying on the street, and took off.

I saw the moment gold-colored scales flew through the

darkened sky toward the two men, but then he turned quickly, landing directly in front of me.

Kit, or Vero rather, leaned down, breathing hot air onto my body, making a shiver of delight roll through me.

Now is not the time to get turned on, Viv. I told myself, but it was difficult. He was here, and goddess, did it turn me on that I could feel his anger through our bond and how he was going to tear those men apart.

Rapid footsteps ran up to us, and for a brief moment, I panicked until Mitsy's voice, strong and sure, spoke to my dragon.

"I've got this, Kit. Get those guys before they get away. I've already called Rayth. I'll stay with Viv until you guys secure things."

I was stunned and stared at Mitsy in awe. She was so put together and wasn't panicking like I was. Usually, I was the level-headed one, but fuck, everything was wrong between my head hurting and my magic fucked.

"Go, my mate. I'll be here when you get back." I said, and once that word, mate, left my mouth, I could feel the desire and excitement from him.

My dragon didn't stick around, knowing I was in good hands, he took flight and resumed his hunt for the two assailants.

Barely a second later, Rayth appeared out of nowhere. Mitsy held pepper spray in her fist and aimed it at the detective.

He held his hands in the air, "It's only me, where's Kit?"

Cradling my head in one hand, I gestured behind us in the direction he had taken off. "He went that way. Two men attacked me."

He nodded, flickering for a moment, his face contemplating whether to stay with me or assist Kit.

"Go," I said, "I'm good here."

He nodded and disappeared.

Mitsy and I moved from the freezing street onto a wooden bench that sat against the side of an empty building across from mine.

There was a huge 'for lease' sign tacked on the wall next to it, and I snorted. Who the hell would want to open anything in this city when things seemed to be spiraling? I had a feeling this space would stay empty for awhile. Only a mad person would take a chance on the chaos that was Mount Hellfire ever since Finn decided coming out from the other side of the Veil was a good idea.

I mean, don't get me wrong, it was fantastic, being out in the open, especially with my best friend, but there were downsides to our presence. And this specific incident was number one among those downsides.

People got bold with attacks.

An ambulance pulled up to the curb, and a few EMTs exited, one of whom I recognized as Kit's friend, Vizek. He had a duffel bag in his hand when he approached, smirking like there was a hidden inside joke he had just discovered.

"You sure do like to get into trouble, don't you?" He joked.

Of course, it made me laugh and then wince from the wound and pounding between my ears.

Mitsy stayed by my side the entire time, and when Kit finally landed, still in his dragon form, I realized I was an absolute idiot for pushing him away. I had a lot of making up to do, and I'd start now.

Boy, was I in the best kind of trouble.

Chapter Twenty-Six

Kit

Vero was an eager dragon waiting for our mate. He had wanted to wait no matter how long it took for her to come home. We knew she said she'd meet us here at nine, but we've been here since seven in case she decided to be early.

She wanted to talk to us, and so much triumph and hope coursed through our blood that we grew anxious and impatient.

I had driven over in my truck, a bag of magically spelled food that would keep warm for hours, while I sat here like the love-sick dragon that I was.

My mate had been rightfully upset with me last night.

I acted like a possessive, not very understandable, asshole. Viv had no choice about the man that her father had paired her with. I knew that, but the jealousy still got in the way of rational thoughts.

Vero had demanded that we assert our dominance over our mate, which was quite out of his character, considering he was an unusually sweet-tempered dragon, much to my father's anguish growing up.

I was very different than those of our kind. And maybe

that's why helping Finn and being around others was so much easier for me than for the dragon species as a whole. We usually stuck to our own kind, every so often venturing out but returning all the same.

My life in the human world and the city of Mount Hellfire had always been considerably enjoyable. And now with my mate residing here, it felt more imperative that my choices led me to her.

Now, I just needed to not fuck it up again. Not to say the wrong things or bring up the male that was a sensitive subject, again. I'd let her tell me what was going on, but I knew most of it.

She was the eldest daughter of a prominent magically family in the coven on this side of the country. Her father was the leader, and she had duties. Those duties were to bind her to an equally powerful magical family and, one day, take over for her father.

But that wasn't Viv. She was a carefree spirit who didn't let anyone or anything drag her down or get in the way of the things she loved and held dear.

She was fiercely loyal.

And I wanted to snatch that loyalty and horde it for myself. Be consumed in her essence and have her look at me like I was her whole world.

So, I waited. And waited.

My phone buzzed in my front pocket as I paced back and forth in front of my truck. The snow that had been sitting there was packed down and nearly icy as temperatures began to drop when the sun went down.

It was Viv; she was going to stop by her store and check it out. Her wards were going off.

Unease crept up my spine, and my scales emerged on my forearms, the itch to fully shift just beneath the surface.

Vero had perked up and knew something wasn't right.

Our mate is in trouble. WE MUST GO!

There was no arguing with my dragon on that. Pricks of agitation made even more scales appear on my human body. He was trying to force the shift. It would be painful if I didn't adhere to his wishes.

So I let Vero emerge. And once I had fully shifted, he roared, taking off into the sky. Our wings beat fast and furious, propelling our body through the air and darkened grey clouds.

When we had made it to town, nearly to Viv's building, our bond echoed her terror and anger.

Two males had hold of my mate and were trying to place her in a dark van.

They were trying to take our mate from us.

My rage blossomed, Vero roared again, and we spewed fire into the air. Alerting the men who touched Viv that a predator was upon them, and they weren't making it out alive. They were about to die once my dragon reached them, and I had to appeal to him to make sure they lived.

I'm going to swallow them whole.

You most certainly are not. We need to question them, find out what they want with our mate, and ensure her safety.

It matters not; they will perish this night. They dared touch ours.

Listen to me, Vero, we need to secure them and interrogate them. Make sure there isn't more out there that would come after her in the future.

He huffed, growls permeating the air as we began chasing the two men down the street, only to turn back to our mate who lay on the cold, hard street.

We'd catch up to them, but we needed to ensure she was alright.

We landed in the street, and Viv seemed disoriented. My

vision swirled red for a moment, and then another woman appeared. She was Viv's friend, Mitsy, and she urged me to go after the men, saying she would keep our mate safe.

I hesitated because everything in me screamed to stay with her, but it also urged I take retribution.

So, with Viv secure, I took off and went for the two men who hadn't made it more than a block away.

I landed in their path, standing tall, puffing out my chest to appear more menacing. In reality, I didn't have to do that because I was a glorious fucking dragon and anyone should shit their pants being on the end of a pissed off mythical creature.

"Oh shit." One of them said under their breath. His face paled, and I knew this was the end of the line for them. Neither one was going anywhere.

We didn't let them get two more feet when we pushed them to the asphalt street and pinned them both under our claws. They gasped, screamed, and one of them pissed themselves as the stench of urine made its way to my nostrils.

I almost reared back; it was so pungent.

Fucking disgusting pieces of filth.

One of the males was struggling harder, and he moved so that his leg was beneath a talon, which I just happened to let gravity take its course, piercing the skin and muscle, digging in as his screech echoed in the otherwise quiet streets.

As I was about to push further in, Rayth appeared, an angry but pleased look on his face.

"Oh, good, you got them both, and they are still alive." He commented, his body flickering, giving away that he was anxious that he'd have more paperwork to do if I did gut them where they lay.

Vero huffed smoke in their direction, and the two men cringed.

"Atticus or Vero, whichever one is in control right now, can you please let them up so we can take them in and integrate them properly?"

He was pleading with us, and my human side rationalized with this request; however, Vero hadn't relented yet. He wanted more blood to spill, so he slowly pushed his talon further into the one man's leg, making him cry out for mercy.

"Oh god please make him stop! I'll tell you anything you want to know!"

Vero, let the humans be handed over to our forces' custody. Rayth will ensure they are locked away where they can't reach our mate.

He internally glared my way, his desires split between letting them loose and returning to our mate or ending them where they lay.

VERO!

DON'T WORRY SO MUCH, HUMAN. I'LL LET THEM UP IN ONE MOMENT. ONE OF THEM HASN'T PISSED THEMSELVES YET, AND I WANT THEM TO SOIL THEIR PANTS IN EMBARRASSMENT.

Laughter echoed in the place where I was watching, inside our minds. I relaxed as Vero lifted one claw from an assailant, drawing his talon from the injured male.

Rayth quickly put him in restraints while another officer from the ISF hauled him into a cruiser.

The only one left was the one who hadn't pissed himself or been injured.

So, we roared in the male's face, letting our spit pour over him.

That did the trick, and he was suddenly wet beneath our claw. I quickly lifted them away before I could get the male's urine on our scales.

Rayth turned to me when the final male was taken away, a grin spread on his face, while he shook his head. "You sure do like to put on a show, don't you?"

Vero dipped his head and started walking back to our mate, ignoring Rayth for now. She was waiting for us to take care of her and bring her home, where I could lavish her in my human form and beg for forgiveness.

If anything, this situation made us even more protective of her.

I'd crawl on my hands and knees, let her use me to her desires, if she'd allow us to remain by her side for eternity.

When we reached the ambulance, where our mate was sitting on the back being looked at, Vero let me take over. He understood we'd need to encompass her within our arms, and I couldn't do that while being a dragon.

So I shifted and waltzed to my wide-eyed mate, smirking while she gazed those eyes up and down my body.

"Oh. My. God. Can you put on some pants or something? That is not for my eyes to see." Her friend Mitsy shrieked, covering her face and turning her back to us.

Viv laughed, "Oh, Mits, it's not like you haven't seen a cock before."

Mitsy turned her head, still shielding her eyes, "I have, but I don't want to look at your man's swinging dick."

Vizek came around the ambulance, took one look at me, and sighed heavily. "In your birthday suit, yet again I see." He opened a hatch and threw some shorts in my direction.

I put them on, just to not scar anyone else in the vicinity, I supposed.

"Hello, my mate." I purred, "How is your head?"

She absently reached for the back and winced. I gripped onto her wrist, pressing her knuckles to my lips.

"Don't—you'll hurt yourself further," I whispered.

My fingers tenderly rubbed against her cheek, touching her anywhere she would let me. It seemed she wasn't opposed and leaned into my palm when I cupped her face.

Mitsy cleared her throat, "I'll be right back. I don't have to tell you twice to look after her."

My mate's friend was protective of her. I was grateful that she had not only Teags as a close friend but also Mitsy, whom I had briefly met a few times.

"Are they?" Turning back to my mate, my attention solely on her, through our bond, I knew she was asking if I killed them. There was hope there, but also fear. She wanted to know as much as I did who was behind the attack.

I shook my head, "Rayth convinced Vero to let them go. He did, but not before inflicting pain and embarrassment on them."

She chuckled, "Thank you for saving me. If you hadn't shown up, roared, and thrown a fireball from your throat in the air, I was afraid they would have gotten what they came here for. Which I'm still not entirely sure why they wanted me to begin with."

Just then, Jorrik and Hawk walked up with their arms crossed and scowls plastered to their green faces.

"Put on quite the show there, Kit. Heard both the males pissed themselves, and that you stabbed one in the leg with your talon." Hawk said jovially, Jorrick remained quiet, peering around like the bodyguards they specialized in being. His nostrils flared, and his head swiveled looking for whatever he scented, his body on edge.

I ignored him, reassuring my mate we'd find out. "Don't worry, my Neesha. Rayth will get it out of the men what they want, and if someone sent them, who exactly it is. He has someone who has their ways to make them talk."

She visibly relaxed, her eyes still glazed from being hit over the head. Viv suffered a mild concussion and wasn't going to be left alone. I'd take her back to her home and remain awake watching over her if need be.

"Can we leave yet?" She asked, and she tilted her head to peer up at me. I could deny her nothing.

"Yes, my mate. We'll leave shortly." I turned to Hawk, "Text me if you hear anything. I want to know everything. I won't leave Viv's side, so I need one or both of you to update me on what you learn."

Hawk smirked, his scowl disappearing when he looked between us. He knew mates were important and came first.

When an Orc mated, they worshipped the ground their female stepped upon and would stumble over themselves to ensure her happiness and comfort.

Hawk opened his mouth, his nostrils flaring like Jorrik's had, leaving him speechless. His eyes widened a moment later, and they were glued to someone around the side of the ambulance.

That someone who turned the corner was Mitsy.

She was completely oblivious to the two green bastards before us who had hearts forming in their eyes as they silently watched her walk up to Viv.

Mitsy reached out, putting her hand on Viv's arm to get her attention, "You going to be okay if I leave you, Viv? I have to finish closing the store. I sort of just left it unlocked when I heard Kit roar and then saw you on the ground."

Viv nodded, a lovely smile just for her friend, "Yeah, Kit's got me. Do you want someone to come with you?"

Mitsy waved a hand, brushing off the offer, "Gosh, no. I've closed my store late at night on my own before, silly. Call me tomorrow or the next day if you want company, okay?"

She turned and jumped; both Jorrik and Hawk had closed in on her without anyone noticing, and it startled her.

"Oh! Excuse me, sorry I didn't see you both there." Silently, they opened up a very narrow path for her to squeeze past, and she hesitated at first, eyeing them like they were going to snatch her up at any moment.

The two Orcs towered over her, and when she brushed past them, they turned, keeping their gazes glued to her while she glanced over her shoulder before making a hasty getaway.

Vizek burst into laughter, "Can you two be more obvious?"

They turned in unison, folding their arms and glaring at my friend. "Alright—alright. Shows over. Jorrik—Hawk, I don't care which one of you does it, but let me know when you have a semblance of an answer on why my mate was targeted."

They nodded, remaining quiet, and glancing over their shoulders one last time at a female who had already disappeared into her store.

I turned to my mate and offered her my hand, "Come, my flame, let's get you home. I have food waiting for us."

"It's probably cold by now." She grumbled, but I didn't say a word. I was just elated she reached for me without further complaint.

We'd find out the answers to what happened tonight, I knew that much. But, for now, I'd bring her home, nurse her back to health, and hopefully put my mouth everywhere I could on her skin.

And talk, possibly, if I could keep my hands to myself long enough for that.

Chapter Twenty-Seven

Viv

I really, really could get used to this.

Why had I been fighting this again?

Oh yeah, that's right, to protect Kit from my father. But, all of that seemed lost as he carried me like I was breakable and he couldn't stand to be apart.

And I had to admit, this was really nice.

My libido kicked into overdrive, breathing in his intoxicating scent. I had always loved the lingering after-smells of a campfire and cinnamon. The kind that seeped into a sweatshirt long after the fire died down and even carried over into the next morning while eating french toast.

It reminded me of something wild. Which, I suppose, if you think about it, Kit was a dragon, and they're part of the ferocious animal kingdom in a way.

I knew one thing was for certain: I was finished fighting our connection. Maybe not fighting Kit entirely because I do love a chase.

Oh, maybe he'd chase me as his dragon, I thought. It was a sinfully delightful idea, one I'd want to explore when my noggin wasn't in complete shambles from being knocked over the head for the second time in the last few months.

Delicious, sinfully naughty thoughts swirled in my mind, and I couldn't stop them the longer Kit was in my presence.

"Neesha, whatever it is you're thinking of, it's driving me mad," Kit growled. Something rumbled in his chest while his nostrils flared and he licked his lips, glancing at me while his fingers tightened against my thigh.

We were in my car with Kit driving, headed back to my place.

I turned, facing him as much as I could, smiling, "Whatever are you talking about?" I said, pretending I had no idea he could smell my arousal. There wasn't anything I could do; our bond and the fact that he saved me kicked everything into high gear.

He pulled into my driveway, and when we cleared the tree-line, I spotted his truck and a large bag that had been seemingly forgotten on the porch. He got out of my car and started to make his way around to open my door.

And while I waited, I stared ahead, sighing with relief that I was finally home and we could eat something. I mean, he did promise me dinner after all and said he had left it here. Which I assumed that's what the bag was. It was likely super cold now, but it wouldn't be a big deal; we could just heat everything.

My door opened, and before I could leave on my own, Kit scooped me up.

"I can walk to my door, you know." I pointed out, not really fighting him but making a protest anyway.

"I'm aware my fire. However, if I don't touch you and remind myself you are alright, Vero is going to resurface and fly to the ISF building and fry two human males that touched our mate."

"So, barbaric. I love it."

The corner of his mouth turned up, and I nearly lost my breath at how it made my heart skip.

He had chipped away at those walls I had built, and they were finally all crashing into dust.

It was too late to turn back; I was going forward, and damn, did it feel good.

"Where are your keys, Viv?" Kit had me cradled in his arms, he reached the porch, and only let my feet touch the floor without moving away. It was like distance wasn't an option. He didn't move as he stared, waiting for me to answer.

"Oh, right," I shook myself out of this trance he seemed to put me in tonight. "They're in my back pocket."

Before I could grab them out, Kit's fingers were already there, sliding into my pocket, his hand lingering over the keys as I gazed into his eyes.

After a few tense and panty-melting moments, he pulled them out, opening the door, grabbing the food, and hauling me back into his arms.

I rolled my eyes because this was getting a little ridiculous, "Kit, I can walk in my own home. No one is going to jump out and attack me here."

"Not that you realize," He muttered under his breath.

I chose to ignore the comment because just then my stomach protested its emptiness and I needed to fill it pronto.

Kit held up the bag he had grabbed off the porch and headed for my kitchen island. He removed several containers, and I went to open the microwave and grab a plate when he shut the open door.

"It's still hot. I requested the food stay heated, a new witch at the restaurant put a spell on it. It might expire soon, so we should eat up."

The thought never occurred to me; I was used to working with water and liquids. I'd have to try it on a coffee and see how it fared with the caffeinated elixir. There were times I would forget about my drink and end up having to remake it because it was too cold for me.

I sat in the chair across from Kit and glanced up to see him staring. "What?" I asked, poking my food with the end of a fork he had handed me.

He smirked, "This would be our first meal together where you're not actively fighting me. I'm just memorizing the moment."

Oh my goddess, he was too adorable. How had I not realized it before? Oh, that's right, I completely rendered any kind of happiness useless to myself—an unfortunate side effect of having Horace Woodward as a father.

"Well," I started, "does it exceed your expectations?"

He nodded, "Absolutely—just being near you, even in silence, exceeds everything I could have hoped and imagined."

"Kit—I'm sorry."

"No need to apologize, Neesha. All that matters is that we move forward. Although I think we need to eventually talk about what being mated to a dragon entails."

I feigned a gasp, placing a hand over my chest, "You mean to tell me there's more to it than just you beating your chest and roaring, 'mine.'"

His brows furrowed, and the look he gave made me burst into laughter. I waved a hand at him, "All in jest. I'm sure you'll tell me all about being your mate and whatnot."

Kit gave me a thoughtful look, "Did you know dragons mate for life and that life is extended?"

I shook my head, "No, I don't know a whole lot about other species. My father never allowed Liv or me to indulge in anything other than what it meant to be a witch in a coven that I'd one day take over."

His throat bobbed while he swallowed, "Viv, about your father."

"Yes?"

"What do you know about the ISF investigating him?"

My eyes widened. This was news to me and, possibly, shouldn't have surprised me, but something deep within started to settle, a calm washing over in a raging sea of justice.

"Really?" I was excited; this was one of the best things that could have happened.

"You don't seem upset."

I snorted, "No, I don't, do I? What kind of daughter am I to hope they find something on my father?" I held up my hand when he opened his mouth, "Let me finish, because if we are going to do this, talk it out, you need to know why I fought this bond for so long. You deserve to know my past sins and decide for yourself if you still want me." I shrugged, my voice cracking with uncertainty.

Kit rounded the counter and gripped my face, gently forcing my gaze to reach his. "Anything you tell me, no matter good or bad, could never make me run. Hell, I've done everything I could, even making a complete ass out of myself to get to this point. Tell me everything, and if you don't want to spill it all tonight, we have many more nights to divulge our secrets. Okay?"

His worried expression wasn't for the information I'd put forth, but making sure I understood he was here for the long haul.

I gripped his hands, pulling them from my face to hold onto while I told him the summarized version of my guilt.

"My father isn't a good man. He forced me to help him torture anyone who opposed his rule as coven leader and businessman. I feared him for so long that I just went along with it. He threatened to use my sister to keep my compliance, and then, when we got old enough, my sister helped me escape. We were a few years out of high school, but she made me swear I'd leave if I got the opportunity. It was hard to accept, but Liv proved she could take care of herself."

I swallowed around the lump that formed, thinking about that night again. The brutality he made me witness and the threat that I'd be the one taking the next life. I couldn't even fathom what that would have done to me. I would have broken into pieces inside.

"So," I continued, "The night I left, it was like any other night; he had me in his chambers, and there was another warlock waiting to be tortured for information. This time, it was regarding a shipment that the ISF seized. My father had no idea it was them at the time until he tortured it out of the warlock, and as far as I knew, he didn't find out who gave them the tip, but he kept me there when he got the information. And instead of letting me leave like he usually did, he killed the man in front of me."

Tears slipped, rolling down my face. Kit's fingers grazed my cheek, wiping away the wetness.

It was tender, so incredibly sweet, my heart ached that I was such a stubborn ass and could have had this for weeks.

"I'm sorry, Viv, he's incredibly selfish for making you do such—"

"That wasn't all," I interrupted, taking a deep breath. I steeled myself for revealing why I left. "I left that night not because he made me torture this warlock or watch him kill the man, but because he told me I would be doing the killing the next day. I just couldn't bring myself to stomach doing that. And I needed out. He's not a good man at all, Kit, and I was terrified that if he found out about you being my fated mate, he'd somehow use you to lure me back in to do his bidding."

I swallowed against my now dry throat. The confession was

uplifting; I could feel the weight dissipating, but there was a tinge of dread at what Kit would say. Luckily, he made it easier to tell him.

"Oh my mate," He cooed, "You are my brave girl, aren't you?"

His fingers brushed through my hair, the motions comforting while they eased the remaining tension.

"I'm so proud of you. You overcame the obstacle that is your father. Do you want me to look further into this investigation?"

"I don't know," I whispered, "Part of me is scared he'd find out I told you or that you're looking into him."

He nodded, "Okay, how about this. I ask a friend to look into everything, and I give him what you told me. Are you okay with that, Neesha?"

I loved the word he called me; it gave me butterflies, even during a serious conversation. "Yeah, that works for me. Just—promise not to confront him or anything."

He grinned; it was stunning and made my pussy roar back up. He groaned a moment later and moved in between my open thighs while I sat on the barstool.

"You make it extremely hard to be good when you have a head injury." His voice dipped and turned husky.

I closed my eyes, putting my forehead against his chest. "I can't help it, you make me forget we're having a serious conversation."

He chuckled, "Maybe we should put a pause on the discussion and get you to bed. It's late, your belly is filled, and all I want to do is hold you in my arms all night."

I pulled away, biting my lip, and gazed up at him while he stood over me, "Is that all you want?"

"Tempting, Viv, but you need to rest tonight. We'll revisit what I want in the morning if you're feeling better." He hummed, nudged my chin with his finger before he left, leaving the space he had just occupied. I shivered at the loss while he cleaned up.

It wasn't long, and he was lifting me from my stool and taking me to my bedroom after I told him where to go.

Begrudgingly, he kept his word, pulling me back into his chest, his hand resting across my stomach as he nuzzled my hair. We were both clothed, although I was in a short pajama set, my sexy lingerie forgotten for now; he had stripped to his boxers.

It was agonizing torture.

We lay there, not getting to any good parts of what a night having a man in my bed should entail. And while his breathing evened out, I was grateful to have him by my side and in my bed. Even if he didn't touch me the way I wanted, this was by far more intimate and fulfilling in our budding bond.

Chapter Twenty-Eight

Kit

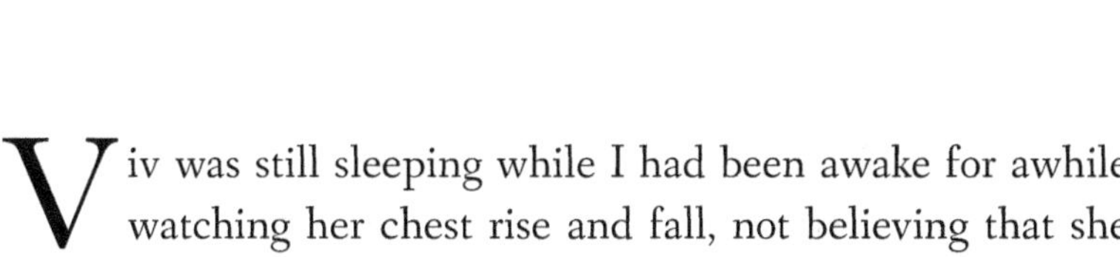

Viv was still sleeping while I had been awake for awhile watching her chest rise and fall, not believing that she was still here. Although I didn't know where else she could have gone, considering I was in her bed.

Last night was a revelation. She finally told me why she had been so adamant about pushing our bond away, and it all had to do with her father.

I'd see to it that the investigation into him continued and remained a priority, rather than being put on the back burner.

Finn would certainly have something to say once I spoke with him about her father's ways of getting information and, of course, finding anything to tie him to any unsolved murders.

I trailed my fingers along Viv's arm and over her hip. The touch was tantalizing, stirring my cock to harden further than it already had been, waking up first thing this morning.

I couldn't help it, though, I had my female—my mate, in bed, her tempting body lined up against mine, her curves fitting perfectly to my front.

What I wouldn't give for her to wake, turn to me, and let me lavish her with all the pleasure she deserved.

I had glanced gently in between the strands of her hair at the wound on the back of her head, and it seemed to be more healed than any normal human's would. Her magic must have something to do with the wound being accelerated in restoring it to how it was before she was bludgeoned.

My fury rose once again at the reminder that she had been attacked and nearly kidnapped. If I had been a moment longer, she would have been lost to me. Without the knowledge she gave about her father, he wouldn't have been at the top of my suspect list. Now, though, now I had second thoughts, and I'd need to voice them to Rayth.

However, that was for another time because I would lie here and wait for my mate to wake.

And it wasn't much longer before she stirred. Murmuring and nuzzling into my bicep, which I had slipped under her neck sometime in the night.

"Viv?" I whispered into her neck.

She pushed her ass back further into my hard shaft, humming with a sigh.

"Am I dreaming, or is there a man in my bed with a delicious cock shoved between my ass cheeks?" Her voice was groggy, with the lingering sleep still keeping her under.

I slid my hand down her waist, hip, and thighs, making her moan.

"This is nice, Kit. Keep going."

I knew she was awake now, and I so wished to continue my explorations, but I wanted to ensure she was well enough for what I wanted to do to her this morning.

"How's your head?"

Viv turned, glancing over her shoulder at me. She smiled sleepily. It was a beautiful sight, like the first rays of a sunrise, while wrapped in blankets, sitting on a porch with a hot coffee in hand.

"It feels so much better." She sighed, turning and lying on her back to look up at me. "What's on your mind?"

"A lot, I was curious. I looked at your wound, and it looks nearly all the way healed."

She flushed, "Oh, that, yeah, I may have spelled something in my water to help. Although it works better in coffee and tea, water was my next best choice since that's all you gave me to drink with dinner."

Chuckling, I brushed a few strands from her forehead, "Apologies, next time I'll make you some tea. Maybe, tea from my homeland."

"I'd love that."

Down the bond, those words felt truthful, like she desired to see my home someday, which I'd want to take her to soon and complete the bond, but for now, I'd let her heal and wait to get some answers once Rayth called.

"So," I lowered my voice, pressing my body against Viv's side. Her gasp was music to my ears. I could already tell I affected her just as much as she did me. The evidence was poking her in the thigh after all. "How would you rate your healing? Good enough for some extra activities?"

"Yes—goddess yes."

"And if I just—" gliding the tips of my fingers, I caressed up from her knee to the edge of her shorts, tracing the lining to her inner thigh. She shifted, moving flatter on her back and parting her legs ever so tantalizingly.

Humming, I continued my exploration back to her hip and up her stomach, pushing her night shirt up as I moved, exposing her already tightened buds to the early morning air.

Moving over Viv, I settled between her thighs, still clothed, and trailed kisses from her navel up to the undersides of her small, perfect breasts. I cupped one in my hand, and it fit perfectly while I licked my way up to her already erect nipple. Rolling the one between my fingers, I covered her other with my mouth, sucking gently at first and increasing the suction until I had her panting.

She gripped the sheet in one hand and fisted the hair on the back of my head with the other.

"Goddess—yes! Kit, I need—"

Popping off her nipple, keeping my face to her chest, I glanced up, "Tell me what you need, my fire, and I'll give it to you."

"Clothes," She gasped, "I need them off, mine and yours."

She didn't have to tell me twice; I pulled her nightshirt off quickly, lingering at her sleep shorts. Slowly, I rolled them over her hips to reveal the gold strap of her panties. I quirked an eyebrow and purred. "What is this, my mate?"

She glanced down in impatience and smirked. "I had a surprise for you last night, but it was ruined." Her breathing picked up as I pulled the shorts all the way down her legs.

The patch of fabric covering her cunt was also gold and had intricate designs in the lace. It was enticing, making my mouth water.

She saw I had been focused on her center, making her shift, "I have a matching bra, but I took it off before bed."

I tsked disappointed I didn't get to unwrap that last night, but I wouldn't have changed how it ended with her safe in my arms after the ordeal. "You'll have to wear the full set for me some other time." So, without another glance, I gently pulled the lace from her while stripping bare myself, my own impatience was winning.

I took a moment to admire my mate. The last time I had her in my bed, it was fast and furious. The tension that had been building between us had exploded. The mate bond sickness had demanded it, but now—now we didn't have to worry about how fast or slow we paced our pleasure.

Nothing gave me greater joy than this moment, watching her chest rise and fall in a mesmerizing rhythm that told me she wanted me just as much as I wanted her. Not only that, but the bond began to flourish the longer we remained in each other's presence.

I couldn't hold back any longer, even though I wanted to continue looking at her; my mouth found its way to her skin. Tasting and teasing with the tip of my tongue, I lavished her breasts with the utmost care that the delectable globes deserved.

Viv had other ideas; she gripped my hair once again and pulled me to her mouth. Her tongue plunged inside, dancing and tangling, shooting my arousal to higher levels as she manhandled me. Which, surprisingly, I enjoyed very much.

Sliding my fingers along her thighs, I trailed them to her center, circling her clit, making her squirm in delight before dipping them to her entrance. I tested the resistance with one finger, sliding it inside before adding another, pumping in and out deliberately slow, stretching her.

She was already soaking wet, which left me with little to prepare her for my cock. I wasn't overly large, but it was enough that if a woman weren't ready, she'd be very uncomfortable. And my mate's body was telling me she was absolutely ready, but I desired to know if she was mentally there with me.

"My Neesha, look at me." Her eyes had closed while my fingers had remained inside her, moving languidly, but I wanted her attention, needed to know she was alright. "Shall we keep going? Or do you want to stop?"

She gripped my wrist as her life depended on it, holding it tightly but still allowing me to move my fingers in and out.

"Don't you dare stop. I need more. Need you, Kit. Fill me, my mate."

Gods, just hearing her call me her mate sent a primal shiver down my spine; some of Vero's scales appeared on my skin, and she gasped at the sudden shift.

"Yes," She moaned, hooking her leg around my waist and pulling me closer. "More."

So, I obliged her, took my fingers from her center and lined up my cock with her cunt's entrance, rubbing myself in her wetness, coating and teasing before I drove in.

I couldn't be slow, I tried, but her tempting heat was like a magnet, and I pushed into her in one thrust. She gasped, gripping onto my shoulder, those nails dug in, spiking a sharp pain that subsided as it turned into pleasure.

"Fuck," I breathed, pumping my hips. I couldn't go slow as my thrust sped up, and kept a punishing rhythm.

Viv screamed my name, her cunt fluttering around my cock, milking it, begging it to release my seed into her, to mark her again with my scent as her sudden orgasm crashed over her.

My hips pistoned in and out, the rhythm more erratic as I chased my own release quickly after her. I covered her with my body, moaning through the pleasure, a first for me, but it seemed to spur her on as she cried out into the room again, and I felt her tighten once more.

I slowed my thrusts, panting against her neck, the urge to bite down on her shoulder shivered through me, but I pulled back.

Now was not the time to complete the bond; I had to do it traditionally, in my home under nature, and in the sacred mating caves.

Reluctantly, I pulled out, lying on my back, pulling Viv to drape across my chest. Vero demanded we keep her close this time, and I chuckled at his persistence to chain her to the bed.

"What's so funny?" She asked, trailing her fingers lazily against my chest as her breath tickled against my skin.

"Vero's insisting I tie you to the bed so you don't leave like last time."

She winced, "I deserve that, but he forgets you're in my house. I can't go anywhere when you're at the one place I escape to."

"I'll keep that in mind if you ever decide to make a run for it."

"I won't." She whispered, "I mean it, Kit, I'm here, I'm done running from this, from us."

Playing with her hair, I smiled against the top of her head, "I'm glad, my fire. Now rest." And I pushed her head to relax on my chest while Vero purred his contentment.

Our mate was here and not running for once.

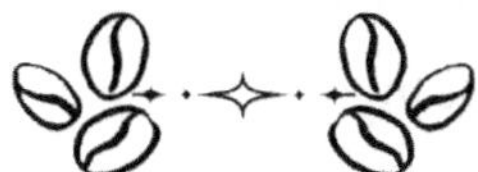

We had fallen asleep after Viv decided to climb on top and ride me like I was taking flight with her on my back.

Which, I'd need to do soon because Vero was hounding me about feeling the breeze on his scales while he glided through the clouds with our mate on his back. It was the one thing he most desired, aside from enjoying the view while I fucked her senseless.

Viv's phone vibrated against the bedside table, and once it started, she groaned in annoyance.

"Why is someone calling me this early?"

I chuckled because it most certainly wasn't morning anymore.

Kissing her shoulder, I reached over, grabbed the phone, and handed it to her. "My mate, it is after noon."

"What!" She bolted upright and scrambled to grab her phone before it fell off the bed. She took one look at the screen and groaned, "It's my sister."

I kissed her arm, unable to stop touching her, even though we had been entangled with one another all morning. "Answer it, my fire." I urged.

She didn't let it ring much longer when her voice answered cheerily, "Hey, baby sis."

I could hear Liv on the other end, clearly being this close to Viv in bed.

"What the fuck happened last night, and why didn't you call me?"

Viv winced, pulling the phone from her ear. "Sorry, Livvy, there was so much that happened, but Kit had it handled."

"Kit?" Liv asked, curiosity lacing her voice, and suddenly she wasn't so angry that my mate hadn't called her.

"Yeah, he's actually with me now. What's up?" Viv's finger traced one of the floral patterns on her blanket while she waited for Liv to tell her why she called.

"Well, I just—" Liv huffed, "I wanted to make sure your dumbass was still alive."

"Yeah, I'm alive and well, thanks to Kit. He rescued me before those two guys could kidnap me."

"Well, thank the goddess. Will you be coming by the coffee shop soon? I've been waiting here for hours. I have a grumpy red male who followed me in and won't leave unless I do." Liv asked hopefully.

"Give me an hour, and I'll be there so you can tell me about this grouchy red male I'm interested in hearing more of. Love you, Livvy."

"Love you too, Vivvy. See you both soon."

They hung up, and Viv tossed her phone, groaning and lying down, snuggling back into my side.

I couldn't help but smile. Her immediate reaction was to reach for me, and I had a slip of worry that it was too good to be true. However, the bond told me otherwise, and she really was seeking my body for comfort.

"Should we get up and get dressed?" I asked.

"Give me like a half hour of this and then yes."

So I did. We lay there for another half hour before getting ready. And now we were walking in through the front doors of her coffee shop hand in hand, and I couldn't help that my happiness was broadcast all over my face.

Several inhumans glanced at us and smirked; they knew my notoriously stubborn mate was no longer resisting my efforts. It was a glorious victory that made my chest inflate with pride. The kind of pride that having my beautiful, stunning, fierce mate's arm draped over mine couldn't be replaced with anything.

"There you are!"

Well, anything aside from my mate's parents.

Viv stiffened, and instead of letting my arm go, she held onto it tighter. Tight enough that little moon indents would be left behind when she removed her fingers from my skin.

"Mom—I thought you and father would have left already. I haven't seen you around," Viv's voice wavered. She was nervous; the bond demanded I shield her from whatever was about to transpire.

"Oh, nonsense, Vivienne. Our goal has been and always will be to have you come home with us—where it's apparent to be a safer option than remaining here. You were hurt yet again." Horace, her father, sternly said.

My mate, being my fierce ember, glowed heatedly before she sparked into my fire.

"I'm not some child you can command, *father*. My life is here—with my mate." She pushed herself further into me. My arm automatically wrapped around her shoulder, pulling her into my side as well.

Horace sneered at the display, "No daughter of mine will mate with a beast—"

"You don't get a say!" Viv shouted. The entire coffee shop fell silent. Not a single word was muttered, nor the clink of cups being placed on tables that had filled the space before. Everyone was still, waiting to see if this was going to turn into something more than just a verbal argument.

"Vivienne—"

"No, you are no longer in control of my life. I am. I say where I go and with whom, and you don't get to defy the goddess either. Kit is my *fated* mate. Our goddess chose him for me and me for him. If you get in the way of that, you know there will be consequences, not by me but by higher powers than we understand."

She stood up for not only herself but for me as well, and that change in her was everything to a dragon, to me. She was my ember that started our fires, and the bond between us flourished even stronger.

Her father opened his mouth to speak when Viv's mother placed her hand on his arm. "Enough, Horace. She's right; we cannot force her to come home. All we can do is hope she will come on her own. And," Her mother looked up, staring into my face, something hidden beneath. "Maybe if we are lucky, she will bring her mate that the *goddess* blessed her with, and he can help where needed."

She was placating him, I realized. Trying to smooth the tensions that snapped like the tightest rope holding two pieces together that pulled in opposite directions.

I gave her mother a very tight, slight nod so she knew I understood she was only trying to help.

And it worked. Horace straightened himself and his designer suit.

"Very well," He gazed from Viv to me. "I expect that at some point you will grace us with your presence back home. If only for a few days."

Viv remained silent, her seething still on the cusp of explosion. My pretty little red-headed female lived up to the reputation, which only made my dick hard.

I stepped up, pushing my hand toward Horace to shake his. "We'll discuss that as a bonded pair, and we'll be sure to send word if and when we plan a trip."

Horace eyed my hand in disdain, but schooled his features, gripping my hand in his. "I look forward to it." Then, he glanced down at his defiant daughter, his brow furrowing deeper before he let go and held out his arm for his wife, Viv's mother. "Let's head home, shall we, Iridia?"

She smiled tight lipped and nodded.

As soon as they were out the door, the heaviness lifted, and everyone, including the silent bystanders, took deep breaths and resumed normal business.

"Goddess, they sure know how to silence a room when need be." Liv, who had been hiding in the back room, emerged, breaking the stillness that had yet to leave fully.

Viv chuckled, breaking away to bring her sister into a hug, "And what were you doing back there, Livvy? Enjoying the show?"

"Of course, big sis. Better you than me at the moment. It seems father has set his sights on getting me to move back and take over whatever jobs he had you doing." She paused, pulling back, smiling at Viv before rolling her eyes, "I suppose if I have to, I will to keep him off your back—"

"No!" Viv and I both said in unison. We glanced at one another, then back at Liv, who held her hands in surrender.

"Okay, it was only a suggestion."

Viv gripped her sister's arm, glancing over her shoulder to ensure their father really left. "Promise me you won't ever agree to do work for him."

"Okay," She replied slowly.

"No, Livvy, promise me, if I have to, I'll invoke an oath."

Liv's eyes widened, and that's when she knew it was serious, so she nodded, whispering, "I promise to the goddess that I will never work for our father." Liv gave her own proclamation, it seemed, and Viv visibly relaxed.

"Thank goddess. There's so much to tell you, but it needs to happen another time, okay?"

"Yeah, I agree."

The sounds of the coffee shop had resumed shortly after Horace and Iridia left, so no one else had even paid any attention to the conversation.

Well, no one except Jeron, who sat in the corner, his red skin rippling and fire dancing between his fingers as he watched Liv walk out of sight with her sister to the back room.

I turned, smirking, I knew that look all too well, because it was one I had bestowed for weeks. That was the look of a man who had the possessive need to protect his mate from everyone included their own flesh and blood.

Chapter Twenty-Nine

Viv

My parents returned home to the coven, leaving Liv and me alone for the time being.

I was inherently worried about my baby sister. If it were true that my father was trying to get her to work for him, I'd have to do everything in my power to keep her here, even if I needed to enlist people to help.

There was one male I knew who would jump at the chance to ensure she stayed. I hadn't officially met him, but caught glimpses of him lurking around wherever Liv was. If I had to, I'd utilize his help.

For now, though, I just wanted to float on my back in the pool with Teags languidly. She handed me a pool noodle, which I looped my arms over so it wasn't so much of an effort to levitate in the chlorinated liquid.

Using my magic, I twirled a gentle current that moved us in a circle, avoiding the sides of the pool so we didn't crash into them, keeping our momentum of utter blissful bobbing.

"Neesha, you've been in that water for hours, aren't your fingers pruny yet?" Kit called out, his voice echoed along the glass and tiled walls, making him sound closer than he was. He was anxious to get his hands back on me, but I wanted more moments with my best friend; he'd have to wait.

Shaking my head, the water sloshed on either side of my face while I hummed, "Nope." Popping the 'p' and fluttering my feet, slowly continuing to enjoy being buoyed in the current I made.

And while Teags and I continued to float, the two men were chatting like girls at the table. I chuckled, thinking about them gossiping, only it was about what was going on in the inhuman community and on the other side of the Veil.

Apparently, Saige still had yet to be located, and it was worrying everyone, especially our King, Finn. He wanted to know if she was okay being in that environment; we all did. It all came down to whether he could one day bring Teags into the Veil as well, since the first human had entered unexpectedly.

If shit ever went down on Earth, he wanted a contingency plan to call everyone to retreat to the safety of the Veil, and that included the human mates that some of the Inhumans had already bonded with.

"So," Teags started, floating on her stomach, propped by the pool noodle nearby, "You and Kit are?" She let the question linger, wanting to ask but also respecting my boundaries if I didn't want to talk about it.

"Yes, Teags, I've fully given into being his mate and not running," I said, rolling my eyes before revealing the biggest grin I could ever have, thinking about the last few amazing days, barely leaving the bed except when nature called or to fill our bellies with sustenance. It was almost too good to be true, but nothing about this felt like an impending doom floating over my head. "He's been incredible, and if I'm being honest,

I'm kicking myself for not trusting he could handle himself against my father sooner."

She grimaced at the mention of the man I called father. "Yeah, how are you doing with all that? Finn said that the investigation into his business and possible murder connections is in full swing. They have someone watching his every move. That includes the many phone calls he's attempted to make with your sister."

I knew about every single one he tried to make because each one ended with Liv texting or calling to let me know that our father was reaching out. She often confided in me about what I thought she should do, especially after I told her everything I had been shielding her from for years.

Liv knew all of the times he forced me to torture other people, inhuman and human alike. And of course about the night she had helped me escape, where he murdered someone in front of my eyes.

"She knows what happened, and Liv's agreed to keep any contact with him to a minimum and never answer the phone unless she's recording their calls or with another person in the room."

And because Finn knew everything as well, that meant Teags did, and honestly, it was such a relief that all my secrets and hiding from the trauma my father inflicted over the years were out.

It made my mind more clear than it had been in years, before my father demanded my servitude.

I waved her off, wanting to change the subject.

"Okay, so real talk," Teags perked up, suddenly interested in what I was going to say next, and I nearly burst into laughter before I could get it out. "How fucking amazing is it that we're best friends, Kit and Finn are best friends, and we're fucking them senselessly."

Teags cheeks turned pink, her eyes widening, "Oh my goddess, Viv, that's so crude."

"Oh, please, you've heard me say worse shit. Admit it, it's awesome because we can hang out often while those two dinglebutts stay out of our hair and do their own thing."

"Yeah, I do love that they can entertain themselves." She whispered, giggling while happily kicking her feet behind her in the water.

"I heard that Firefly," Finn called out.

Then Kit piped in, "I heard what you called us, Neesha. Shall I redden thy bum later?"

She gave me a wry smile, "Oops."

I shrugged, and then we were thrown into fits of laughter, ignoring their pouting.

All felt right in the world; nothing could disturb the peace and fun we brought to this space.

Except that wasn't nearly close to true after I had thought it into existence.

"Viv—"

I screamed, nearly jumping out of my skin and the water as Rayth appeared at the edge closest to my floating body.

"Rayth! I could throw a wall of water at you right now!" My heart thudded in my chest, and the lingering adrenaline coursed through my body. If my hair weren't so drenched, every strand would be standing up from being frightened by his sudden appearance.

Turning my head, I caught sight of both Kit and Finn trying to hide smiles behind their fists. I frowned, "You think this is funny? Finn, don't you have like some super duper magical security system or something to prevent people from just waltzing in here and snatching up your pretty mate?"

Finn's smiling face dropped, and he growled, "Only those permitted under the spell are allowed just to show up. And that's usually just Rayth, considering he hardly walks anywhere. Everyone else has to use their own two feet."

I sighed, turning back to Rayth. "What is it, ghost man?"

"I'd like to speak with you and Kit."

I waved my hand in the direction my mate was seated, "He's right there and can hear you with his dragon eardrums. And I am right here floating in what was supposed to remain blissful peace before you poofed yourself in."

"I'd prefer if you exited and began drying yourself." Rayth ignored me, flickering in irritation, and then disappeared from the edge of the pool only to appear next to the two males.

Our time in the warm, relaxing water was over. Teags was nearly out already, leaving me alone on the other end of the pool before I begrudgingly swam over.

Kit wrapped me in a towel, and without caring that my ass was still drenched with chlorine water, he sat me in his lap.

I smiled, internally screaming like a schoolgirl because I had never had enough attention span for other guys to interact like this. It was usually foreplay, fuck, and then dip.

However, that all was changing now as I continued to accept Kit as my mate. Something was still missing, though, and we hadn't talked more about our bond as witch and dragon. I wondered if it was different than that of a dragon pairing with another of their species.

Rayth remained standing, which made me uneasy, and I couldn't stand it any longer with his staring sweeping across us.

"Well? We're waiting."

"Right, yes, first of all, we have been interrogating the two men who attempted to kidnap you, and even though one said he would talk, they are both very tight-lipped," Rayth explained.

Kit gleefully butted in, "You need someone to come get them to talk? I can certainly help with that as long as you put them in a big enough space. I can shift and make them spill their guts or maybe piss themselves again."

Rayth held up his hand, "No need for that. We'll eventually get them to talk. They did, however, present that the person who paid them to grab you said you were to be forced to use your magic to help them do their dirty work, and he was of the paranormal sort."

I got this sick sensation rolling through my gut. "Boy, that doesn't sound familiar or anything." I snorted. This had to be my father's work, and Kit agreed.

He turned my face towards his, "You thinking it could be?"

I nodded, "I wouldn't put it past him to pull that kind of rouse, especially since I refused to go back home with him and my mother."

"It's plausible, however, my mate, he seems extremely fixated on your sister." Kit pointed out.

"Yeah, now he is, but you're right, he has seemed rather eager for her to come home now that I'm mated and it's been announced to the community. Liv, unfortunately, isn't mated, nor does she have one lurking around that we know of." I couldn't fathom my father would continue to pursue getting me to do magic when he had another daughter he could use who wasn't protected like I was.

"I wouldn't be so sure about that, my mate," Kit said, grinning like he knew exactly who would be lurking. He nudged my chin, "I'll tell you about it later."

I smiled at the promise because I knew he would be good on his word.

Rayth's corporal form flickered, and he looked lost in thought, "We'll keep someone close to her without rousing suspicion from your father."

"Oh, Liv is going to love that." I chuckled. My sister was a Woodward, after all. Our stubbornness ran in the family, and whoever they had watch over her, she'd give them a run for their money, so to speak.

I'd have to ensure that she understood she was now a potential target; she would have to protect herself until this so-called mate came forward to claim her. Although I possibly had an idea of who it could be. I'd just have to wait for my mate to confirm my suspicions.

Glancing back to Rayth, he tucked his hands into the front pockets of his jeans. I quirked an eyebrow when he suddenly looked shy. "What?"

"I have a favor to ask of you," he seemed uncomfortable muttering those words, and I was sure it was a big ask. "As you know, we can't locate the human female Saige in the Veil, and we are becoming increasingly worried about her safety. Not only for the mere fact that she's the first human in history to enter the Veil, but also because there is some unrest amongst the Vampire community. If they found her wandering around, I'd hate to find her either dead or unwillingly turned."

Feeling like I needed to do something with my hands, I grabbed a red gummy rope from an open package that I had brought along. Taking a bite, I whipped the sugary strand around, pointing it at him, "Okay, so what's the favor you need from me? I'm guessing it has to do with a spell."

Rayth nodded, and Kit wrapped his arm around my waist, squeezing lightly, "We were hoping you'd be able to enter the Veil, with Kit as your escort, and locate the human and bring her back. I hear that your mate has already been making plans to take you over at some point, but I'd like to elevate that trip."

I glanced over my shoulder at my mate, who looked sheepishly at me. "You don't say, huh?" I poked Kit's chest and smiled to display that I wasn't displeased with the knowledge that he was planning a honeymoon of sorts.

I mean, we weren't married or anything, but pretty damn much.

"Sure—no problem, you guys could have asked sooner, you know, like when she disappeared."

Finn spoke up, "That is true, Viv, but we didn't want to burden you with this because we know how much larger spells can weigh down on a single witch. We must keep this on a need-to-know basis. No one but a small group even knows there's a human in the Veil. The human government certainly isn't privy to that information."

"Alright, I'll pack a few things, and we'll head to the portal tomorrow, if that's okay with you, Atticus." Rolling my mate's full name off my tongue set him on edge; With that, Kit knew I would be in charge, and I think he secretly loved it. Or at least that's what I interpreted from our bond that kept growing every day.

"Yes, Neesha. You *are* calling the shots."

"Oh, I want Teags and Finn to come with us as well. Make it a double date vaca thing, since we already know humans can enter."

Just as I glanced at Teags, she winced while Finn shook his head to say no.

"I can't, Viv."

"Why the fuck not?" I asked, frowning.

She took a deep breath, reaching across the table to grip my hand that wasn't holding the gooey red sugar string.

"While we know humans can enter, we don't know what it'll do to a human who is carrying a child."

I snorted, "Girl, you won't be carrying anything but a cup of iced chai."

Finn chuckled, and Teags bit her lip. It seemed I didn't fully grasp what she said until my eyes widened, and it finally dawned on me.

"Shut the hellfire up!" I shouted, then lowered my voice, leaning forward and pulling her toward me, "Are you preggers, girly pop?"

Her eyes welled with tears, and she smiled, "Yeah, I am."

I squealed and jumped up from Kit's lap, "I'm going to be Auntie Viv?"

"You are. I'm sorry I wanted to tell you sooner, but everything has been sort of chaotic lately."

Pulling her out of Finn's lap, I wrapped her in my arms. "I don't give a shit if you told me the day after you fucked, Finn, or right before you started showing, I'm so happy for you!"

Kit leaned over, clapping Finn on the shoulder while Rayth stood back and said his congratulations.

Then, it was Finn's turn to slap Kit's arm, "You're next, my friend."

"Whoa, whoa, whoa." I held up a finger and wagged it at the two males. "Unlike my best friend, who has always wanted someone, aka you Finn, to love her and make babies, this bitch has a no children zone placard boarding up her cervix. Got it? That means no litter of dragon offspring will come out of my vagina."

Kit rose, gripping my hips, "I wouldn't dream of sharing you, Neesha. Only if and when you want children will I gladly give them to you, fill you up, and make sure you can't walk for a month to ensure my seed takes root. Otherwise, I'm content in just being the two of us until the end of time."

"Uh-huh," I said, narrowing my eyes. "As long as we are on the same page."

"We are, my fire."

Rayth coughed, "Gross, I feel like the fifth wheel right about now."

"That's because you are, ghost boy." I pointed out, "Alright, no Teags or Finn. I guess that leaves us. We'll let you know when we find her."

Kit and I stayed for another few hours while I gushed over my pregnant best friend, leaving the men to get a plan going, not only to protect my sister, but also to determine where we would be staying in the Veil since Kit's homeland was hours from the nearest portals. We figured she would have stayed close to wherever the magical entrance into our paranormal world had spat her out, if we could find the moving one that had likely sucked her in.

Don't worry, Saige, I'm coming to find you and bring you back home.

Poor girl was probably shocked by how different the Veil was from Earth. I had only been there once when I was younger, and even that wasn't nearly enough exposure to what that place was as a whole.

There were vast lands that could still to this day remain unexplored, along with whoever inhabited them.

Chapter Thirty
Viv

Kit and I stood outside the portal that had appeared near the event stage in the park. Not only was it not supposed to be there, but we were worried another human would find their way unsuspecting into the Veil.

Rayth's body was flickering as he seemed to glide around the portal, looking on the ground and around the area for any other signs or indications on why it appeared where it did.

He glanced up at me, tapping the end of his pen against his notepad, "Do you have any knowledge of portals, Vivienne?"

I rolled my eyes, "Rayth, I've told you several times, call me Viv. Only my snobbish father and meek mother call me by my full name; I despise it."

He looked up, his flickering face expressionless, "Noted."

"But, to answer your question, no, I don't know a whole lot about portals," I replied.

He sighed at my response, "That's unfortunate. We're trying to find someone to flesh out why the portal is jumping around. Finn's never heard of it happening, and we're wondering if having so many coming and going is affecting it. But, this seems to be the only portal acting up."

I tapped a finger on my chin, lost in thought. "You could ask my sister. She was afforded a better education and understanding of all things magical. She might know where you can start your search if she doesn't have an answer."

He grinned, which was rare for him, while jotting a few things in his notepad, "I'll do that, thanks, Viv." Rayth turned to Kit, placing a hand on his shoulder, "Have fun over there. Don't forget to update us if you find Saige."

Kit smirked, wrapping his arm around my waist and pulling me flush against his side, "Will do, Detective. I'm sure it won't take us long to locate the elusive baker."

We stopped at the edge of the portal, and I suddenly had butterflies dipping and diving in my stomach.

The urge to turn around was like nothing I had ever felt before. What would happen once we entered the portal? Would the one we came through just disappear, and what happens if we couldn't find our way back to another one?

I mean, Finn wouldn't have come over if he had known the portals would become wonky, right?

"You're thinking too hard about this, my fires. We'll be able to find another portal in the Veil that won't move around." Kit reassured me.

Hands gripped my waist as the familiar press of his chest warmed my back. I leaned into him, closing my eyes and taking all the comfort he could give.

"Are you sure we can find a way back?"

"I am, and if we can't, would it be so horrible to have an extended vacation just the two of us while we explore the Veil?" He was right, it wouldn't be horrible, but I just hated to be stuck in a place I couldn't escape.

It reminded me of the prison I had been confined to with my father in the coven mansion.

"As long as I'm with you, I know things will be fine. I'm just —" I shook out my hands and then my body, wiggling against the front of Kit. He groaned, tightening his hold on my waist, making me smile.

I loved it when I affected him, and then when he voiced it with his moans and groans; there was something so incredibly hot about a man making sexy noises.

Kit's face pushed into the side of my neck, and he inhaled. "We could come back in a few hours, after you let me have my way with you."

"If we wait a few hours, this portal might not be here, and then we'd have to go searching for another," I said, tilting my head to the side, giving my mate more access to trail his lips along the column of my neck.

When I had been a hit and quit it girl, I had hated public displays of affection or anything in the realm aside from a quick romp in the sheets. But with Kit, I languished in his attentions and was greedy when he couldn't keep his hands to himself.

Right now, though, we needed to help find Saige; she was our main priority. Once we located her, we were free to roam the Veil and do anything we wanted to each other.

"We should go before the portal closes in front of our faces." I urged, hesitantly extracting myself from Kit's hold.

"Fine," He growled, clenching his jaw in defeat.

I rolled my eyes. He was being extra dramatic today, "We'll have plenty of time to mess around after, I promise."

That helped lighten the mood.

So, we entered the portal, hand in hand, and when we emerged on the other side, I gasped.

My eyes widened as I took in the sky; it wasn't the blue tint of Earth, but purple, almost like eternal night without the complete darkness.

A sucking thud made Kit and me stiffen, and when we turned around, the portal had winked out of existence.

"Well, no going back now," I muttered.

Twirling, I breathed in deeply. There wasn't a hint of the city air that Mount Hellfire had. And although it was still a fairly small city, not overly crowded, it had that tinge of industrial metals mixed with the natural elements of grass, trees, and flowers.

The air here smelt of all the elements of nature, tinged heavily with magic and mystery.

It awakened the innate, integral part of my being as a witch. It was nearly intoxicating and stifling.

Kit took my hand and squeezed, the sensations heightened along with my magic, "It's a lot to get used to at first. Are you alright?" He asked, concern sparkled along with a mischievous streak that was gone just as fast.

I nodded, continuing to inhale and glance at our surroundings.

My eyes snagged on the flowing waters of what I could recall to be the Veil's river of inhuman souls. It glowed brightly with a tinge of blue hues that morphed into indigo, which I presumed would be the deepest part of the river.

It was breathtaking and nothing like I had ever seen before, as was everything else.

I glanced around. We were currently in the woods, away from any villages or towns I had seen mentioned in the textbooks my father forced on Liv, mostly, but also on me.

Holding a pouch of crumbs from the last pastry Saige had baked, I poured a small pile into my palm. It was old, hard, and crusty, but it was the best we had, considering her personal belongings were with her, or so we hoped, in her bakery truck, which would be her savior. The crumbs were the next best option for the spell.

Kit stepped away to give me room to perform the spell. I could feel his absence, and while I knew he was right there, a small part of me worried he'd disappear from my sight.

Crumbling the pastry further in my grip, I allowed a drop of water that I called out of the dirt to penetrate my fist. This spell required something from Earth and something from the Veil, and it was the best thing to mix.

I let the dust mix with water, and when I felt enough magic laced and entwined with the food, which didn't take me as long as it would have on Earth, I scattered the pieces in the wind that picked up.

We sat back, watching as it twirled, spiraling like a sugary tornado until it floated in one direction.

Kit and I glanced at each and I grinned while he asked, "I take it that's a good sign?"

"Absofuckinglutely. She's nearby."

We only had to walk for maybe what felt like twenty minutes when we spotted the edge of Saige's food truck nestled beneath a large weeping willow. On the other side of the willow was a very large building that almost seemed like a broken-down castle; the bricks were blackened, as if a dragon had burnt it to a crisp. But the closer we walked, the more it seemed to be just a very dark stone used to build the enormous castle ruins.

"I sure hope she's in or around the food truck. This was easier than I thought it would be. We'll get her back to Earth by dinner—" I didn't finish what I was going to say when a muffled feminine moan cried out.

We froze before moving closer to the food truck, and that's when we saw the slight rocking, more grunts and groans that were most definitely coming from a male, and then, "Yes—right there. Don't fricken stop." That would be Saige, and she was having the time of her life.

I covered my mouth from giggling out loud because, oh boy, did we almost interrupt something that I was sure my baker friend would use a knife to fillet me if we did.

She was obviously not very concerned about getting back to Earth, and I was very confident that the man with her could get her back if she really wanted to go home. And by the sounds they were both making, I didn't think that would happen anytime soon.

We moved away from the creaking and rocking of the bakery truck back the way we had traveled.

Kit already had a specialized phone that worked just like a regular cell phone, except it transmitted between the Veil and Earth. Human cell phones wouldn't work in here, which was why Saige hadn't been located yet. And the only people who were authorized to have them were the king and his close operatives.

Kit snapped the flip phone shut and shoved it back into the backpack he insisted on carrying.

"Rayth and Finn have been updated on the whereabouts of Saige, and they have also been warned that there's a male with her and to approach with caution if she still hasn't returned to Earth in a week or two."

I glanced at Kit, unsure whether someone should wait that long to check back in with her. But he held up his hand when I opened my mouth, only to close it again.

"They're in the throes of his rut right now. I smelt it before the truck came into view. I wasn't sure at first that that was what it was, but it's heavy in the air. Any interruptions will cause him to go caveman, as humans say, and he'll take her far from where they are safely located right now." He explained. And I had to wonder what kind of inhuman would go through a rut. Several species could, but hardly any had come to Earth. They kept themselves in the Veil, where they could cycle through their heats without humans using them as spectacles. Most of the time, the inhuman male in a rut wouldn't care about when or where the action happened.

I most certainly hadn't read anything about the ruts of some males just so I could possible coax one from Kit. Nope, certainly not.

Of course, dragons didn't go through one of those, and so I wouldn't be graced with hours and days of a male worshipping me between my thighs or fucking me senseless anywhere and everywhere.

Saige was one lucky bitch in that aspect.

But I was also blessed with a dragon who would let me ride on his back, which is what I wanted at the moment, to get a better view of this world.

Kit quirked his brow like he could read what I wanted, and okay, he could sense it well since that was something dragons were known for. Not that I had read that in that so-called book either. Nope—not at all.

He held his hand out for me to grasp, and when I did, he pulled me into his chest, making me squeak, a very undignified sound in the quiet forest of the Veil.

He spoke low, breathlessly in my ear, "You want me to take you for a ride as my dragon?"

I nodded, and when he felt the movement, he growled, "Vero is very pleased with this. He'd love nothing more than to have you sit on his back. Naked?"

Smacking his chest, I laughed, "No, sorry to both you and Vero, there will be no naked dragon riding today."

"It'll make it easier to climb between your legs when I shift back." Kit wiggled his brows, holding me against his chest.

He nuzzled his nose against mine before his lips took the

liberty to devour mine. I leaned further into him, moaning at the pressure. He sure knew how to kiss, leaving me breathless every single time.

But that passionate embrace was short-lived when he pulled back, our chests rising and falling against one another.

"Here, you're going to have to strap this to your back. I'll undress, you can put my clothes in the bag, and climb on. I want to show you something in my homeland, if you're up for it?"

He asked the question eagerly with a smidge of shyness.

It was important; I understood that much, and I couldn't deny those dragon eyes that reminded me of puppies giving people the pet-me look, otherwise known as puppy-dog eyes. It made me giggle and roll my eyes in exasperation.

"Of course, I'd love nothing more than for you to show me your homeland." I wrapped my arms around his neck, pecking his lips quickly. "You are my mate after all, we are still learning one another, and I want to see this part of you."

He sighed heavily, relief that I didn't shut him down echoed in our bond, and I nearly wept from the love that flooded it afterward.

Kit stripped, stepping away far enough that I wouldn't be crushed beneath his talons and weight.

I'd never get used to the shift and the sheer size of him. Kit, or Vero, I supposed, scales shimmered beneath the purple sky and blue-tinted lighting from the river behind me. His golden colors brightened, almost as if little flecks of diamonds were ingrained in each scale.

He took my breath away.

"You're marvelous in this light, Vero," I said, approaching my dragon. "Maybe you should allow some of these scales out while Kit is in his human form, while we are here. I'd love to see the glow reflect while—"

My cheeks heated, and suddenly I was embarrassed by where my mind went. But Vero nudged my stomach, and I could feel amusement through our bond.

I chuckled, "Okay, anyway, let me get this backpack on, and I'll climb up."

I didn't have far to clamber when Vero flattened his body, angling it in such a way that it was effortless to get on his back. "Thanks," I whispered, adjusting myself between his shoulder blades until I was comfortable and could grip and hold onto a few spikes at the side of his neck.

"I'm ready, but promise to take it slow until I get used to it. Then, I want you to let go and show me how you really fly."

Vero wouldn't risk my safety, but I knew he craved the open sky of his home and the magic that coursed through the winds. I thirsted for it as well, opening my heart to the possibilities of what the magnetism could hold.

Chapter Thirty-One

Viv

The fresh, magically charged breeze whipped the red strands of my hair loose from my pony as Vero dipped, dived, and plummeted through the skies of the Veil.

My grip tightened on his side spikes, bracing for the inevitable drop I could feel coming from the muscles tensing beneath my spread thighs.

He pulled his wings close to his large body and dove towards a very large lake surrounded by willows. Just before we hit the surface of the glass-like water, Vero snapped his wings open, making me squeal in delight from the rush.

Being on the back of a dragon was unheard of in itself, and it was nothing short of amazing, but knowing this was my mate, Kit, and his inner dragon, Vero, left the rolling emotions to clog my throat. I couldn't help but swallow around the lump that formed because I had this, had them, and the love they threw at me like Cupid shooting his arrows.

At times it was overwhelming, but when I thought about it, Kit's devotion and Vero's reflection of that was exactly what I needed. I had been starving for affection all my life, and now that I had it, it was addicting. But, only with Kit and Vero, of course.

I was still trying to get used to the fact that the dragon beneath me was Kit as well as Vero. They were two separate entities, but mashed together. And Vero was incredibly gentle with me as well. Not as possessive as you'd think dragons would be of their mates, but incredibly loyal.

When I tapped the side of Veros' neck, indicating I wanted to go this way or that way, he obliged, and I found myself using his spikes to steer him. Which only made me laugh harder, because it was odd to tell a ginormous dragon what to do and where to go. I loved it, though. *Loved them.*

The realization made me gasp, because it was true. I had been trying hard to keep my distance from Kit for so long that once I finally gave in, that love was shoved down my throat and gripped my heart so fast it was intense.

I hadn't said those three little words out loud to Kit yet. I knew he could feel it down the bond just as I felt his and Vero's feelings, but there was something about needing to say and hear the words out loud.

I'd find the right time to say it to him, after all, he put up with chasing after my stubborn ass for months before I finally gave him a chance.

And all because he saved me from being kidnapped, too, who knew?

Looking over the landscape, it began to change drastically, from weeping willows surrounding lakes and grassy fields filled with flowers to crags of rock, mountains so high they could have rivaled Mount Everest on Earth.

That wasn't what was so mesmerizing, though, as a gasp left my throat when Vero flew through a thick cloud. On the other side were several floating isles of different shapes. Some of them had water flowing freely down, while others had hanging vines.

Each one also seemed to have some kind of housing structure, with small figures milling about, doing chores or tending to sprawling, lush gardens.

"Wow," I said, gazing all around us, "It's stunning. Is this where you grew up?"

He didn't answer, of course, because he couldn't, but I felt a tinge of sadness through the bond mixed with contentment. Immediately, I felt terrible for asking, remembering what he said about his departure with his father. So I rubbed the side of Vero's neck in comfort, which elicited a purr to vibrate beneath me.

I kept swiveling my head to take everything in when I realized we were headed straight for an isle that held many vines dangling beneath the rocky underside.

Vero landed in a large grassy field, where he tilted himself to allow for an easier landing while getting off his back. I pulled the backpack off and rolled my shoulders. I had no idea what the hell Kit had put in here, but it wasn't light by any means.

I pulled out his clothes, eyeing him appreciatively before he quickly dressed, smirking in my direction.

"Later, my mate, I have another special place to take you, but first, I wanted to show you the home I grew up in. I'm not sure if anyone is home, but fair warning, they might not be happy to see me."

"ATTICUS!" A woman shrieked, dropping the basket of clothes she had been carrying to a clothes line. She was older, but still possessed that youthful grace.

Her eyes watered, and then streams of tears ran down her cheeks as she took Kit in her arms. "My baby boy! You've come home! Finally, and with a female, too."

"Hey, ma, missed you too." He chuckled, his arms wrapped around her smaller frame.

She held his face in her hands, smiling with so much motherly love that it made a small piece of me hurt, only because I had never been shown as much affection as Kit was getting in that moment. It was evident he grew up loved and wanted.

His mother turned her head and gazed at me. Her smile widened, and she launched herself at me. I nearly stumbled to the ground, but Kit was there to catch us.

"Be careful with my mate, ma. You don't want to scare her away, do you? Took me long enough just to get her to stop running from me." Kit joked. There wasn't any kind of gloom to his words, only satisfaction and mirth.

"Well, I'm sure she had her reasons for absconding from the goddess's wishes." She brushed my hair from my face, taking in my features, "My, you are beautiful with this red hair and your stunning, different colored eyes."

"Thank you, Mrs. Hart."

"Oh, please call me Lydia or Mom. You are, after all, my only daughter for now." She turned to Kit and laughed, "If only your brothers would leave the nest and seek out their mates. I'm glad you went with Finn when he asked; otherwise, you wouldn't have brought me back a female to keep you boys in line."

Kit grabbed his bag, slinging it over his shoulder, glancing past his mother. "Where are my brothers? And father?"

"Your brothers are off for the weekend, gallivanting with the other single lonely dragons. If you're not planning to stay that long, you won't see them. And your father—well, he is in the house." She winced, "He'll be unhappy you're here, but pay him no mind, Viv. They can squabble on the porch if that happens. Come, come, let me make some tea and get you two snacks."

Kit didn't say another word as he gripped my fingers, his mother glanced at my exposed shoulder, and hummed. "I take it you are here to take her to the cave?"

He nodded but didn't say another word.

So she knew of this special place he wanted to take me. It made me contemplate if this were one of those dragon things that may or may not have been in the book I had been trying to study before Kit decided he wouldn't leave my side. I hadn't glanced at it in days because, well, I was getting fucked often and we only had time to eat and sleep in between.

My face heated at the dirty thoughts while we were with Kit's mom, which made my dragon squeeze my hand after taking a deep breath, flaring his nostrils. I knew he could smell me.

I mouthed 'sorry,' and he smirked, completely cocky, knowing he just did it for me and could rev my engine without even trying.

Just as we reached the house, a man who looked almost eerily like my mate exited in a huff, scowling and staring at Kit with a snarl on his lip.

I held tightly to my mate's hand because this could only be his father; after all, his mom had warned us he wouldn't be happy to see Kit. And well, she was right, plus they could have been twins if Kit wasn't the younger version of his dad.

"I told you never to come back here, boy. That the moment you left, you were dead to me." His dad growled.

Lydia stomped up to Kit's father and brazenly poked him in the chest, "You knock that growling off right now, Marcus, or I'm gonna make you sleep in the barn with the animals you act like."

He frowned down at her, "You threaten me, woman?"

She folded her arms and cocked her hip to one side, "I sure the hell am, *male*."

Oh my goddess, I already love his mom. She has fire in her.

It made me curious if she was also a dragon or if it was his dad who had the genes. She was hellfire fierce, that was for sure. I'd hate to be on the end of that finger she was still poking into his dad's chest.

Marcus huffed, his shoulders slumping in defeat as he grunted and sat down in one of the lawn chairs on the covered porch. He glanced over at us, "Well, don't just stand there, come sit down and bring your female."

I leaned into Kit, rubbing a side boob against his arm to distract his rising ire. "It'll be okay, I'll sit in your lap if that helps."

"It would." He muttered.

So, we walked, Kit, very reluctantly, and me, with pep in my step, the rest of the way to the house.

We all sat, and as promised, I used Kit's lap as a seat. It seemed to ease the tension in his body, even if his father still sat poised with a stick up his bum.

Lydia clapped her hands. "So, tell me what brings you back home to Kreli Kit?"

"Viv and I were looking for her friend, Saige, around the old castle ruins near the village of Muria. She's human and somehow ended up in the Veil. Luckily, she was found but indisposed, so I suggested that since we were already in the Veil, I'd take my mate to see my homeland. And I plan to take her to the caves once we leave here."

Kit's father peered over at me. His gaze softened as he took in my shoulder. The same one his mom, Lydia, had eyed just a moment ago.

There was something big I wasn't understanding that had to do with my bare shoulder and Kit being my mate. I went to open my mouth to ask when Marcus spoke.

"Well, Atticus, I expect that you take your mate to the

caves as soon as possible instead of lingering around here with your bickering parents."

"Of course father, I only wanted to show Viv around before getting to that. And I knew if we didn't stop, mother would pinch me by my ear."

I glanced over my shoulder, and Kit's face beamed with pride and giddy, excited energy.

Lydia had a cloth in her hand and shooed us up from the seat. "Go on you two, time's a-wasting. I expect some grandbabies in the future."

"Mom, Viv, and I don't know if we want kids now or even in the future."

She was still smiling brightly even with the news she might not get grandchildren, and for a moment I felt guilty until she giggled, "Oh, well, no worries, I have your brothers to count on for that then, you two just go enjoy the bliss of an official bonding. Go, go, shoo!"

I hugged her goodbye, relieved she wasn't one of those mothers-in-law who pestered the couple for children. I nodded to Marcus because I didn't take him for the hugging type, and we left.

Kit and I stood in the open grass while he stripped again, making my mouth dry from all those rippling muscles and tight buns.

"Don't worry, Neesha, soon we'll both be unclothed for days, you can have your fill then."

He shifted suddenly. I didn't have time to move back, but Vero emerged and towered proudly over me, casting a shadow to protect against the lavender-hued sun.

I stood beneath his chest, raising my hand, I rubbed his scales, making Vero shiver.

He leaned down and tilted again, allowing me to clamber on his back with the heavily laden backpack.

Then, he took off without warning towards the largest mountain within eyesight. There were several dark holes that, upon closer inspection, proved to be large cave openings. A few were lit up with a bright blue glow that pulsed like a heartbeat.

My own heart raced against my chest. All I could comprehend was the thumping and pounding in my ears.

Vero aimed for a higher darkened cave landing softly near the edge. He tilted his body furthest away from the opening, and I climbed down.

Within a breath's time, he shifted, and my eyes didn't leave the hard dick that bobbed when he strode over to me. I absently reached for the backpack and unzipped it all without taking my eyes from his cock.

I licked my lips, and before I could pull out his clothes, he was standing in front of me while I was on my knees.

Goddess, what a specimen this man is.

He stepped closer, his hand reached down to cup my chin and pull me to my feet. His eyes never wavered from mine while he silently scooped me into his arms. I wrapped mine around his neck as he walked further into the cave, the backpack dangling beneath me.

It was pitch black for a moment, then a very faint pulse of blue light guided Kit to a hidden alcove that was dim but easier to see than when we had been outside. In the middle of the room was a large bed of moss that Kit lay me on. He pulled a few vacuum-sealed packs out of the bag and ripped them apart.

Large, thick blankets expanded, and he gingerly laid them out like he was making a nest.

I remained quiet, watching Kit work because this seemed to be important; he didn't speak either.

My stomach flipped, a dull throb began at my core, and grew the longer I watched Kit make us a space to lie together in because that's what this had been, hadn't it? His little comments, the eagerness from his parents, and their stares at my barren shoulder.

Was he meant to give me a mark like Finn had given Teagan to bind her to him?

If that's what this was, I was all the way in.

Standing from the soft moss, I peeled my sweatshirt and undershirt clean off, nearly ripping my pants in the process. I stood near the edge of the blankets in my sexiest bra and lace panties on the edge of anticipation.

Kit didn't need to say another word when he hauled me to his chest, lifting me so I gazed down at him.

"I know I haven't explained a lot about being mated to a dragon, Neesha, but this is the beginning of it. Well, mostly the beginning, we've already skipped over having sex to quell the bond sickness. This, though, this is where our forever will start. Where I'll bind you to me if you wish." He looked earnestly at me, a plea in his gaze.

I nodded, "Of course, Kit. Tell me what it entails. I tried reading up on a few things, but your kind are very secretive. I want to know everything."

His lip quirked to one side, "You tried learning about my people?"

"Of course I have, you big scaly dope," I said, rolling my eyes.

He pulled me in harder, nuzzling my nose as he lay me in the middle of the blanket nest. It was incredibly cozy, and I could see us spending lots of time here. Maybe we could take a few days before returning to Earth.

"That pleases me to no end, my mate." His lips trailed along my neck before he lifted his head, hovering his body over mine. All I wanted was to feel the weight of him pushing down against my body while I cried out in pleasure.

"Dragons mate for life, and the only way to bind you is for

me to bite you here," He trailed his finger along my shoulder. "While in the throes of pleasure. And once I have bitten, I will blow flames onto your skin to complete the binding of the bite. And since it's tradition amongst my people to bring their mates to these caves, I brought you here. Once we have consummated our bond, the living creatures in this cave will light up brightly, and we can spend days lost in each other until their light dies back down."

I liked this idea very much, though the fire on my skin scared me a bit. "Will it hurt, the bite and flames?"

He shook his head, eyeing my shoulder like he was eager to sink in already, "It will only sting for a moment and turn into something akin to coming home, or feeling whole."

I hummed, tapping my finger as I took in the information, but needing more, "So, those other caves that are lit?"

He nodded, "They have other dragons in them that have completed the bond."

"Kit?"

"Yes, my fires?"

"I need you."

He didn't wait for me to change my mind when he nestled himself between my thighs, his lips finding mine, and getting lost in each other.

He took his time trailing kisses all over my body, each one heightened into the next until I was wiggling uncontrollably beneath him, seeking any kind of friction I could get.

Kit worked his lips and tongue down my body, removing my bra and panties as he descended.

Spreading my thighs, his head closed the distance, and he inhaled deeply, groaning before gazing at me, sticking his tongue out, and taking one long swipe up from my entrance to my clit.

Letting the sensation roll over me, I cried out his name. He continued to lavish between my thighs so thoroughly that I was soaked by the time his fingers entered my pussy. He pumped his digits once, twice, before he turned his head, nipping the inside of my thigh.

And then, Kit climbed up my body, and without further notice, impaled me on his thick, throbbing cock, pumping his hips like he was a man starved for friction.

Every thrust pushed me higher in ecstasy and in the blankets, panting and lost for words as our pleasure threatened to tumble over.

"Kit! I'm so—"

I couldn't finish the nearly incoherent thought when Kit's mouth closed over my shoulder, and he bit down hard.

Crying out, I saw stars as pain mixed with pleasure, my release rushed over me and lasted for what seemed like forever. I closed my eyes as it blinded me with the brightest blue light I had ever seen echo through my lids.

Kit released my shoulder after I came down from the euphoria, his hips pistoning erratically until he tumbled over when another orgasm made me clench around his cock. He roared, and the lights that had lit up with my first release pulsed to our now synced heartbeats.

He slowed his hips, peppering kisses all over my face, neck, and chest while avoiding the tender bite he gave.

My mate rolled us so I was on top with his cock still pulsing inside my pussy. It was utter bliss and by far the best thing I had ever experienced.

We panted, sweat coating our bodies, making us slick against one another, while we lay silently as the cave continued to pulse.

Every blip dimmed little by little but remained brighter than it had been when we first entered.

Our mating was complete, my soul finally felt settled, and our bond was like concrete.

I love you so much.

Kit stiffened, making me lift my head. "What is it?"

"Say it again." He rasped.

I chuckled, "I didn't say anything."

"You didn't out loud—" *But, I heard you within.*

I gasped, sitting up with his cock still lodged inside. I narrowed my eyes and thought of the most ridiculous thing I could think of in that moment.

If you can hear me, then I want you to give me all your seed and give me babies.

He snorted, "You told me you don't want children, my fires, have you changed your mind? I certainly will enjoy the act of making them."

I slapped his chest, "No, I haven't changed my mind, Kit! You can hear what I said?"

The grin he gave was panty-melting, if I were wearing any and not on top of him. "Yes, I wasn't sure if it would happen for us since you're not a dragon, but we can speak to one another, and you can even hear Vero."

Hello, female. It is a pleasure to finally hear you within us.

Uh hey? I said, wondering why in the world I was so nervous to speak with Kit's dragon.

It is alright, sweet fires, you are not used to conversing with me as Atticus is. I am content to wait for you to feel comfortable enough. I like sitting back and watching, too.

There was a purr that left Kit's chest that made me laugh out loud.

"I think Vero is a naughty dragon."

Fingers gripped my waist while I caught the mischievous glint in his eye.

"As am I, my fires."

Kit began moving below me, making his cock harden inside again.

I couldn't believe I had spent the last few months denying this man and myself the pleasure we shared. Not only physically but spiritually as well, while our bond had thrived, flourishing beyond measure once we completed it.

We'd protect one another for eternity and continue learning new things about each other. After all, there was no rush. And I planned to do many arousing, provocative things in the near future.

"I love you, my dragon." I panted against his mouth when he sat up to kiss my lips while I straddled his waist.

"And I love you, Neesha, my fires. You're forever mine."

And I would be, I'd never run from him again—except if it led to him fucking me up against a wall or tree. Then, I'd sprint as often as I could.

Sneak Peek into Heartstone Crumbs

Saige

Before the Veil

You'd think I'd learn to use modern technology and utilize the map app on my phone. I was most definitely determined to keep my younger years, with less techy stuff and more roll-with-the-punches, as I glanced over the paper map.

I had several towns and smaller cities marked, the more desirable ones at least. There were thousands of options, but I'd done some research on each one.

My heart could never quite settle on a place to call home. Instead, I traveled from town to city in my renovated large food truck-slash-home.

It was the perfect dual purpose, with a bed, bathroom, and small closet in the back where I kept my personal items, and the majority of the truck where my mobile bakery had several smaller stoves, fridge, a good-sized flat counter, and storage galore for my mixers, sheets, bowls, and covered containers.

I had done the odd job here or there. Put up flyers for

specialized orders, and it worked for awhile until my soul felt restless and I decided to move on.

The need for money never crossed my mind as I had significant savings. All because both my parents died in a plane crash while headed to their villa in Italy for a vacation, while I stayed with my grandmother.

And then my grandmother, who had raised me since then, passed a few years ago, also leaving me a lump sum on top of selling all the properties that had been placed into my name.

I considered them burdens and wasn't going to use them anyway. Plus, there were no siblings or aunts and uncles to whom it could have gone to, so it was all stuck to me, which is likely why I felt the need to move so much. I didn't want to be weighed down while also searching for something.

Which brings me to today. Biting my lip, I closed my eyes, trailing my fingers over the paper map until I could feel something—anything.

I was just about to count when I felt it. A shiver ran up my spine the closer I got to the spot my senses wanted me to stop at.

When I felt the familiar tingle at the back of my neck, I quit moving my fingers and opened my eyes. My index had landed perfectly on a city called Mount Hellfire.

I snorted at the name because not only did that sound ominous, it also sounded magical. Which, I knew, magic and all things make-believe from fairy tales didn't exist, even if I wished they did.

Putting the map down in the empty passenger seat, I clicked my seatbelt in place before starting the engine. I had all the windows open, including those in the 'kitchen' area of my truck. The last of the cupcakes Mrs. Mildred ordered for her kindergarten class sat neatly packed, already frosted, decorated, and sprinkled with edible glitter, waiting to be delivered for their first day at school.

I'd drop them off and get on the road to my new destination of Mount Hellfire. It'd be a few-hour drive, where I'd have to stop somewhere overnight, but that never bothered me.

Having a mobile home and job was almost like taking a cross-country road trip, only some places I'd stop for days, while others would be months. I was what some older folks call a wanderer.

And until I found what called to my heart, I'd keep on wandering, traveling, and roaming this world until I stumbled into whatever would make that beating thing in my chest sing happy tunes.

I glanced up, tapping the metal bat necklace my mother had given me before she died. It never left my bakery truck, as I feared it would go missing, and it was one of the last things I had to remember her and my father.

I loved bats, specifically the fruit bat. They were so adorable, and their wings were fascinating. The strength of those membranes in helping propel them into flight was magnificent. I'd always wanted a pet bat, but I knew I could never have one since living in a bakery truck with an animal violated so many food codes.

My eyes gazed outside the front windshield just as Trent rounded the corner. His scowl deepened when he saw me in the driver's seat.

"Oh fizzlesticks." I quickly put my truck in gear, speeding towards the elementary school where I'd have to be as fast as lightning, dropping these cupcakes off and zipping out of town before he could catch up.

In the rearview, I saw him jogging back towards his vehicle, which was a block and a half away from where I had been parked.

The guy couldn't take a hint. I had purposely stood him up last night. I wasn't trying to be mean, but he wouldn't take no for an answer, and when I finally said yes to last night's date, I hoped I'd already be gone, but then Mrs. Mildred asked for last-minute cupcakes that she'd paid extra for.

And me being me, I was too nice to say no to her.

So here I was, power walking into the school, dropping off the cupcakes, and dodging a man I didn't feel any kind of instant spark with.

After driving for a few hours, my body relaxed, and I hummed in time with the radio, heading toward my new temporary home.

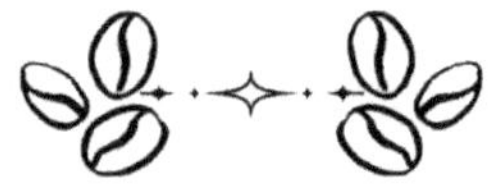

It took a few extra days to get to the edge of Mount Hellfire's city limits, as I didn't feel the innate sense to rush. It was early, with the sun just peeking above the horizon, as it wished everyone a good morning.

And here I was, Saige Lancaster, short and curvy baker with locks the color of light-roasted coffee beans and eyes as blue as the Caribbean Ocean, on a new adventure where anything and everything good could happen.

However, at the moment, I desperately needed some caffeine before exploring the city and finding a good place to hunker down and set up a temporary post.

And as I drove down the main road, I nearly passed a large older building that had a coffee shop next to an empty storefront. I gazed longingly at the empty store, daydreaming about opening up a more permanent bakery.

Someday.

Once I found that place that stuck to me like caramel, then I'd spread some roots. For now, my truck was all I had.

Entering the coffee shop called The Molten Java, I took a deep breath as I walked to the counter. I didn't want to just stop in the middle of the store and act like a weirdo in front of the few people already at the table. Their laptops, tablets, and phones were shoved in their faces as the delicious aroma wafted through the room.

"Morning, gorgeous. I'll be right there."

A woman who I would deem a goddess was the only one currently behind the counter.

She was smiling and dancing while whipping up some espresso shots and frothing milk. Her hair was the most vibrant red I had ever seen, and when she glanced up, she had one green eye that reminded me of the fronds of aloe, while her other was light brown like warm honey.

She was stunning, and I immediately felt a kinship with her. Something pinged in my heart, like she was part of coming home, but only a stepping stone.

I'd need to assess this more. Find a way to come around often without seeming like a desperate stalker.

"What can I get you, girly pop?" She asked, and when I looked for a name tag, there was none. It was a bummer because I was too nervous to ask for one.

"Uh, what do you recommend?" I asked, like a dunce.

She must have noticed I was looking for a tag when she smiled, it was friendly and welcoming, "I'm Viv. You're a new face that I haven't seen around. Are you allergic to anything?" She asked, already dispensing beans into a container to make fresh espresso.

I shook my head, "No, not that I know of at least."

"Perfect, since it's transitioning from summer to fall, how about something hot, spicy, but sweet?"

"Sure, I'm Saige, by the way. It's nice to meet you." Telling her my name felt like the next step. And while I waited at the counter to pay, I glanced over, noticing there was a display case but no pastries or fresh food. Only packaged goodies. I thought this might be a good way to offer my services for fresh-baked goods that might further this feeling that enveloped my body.

"I see you don't have a whole lot in your display case," I said over loud hissing that echoed in the store before it quieted.

"What's that? Sorry, couldn't hear over the frother."

"Oh, I said your display is a bit bare. Do you have anyone who does fresh pastries?"

She shook her head, pouring steaming milk into the cup over espresso and then shooting some kind of syrup I couldn't see the name of in the cup.

"Nah, the bakery that was across the street closed a few months ago, and no one else has opened one up in the city. It's hard getting anything fresh from other towns, so it hasn't been a main focus for me."

Viv placed a lid on top of the cup and handed it to me.

"How much?"

"Oh, on the house for the newbie. You only get one, though, so enjoy it and don't throw it out. I added a little something extra that should help wake you up better."

Well, poop, she made it just for me. That warmth I felt before exploded. I had the urge to cry, but held it together because that would surely be awkward in front of a stranger.

"That is so incredibly sweet, Viv. Thank you so much. Although I'd like to pay somehow, and if you don't want to take my money, can I bake you something? I own a mobile bakery truck."

Her eyes widened while she licked her lips.

"Oh fuck yes, you can. I'm a sucker for sweets."

Bingo-dingo!

"How about this, I'll make you a few things, and if you like them, maybe I could be the one to stock your display case?" I said, gingerly sipping on the hot drink so I didn't burn my mouth.

The first taste had my tongue dancing like it had a shot of adrenaline. "Wow." I turned to look at Viv, and she was watching me intently.

"What do you think?" She asked, eager for my answer.

"It sure has my tongue dancing for joy. This is exactly what I needed after my long drive."

She did a little dance and went to clean up the mess she had made. I stuck around, glancing at the tables, walls, and open ceiling. In the front was a large bean roaster, along with a largely empty counter space.

I wondered if things went well, if she'd let me prepare everything here and then bake in the truck. Things were sometimes cramped in there, but I made do.

While I was busy peering over the counter at the space, Viv was finished cleaning and came over.

"So, what kind of things do you make?"

I shrugged, "Mostly cupcakes, cookies, and my family's signature cinnamon rolls. I can do cake orders, but those are tedious and require hours of my time and cooling."

She rubbed her belly, humming, "I could so go for a cinnamon roll. If you have any of those, I'll definitely try one; otherwise, give me whatever you want me to try."

"Oh," My face fell. With traveling, I usually made sure everything that had been baked found a home, so I didn't have to worry about forgetting it in a storage bin somewhere. That happened once, and I ended up throwing the whole container away. "I actually have to bake everything. So, it might be a few hours or even tomorrow before I find a place that will allow me to use their electricity."

"Oh, easy peasy, just park out back and I'll run a cord out to you. Even if we don't work out, which I'm sure we can come to some kind of agreement, you can stay parked there."

It almost seemed to be too good to be true, but deep in my soul, I felt her truth. It only presented me with a hopeful future here in Mount Hellfire.

Maybe this place was sent in my direction by some kind of higher power.

"Thanks, Viv, first the coffee and now a space to park my bakery truck. You're amazing, and I'm so grateful to have you be the first person I met in this city."

And I was indebted to her. I'd make her the best fizzle-sticked cinnamon roll she'd ever eaten so she couldn't resist the rest of my baked goods when I presented them.

Ever since entering the city, I've just had this profound sense of belonging. It was the first time my intuition had ever screamed, 'YES THIS IS WHAT WE HAVE BEEN SEARCHING FOR!'

And for the first time in forever, I looked forward to seeing if this feeling would continue to grow, allowing me to put down some roots and call this place home.

A note from the Author

Thank you for taking the time to read Brewing Fire. This is my 5th book I have written since becoming an indie author and I'm forever grateful I can continue to share the stories that brew in my head.

This book took a bit longer than I normally write because in December 2025, I lost my dad. He was 60 and died suddenly. It was and still is a shock that he's no longer around. I still struggle immensely to get over the fact that I can't video call him right now and say 'hey dad, guess what?! I just finished another book.' He'd always tell me how proud he was that I was chasing my dreams. I was a daddy's girl through and through.

But, enough with the heavy!

I couldn't wait to write about Viv and her unending ire towards Kit, who only wanted to love her, among other things. And Viv's and even Liv's growth into sticking up to their father.

There were lots of hints as to future mates, but one thing I didn't give away too much was who would be mated to Saige.

I hope you enjoyed Brewing Fire. Make sure to leave a

review, whether you liked the book or not. Those are for the readers to discover, not for me!

Happy reading, AnderSinners! XOXO

About the Author

K.L. ANDERSEN is a multi-genre romance author and avid reader. Whether it's heart-wrenching or silly, she likes to write and dream up different worlds and the not-so-human men in them. She is a fierce Scorpio who lives in the Northern Midwest with her husband, two kids, two dogs, two cats, a bearded dragon, and the many chickens who roam around her home.

You can find her being a goober while enjoying writing, reading, gaming, or hanging out with those she loves.

Books by K.L. Andersen

The Ashfieran Duet

AshFiera

Ashix Rising

Ashoween

Mount Hellfire Mates

Infernal Hearts

Brewing Fire

Heartstoned Crumbs

www.ingramcontent.com/pod-product-compliance
Lightning Source LLC
LaVergne TN
LVHW010639110826
845149LV00014B/2886

* 9 7 9 8 9 9 1 1 8 0 0 9 2 *